(WARNING)
This book might not be for the faint of heart, especially
if you're some *extremely* woke person. So grab your
blanket, helmet, pillow and strap-in
you snowflake.

Introduction

What you're about to read is shaped by my biases, opinions, and observations from over the last few years, with some input from like-minded people. Some of you will nod along and chuckle, others might think I'm way off while laughing, and a few might end up with *their pissy feelings hurt.* That's life.

The world's speeding up, and Common Sense? Well, let's just say it never received the wifi password. Things are getting stranger by the day, and it's confusing to make sense of it all.
So, prepare for some *TRUTH,* mixed with perspectives that might not line up with your own, but again, *that's life.* All I ask is that you keep an open mind as we tackle some of today's more "controversial" topics.

And life's pretty simple: we're all stuck on this big spinning rock floating through space, so it's just *Common Sense* to try and get along. Try not to be a pain, and aim to have at least some integrity—not just for others, but because it makes your life smoother. As you figure things out, you'll realise it's all about connecting with people and learning to compromise without losing your mind or getting your feelings mixed up in places where they don't belong.

Also, with over 130 chapters to dive into—messy and unpredictable, just like life—you're bound to find a few that hit home or ruffle some feathers. That's the point: if it sparks a reaction, you're thinking. And thinking, as rare as it seems these days, is worth celebrating.

You'll spot a few poems sprinkled throughout too—quick pauses to make you laugh, cringe, or maybe even reflect. Yes, *Common Sense* might get a bit repetitive here, but let's be real, if it were exciting, we'd all be using it more often.

So, dive in and embrace the chaos—because that's where the fun begins, and who knows, you might even find some sense in all this madness.

Enjoy

Chapters

Where's the Common Sense today?

Picture someone who's always talking about how they're on the verge of greatness, promising they'll finally get their act together. Yet, when you look closer, they're stuck in the same old routine, hoping for a miracle to happen. It's like waiting for a pizza delivery while refusing to order one—*Common Sense* says you've got to put in some effort and believe in yourself!

Now, envision a person who strolls into any gathering, ready to stir the pot because they think they must show off how much of a billy big bollocks they are. They're like a bull in a china shop, completely oblivious to the vibe around them. It's a classic case of a big ego with a side of zero awareness—*Common Sense* clearly took a vacation!

Think of someone you know who thrives on being a sofa potato, perfectly content in their little bubble of no pursuit. When you try to show them a path to something greater, they act like you've just suggested they swim with sharks. All they can muster are excuses and complaints before even giving it a shot. It's a prime example of missing the *Common Sense* memo about growth and taking action!

Then, imagine a person who's lost in the maze of life, standing up against every injustice they can find, even if they have no clue what they're talking about. It's like watching a toddler throw a tantrum over a toy they don't even want. This is a soul adrift, misusing their voice for misguided causes, and it's a glaring lack of *Common Sense* that's hard to ignore!

Think about someone who seems super into you, says all the right things, making you feel like they're the best thing since sliced bread. Then, suddenly, you realise they were just after an ego boost, and they're out the door. This is a prime example of someone lacking *Common Sense,* leaving you a bit battered but possibly stronger in the end.

Now, picture someone who has access to a shower and a washing machine but still smells like they've been living in a landfill. You know them, but you find yourself sitting three seats away, trying to avoid the stench. This is a classic case of lacking *Common Sense*—just because you don't notice it doesn't mean others aren't smelling it.

Or imagine a group with some pretty extreme beliefs. They're so absorbed in their own activities that they push these ideas onto anyone who isn't part of their group. The lack of *Common Sense* here is that they focus only on their own interests and ignore everyone else.

Consider having a busy day with work, kids, or just life in general. You come across something you need to do but decide to put it off. This is a classic lack of *Common Sense*—delaying now just means it'll be a bigger hassle later.

And if you ever say you don't have enough time, but you spend hours scrolling through your phone, take a look at your screen time. It's a perfect example of a lack of *Common Sense*—failing to see where your time actually goes.

Picture someone brimming with misunderstood anger. These people live for a fight or a good riot, grabbing any excuse to break stuff and unleash their rage on the world. It's a classic case of lacking *Common Sense,* simple.

Now, think about those people who hoarded all the toilet paper at the start of the pandemic. Years later, I still don't get it. I guess they just wanted to make sure their arses were extra clean, but where was the *Common Sense?*

Or maybe you're the type who struggles with sleep but doesn't have any serious issues. You know the drill: turn off the phone, and the TV, and stick to a bedtime. *Common Sense* says you'll function a lot better with some decent sleep. So, how about actually getting more *SLEEP?*

Next, consider how great it feels to eat well and stay healthy. It's pretty simple—good food and a healthy lifestyle make you feel amazing. The *Common Sense* here is to notice how great you feel once you keep up with it… that is.

Also, there's the person who's so wrapped up in their own feelings that they think they've got emotional intelligence all figured out. They're only concerned with how things make *THEM* feel. The real lack of *Common Sense* here is not being able to control your own emotions and being completely clueless about how your actions affect others—definitely, not a shining example of so-called *"Emotional Intelligence."*

Picture someone who'd rather stay sad than make an effort to move forward. It's like they've decided to be the main character in their own pity party. *Common Sense* would say, "Life's a journey, not a checkpoint—keep moving and give it your best shot." Cliché, right?

Now, imagine a group of adults parading around naked, calling it body positivity while waving the banner of free speech. Meanwhile, kids and their parents are on the sidelines, taking it all in. The glaring lack of *Common Sense* here is thinking that this kind of parade is appropriate for children. Blatantly.

Or consider how some people have their freedom of speech restricted because others can't handle a challenging conversation. It's like they're trying to drag everyone down to their level of sensitivity. The real lack of *Common Sense* here is not understanding that growth comes from facing difficult discussions, not by making the world fit your comfort zone.

Imagine people glued to their devices, barely noticing the world around them. You see them crossing streets without looking, missing real connections and experiences in favour of endless scrolling. *Common Sense* says: lift your head and look at the life around you!

Lastly, there's always that person who offers unsolicited advice on everything, thinking they're doing everyone a favour. I'm guilty of it too—who hasn't jumped in with advice, convinced it's helpful? *Common Sense* says: sometimes, just listen. And yes, I'm also guilty of ignoring good advice now and then.

Thinking we don't need each other as Men&Women

(How can we make love, if we can't make amends?)

We *need* each other as humans on this earth, and we've always needed each other—men and women—for centuries, and that need will never disappear as long as we share the same space on this planet. If, for some reason, we were ever completely separated, we'd quickly realise how much we miss and rely on each other. When men and women are together, we tend to act on our best behaviour, striving to be better versions of ourselves—that's no secret. The goal is to grow together and to understand each other on a deeper level. After all, what's the fun in a relationship if it's too easy, right?

The misconception swirling around today is that we don't really *need* each other anymore. This modern notion tries to convince us that men and women are completely self-sufficient on their own, and somehow that's supposed to be progress. The result? We've got people trying to replace meaningful connections with the latest self-help trend or some over-glorified sense of independence. Sure, we're equal under the right conditions, but that doesn't mean we're the same.

This idea that we can do everything alone strips away the natural balance—the masculine and feminine roles that have always complemented each other. Modern feminism, for example, can sometimes come off like it's saying, "I've got balls too!" Great, but that doesn't mean men suddenly don't matter, or that mutual respect between the sexes is some outdated concept. And on the flip side, there's toxic masculinity, where men are taught to suppress emotions and act like they don't need women for anything more than surface-level interaction. Both extremes miss the point entirely.

It's almost as if we're allergic to admitting that we *need* each other. Men have been conditioned to think that showing emotion or asking for help is weak, while women are pushed to believe they need to prove they can handle everything on their own. The truth is, though, we're not supposed to be superheroes. We're supposed to support each other, acknowledge each other's strengths, and fill in where the other lacks.

When we ignore that and try to act like lone wolves, it only leads to frustration, misunderstandings, and a deeper sense of isolation. Society's new motto seems to be, "Who needs the opposite sex when I've got me?"

Well, let's be honest—there's only so much self-love and empowerment can do before you realise it's okay to need someone else. Wanting connection isn't a weakness; it's human.

And then, there's the blame game. Not every man or woman is responsible for your personal baggage, yet somehow people think it's okay to blame an entire gender for their own bad experiences. Just because someone has a trait that reminds you of an ex or someone who hurt you doesn't mean they'll do the same. But instead of learning from these experiences, too many people chase excitement over stability, get burned, and then decide the entire opposite sex is trash. It's a vicious cycle that makes healing and building trust nearly impossible. Let's face it, thinking like that isn't just unproductive—it's downright self-sabotaging.

The truth is, true equality isn't about tearing each other down or competing—it's about acknowledging and respecting our differences, supporting each other's strengths, and finding a balance between masculine and feminine energy. Historically, men and women worked within traditional roles that allowed society to function smoothly. There was more respect, and we didn't see the opposite sex as an obstacle to "deal with." Instead, we were more competent in navigating relationships.

But now, with changing mindsets and societal shifts, we've lost that mutual respect and understanding. It's like we've overcorrected ourselves into a corner, and now some people genuinely believe we don't need each other at all. That mentality not only hurts relationships but also weakens the very fabric of society. Relationships are the backbone of families, and families are what build communities. When we lose sight of that, we lose sight of everything that makes us stronger together.

Common Sense tells us this: don't underestimate or disrespect the opposite gender. Not everyone is responsible for your past hurt, and not every interaction is an attack on who you are. We're different, and that's the point. Learn to work with those differences instead of letting them divide you. We're better together, and pretending otherwise is just a waste of time and energy—and makes you look stupid.

It is a ridiculous notion, never needing each other, don't you think?

Confusing Times

The way *Common Sense* has been eroding over the past two decades, especially in the Western world, is deeply concerning. We're in a time when people are so overwhelmed by their emotions that they can't even process them properly. Meanwhile, others seem blissfully unaware of the chaos around them, happy to live in their bubble of ignorance.

This has led to people spreading misguided ideas, forming groups based on shallow connections, and promoting illusions of belonging just because they're *"bored."* People are standing up for anything these days—not because it makes sense, but because it gives them something to do. Maybe it's protests with no real solutions, virtue-signalling campaigns, or jumping on the latest internet outrage. Everyone's got a cause, and half the time, it feels more like a hobby than an actual passion.

It's like being one of the last people who still sees value in a bit of old-fashioned decency, while others label you outdated for sticking to what's really just *Common Sense.* They call themselves *"progressive"* but often overlook the practical wisdom that keeps things from falling apart. Over the past 40 years in the West, the primary lessons have been to have fun and accept every liberal viewpoint—right or wrong—just so you're not seen as an *"oppressor."*

On top of that, countries—especially in the West—have become like vacation spots for anyone. We're told to accept whatever flows in, without question, no matter how much it might disrupt our way of life. It's gotten to a point where simply having an opinion that doesn't align with the latest trend makes you a target. It's ridiculous. We've grown too comfortable, too lenient. People are more concerned with being *liked* than being *right.* And social media? That's only made it worse.

Social media has turned us into validation addicts. People are obsessing over likes and shares more than real, tangible relationships. It's made us hyper-connected on the surface but deeply isolated at our core. We live in echo chambers where the smallest disagreement feels like a *personal attack.* Human connection used to be about empathy and understanding, but now it's reduced to emojis and hashtags. Instead of real conversations, we're stuck in cycles of outrage and mob mentality, where one mistake can ruin someone's life forever.

At the same time, people seem terrified of being wrong. Nobody wants to admit when they've messed up because apologizing is seen as weak. But here's the thing: being wrong is human, and apologizing shows strength, not weakness. Instead, we double down on bad takes and turn minor disagreements into full-scale battles, all to protect some fragile idea of pride.

And what's with this obsession with entitlement? Everyone seems to think they're owed success, respect, or attention without doing the work to earn it. It's like just existing should come with a standing ovation. But when the world doesn't hand over what they think they deserve, they lash out—blaming the system, society, or literally anything except themselves.

We've also lost the ability to focus on what matters. The environment's falling apart, inequality is everywhere, and communities are breaking down, but people are arguing over who wore it better or what some random celebrity tweeted five years ago. It's like we've replaced substance with triviality, and we wonder why everything feels so hollow.

Then there's this strange trend of treating kids like mini-adults who can handle decisions they're not remotely ready for. Childhood is meant to be a time for growth, learning, and figuring things out—not for carrying the weight of debates they barely understand. Yet, we expect them to take sides on complex issues or define themselves in ways they're not equipped to. It's madness.

And let's talk about this obsession with being offended. These days, people jump at the chance to be outraged, even when they don't fully understand the issue. Every little thing becomes a battle, and it's exhausting. Picking your battles is *Common Sense 101,* but apparently, we missed that memo.

Common Sense? It's the thing that reminds us to focus on what matters, to look past the noise, and to connect with what's real. It's not about being perfect or having all the answers—it's about having the clarity and courage to recognize what's true and act on it. If we stopped living in distractions and started listening to the voice of reason, we might finally find our way out of this chaos. It's not rocket science. It's just *Common Sense.*

It's just unnecessary chaos really.

Instinct to pull your Phone out

Ever find yourself reaching for your phone without even *thinking* about it? It's like some kind of bizarre reflex that kicks in the second there's a moment of downtime. Waiting in line at a coffee shop? Out comes the phone. Friend's running late? The phone's already in hand. Just finished watching a movie on Netflix? Time to check the other screen. And let's not even mention how many times you try to turn the phone on when it's dead. It's almost like people are *terrified* of being alone with their own thoughts for more than five seconds—and honestly, that's a bit of an error in the majority of modern humans.

And it's not even about being bored—you haven't had a chance to *get bored* yet! But there you are, scrolling through the same Instagram feed you checked two minutes ago, hoping something interesting magically appears. It's as if the phone's become this *lifeline* we all cling to, even though, let's be honest, most people would survive just fine without it—after a few panic attacks and maybe some therapy.

What's really hilarious is that people treat their phones like they're some life-sustaining force, yet they managed to exist perfectly well in the days of dial-up internet and flip phones. Think about it: humans built civilizations, crossed oceans, and, oh yeah, survived millions of years without needing to check notifications every two seconds. But now? Forgetting your phone at home is treated like a *life-or-death* crisis.

The second you realise it's not in your pocket, there's that moment of sheer panic, like you've been cut off from oxygen. Meanwhile, the rational part of your brain is screaming, *"Hey, it's just a piece of metal and glass! You're not gonna drop dead!"* But no, you still make a U-turn back home like it's an emergency retrieval mission. How did we go from thriving without even landlines to acting like we're one missed notification away from oblivion? It's absurd.

I looked into it, and it's wild how much phones have actually changed us. For starters, constantly checking them has *rewired* how we process information. The ability to focus for long periods is shrinking because we've trained our brains to crave quick hits of dopamine from notifications and social media. This scatter-brained way of thinking has made it harder to stay engaged with anything that doesn't deliver instant gratification. And don't even get me started on how attention spans have taken a nosedive.

Then there's how it's affecting human connection. People have become more withdrawn in real life, preferring the *safety* of a screen to the unpredictability of a real conversation. Phones have given us the *illusion* of being connected while actually pulling us further apart. It's easier to send a text than to sit through the messy emotions of a face-to-face talk, but that's making us lose touch with what it means to be truly present with someone else.

Put your phone down, not even a peek,
The real world can be fun, for a charger there is no need.
That reel or meme can wait, trust me, it's fine,
Life can be way more exciting, when you're offline. *(Sometimes.)*

But here's some *Common Sense:* the phone isn't life support—it's just a gadget. A really useful, really addictive gadget—but still just a gadget. People treat it like it's their entire world, but the truth is, they'd be fine without it. It might take a day or two of detox and a lot of fidgeting with empty hands, but hey, life would go on.

Try ditching it for a bit—embrace the silence, the awkwardness, and maybe even the *horror* of standing alone in a public place without a screen to hide behind. Because the world didn't end before smartphones, and it won't now. You might even realise the real world is kind of cool—quirks, flaws, awkwardness, and all—even if you have to face it without your tiny digital security blanket.

The irony is, that you'll probably Google a way to stay off your phone.

Clear Conscience

Ah, the elusive clear conscience. You know, that thing everyone talks about but not many seem to actually have these days. It's like trying to find a unicorn—*everyone says it exists, but no one's really seen it up close.* In a world where we're bombarded with distractions, responsibilities, and expectations, it's easy for your conscience to get clouded by all the noise. We're constantly juggling our personal ambitions, relationships, work drama, and let's not even get started on the digital world. So, *how many of us can honestly say we go to bed every night with a squeaky-clean conscience?* Not many.

Having a *clear conscience* isn't just about being morally pure or never doing anything wrong. It's about being *in tune* with your own sense of right and wrong and being able to live with the choices you make. That *inner voice* that either gives you the thumbs up or nags at you like a disappointed parent? *Yeah, that's the one.* The problem today is that most of us don't give it the time of day. We're too busy with *quick fixes,* chasing goals, or trying to live up to some external standard that we forget to check in with our own *moral compass.* And without that check-in, life becomes this constant internal struggle—like walking around with a *stone in your shoe* but never stopping to take it out.

The importance of a *Clear Conscience* can't be overstated. It's the key to living a life with *less stress, fewer regrets,* and a lot more *peace of mind.* When you can look yourself in the mirror and know you've done your best—even if things didn't turn out perfectly—it's liberating. It doesn't mean you're perfect, but it does mean you're in *harmony with yourself.* And in a world where so many people are *conflicted, guilt-ridden,* or just plain *confused,* a clear conscience is basically the *secret to a happier life.* So yeah, it's pretty important. You might want to dust yours off and give it a little attention.

And do you know what comes with a *clear conscience?* That would be *Common Sense,* ironically.

A clear conscience is a quiet confidence.

Today's Distractions

We are so distracted from banding together by everything around us that the phrase *"we are more connected than ever"* sounds almost laughable. Sure, language barriers have been broken, and the internet lets us reach across the globe in seconds, but the truth is, this connection is *surface-level.* You can be yourself, create what you like, sell it, or share it with the world, but that same access to *everything* is what's distracting us from *real unity.* People today spend too much time indulging in *instant gratification* because *everything* is so attainable. That's not necessarily bad, but life isn't just about *fun,* nor is it about working yourself into oblivion. It's about *balance,* something we seem to be missing but that's so *obvious.*

Too much fun can easily turn into addiction, where people chase highs and *dopamine hits* without looking for *deeper meaning.* It's like constantly feeding a sugar rush. Over time, this overindulgence can cause real harm, leading to a *chemical imbalance* in the brain. It's easy to get caught up in this cycle when *everything*—from social media to entertainment—is designed to *keep you hooked.* Scrolling on social media becomes a drug in itself, with endless posts and videos sucking hours from your day. You don't even notice the *time slipping away.* Common Sense says, *"moderation,"* but it's easier said than done when *everything's* tailored to keep you *distracted.*

On the flip side, too much work without balance also strips away your *humanity.* You may become a workaholic, throwing yourself into *robotic tasks* without taking time to live. Sure, if you love your job and find joy in hard work, that's ideal, but most people aren't that lucky. Grinding nonstop without room for *anything else?* That's a fast track to burnout. You need a balance between work and play, between *effort* and relaxation, but today's distractions make it difficult to find that *sweet spot.* We're either obsessed with doing *too much* or doing *nothing at all.*

And let's talk about *phones.* They're basically the *forbidden fruit* of modern life—like the apple that Eve bit into, tempting and full of promises.

Just like the *apple* on the back of so many phones, it's a symbol of how something small and *alluring* can change *everything.* You have access to *all the world's knowledge* in your pocket, yet what do most people use it for? Scrolling endlessly, consuming nonsense. The problem isn't the phone itself—it's how we *use* it. Our attention spans have *shrunk* because we can easily hop from one thing to another, never truly engaging with *anything.* We consume quick bits of content, but *none of it sticks.* It's a distraction from learning *real-life skills* or exploring *deeper ideas.*

The *algorithms* on your phone aren't innocent, either. They're built to keep you *glued to the screen,* feeding you more of what catches your attention. Every tap, click, and scroll is recorded and monetized by someone else. While you're scrolling, others are profiting, and all you get is a *fleeting* sense of satisfaction that vanishes as quickly as it came. What does that do to your ability to *focus?* It chips away at your patience, making it harder to concentrate on *meaningful things.* We're training ourselves to have the attention span of a *goldfish.*

We've been *distracted* from our real *missions* in life. Instead of connecting *deeply* with each other, we've become *consumers*—of things, of ideas, even of people. Relationships are now treated like *commodities,* where we take what we want and move on to the next without building any *meaningful bonds.* It's no wonder people feel more *isolated* and disconnected than ever, even though we're supposedly *"more connected."* And those at the top? They knew this would happen. They've tapped into our psychology and figured out that the fastest way to keep people *content* is with quick mental thrills at the *tap of a finger* but obviously, you can't blame *everything* on others—there is a thing called *accountability* for your actions that's essential to have, *let's be honest.*

The *Common Sense* that's missing here? It's knowing when to *step back.* It's maybe realising that life is about *balance*—between work, fun, and *meaningful connections.* If we keep letting distractions rule us, we'll lose sight of what *really matters* and might feel trapped in *limbo.*

Why be such a Pussy?

What we're seeing today is a world that seems *allergic* to a firm backbone, where *Common Sense* has been swapped out for *emotional hypersensitivity.* It's like the entire population is being taught to *play it safe,* to avoid any conflict or discomfort at all costs. This *"don't rock the boat"* mentality is dressed up as tolerance and progressiveness, but underneath it, people are *afraid to say what they really think* or even stand up for what's right. It's no wonder we're turning into *soft, fragile versions of ourselves.* Being told to tolerate every extreme viewpoint or lifestyle, even when it clashes with your core values, is not only exhausting but downright oppressive to those who still believe in a bit of *old-fashioned decency, respect,* and *Common Sense, are labledd outdated?*

One reason for this *mass pussification* is the over-saturation of political correctness and the internet. You're constantly being told *how to think* and *what to accept,* and if you don't comply, you're branded a bigot or a hater. Even when you have a *valid point,* voicing your thoughts against a prevailing liberal agenda gets you labelled. What kind of *bollocks* is that? It's like *walking on eggshells* everywhere you go. This isn't just an issue of free speech, it's an issue of being able to have a *real conversation* without fear of being publicly shamed or ostracized. People are so terrified of offending others that they'd rather stay silent, contributing to this *growing culture of wimps* who are scared to even have opinions.

Take standing up against extreme religious views, for example, or suggesting that immigrants adapt to a more *open-minded society,* and suddenly you're the enemy. No one's suggesting being a *dick* to people who just want a better life, but when it comes to *extremists?* It's *Common Sense* to put your foot down and demand proper integration. But say that out loud, and you'll find yourself labelled *intolerant* or *xenophobic.* Somehow, we've lost the ability to have *rational discussions* about real issues without everything turning into a drama-fueled fight. *Stupid, really.*

We live in a time when a *flood of information* is constantly being shoved down our throats, especially through social media algorithms designed to give us more of what we already believe. The result? We're stuck in *echo chambers,* only hearing opinions that match our own and becoming more polarized in the process. This makes it easier for governments and corporations to *manipulate public perception,* whether that's through sneaky additives in your food or distracting you with whatever viral trend is happening that day. And it's working—just look at how easily people get *distracted from real issues* by the next flashy piece of clickbait. Social media was supposed to be about *connection and enlightenment,* but instead, it's turned into a breeding ground for *wet wipes* too scared to stand up for anything real. But of course, it's not all people; *some still try and hold it down with a bit of Common Sense.*

The internet has become a *toxic stew* where extremist views, whether *far-left or far-right,* are amplified to the point where those in the middle—the ones using *logic and Common Sense—*are now the minority. *How insane is that?* You'd think in a supposedly *"progressive"* world, standing up for what you believe in would be the norm. Instead, it's become some kind of *rebellious act* to just have an opinion that isn't *pre-approved by the internet police.* It's as if being *sensible and balanced* while expressing a point that people could somewhat agree on is a dying art, reserved for the *rare few* who still have the guts to speak their minds.

The real issue at the heart of all this? People are *terrified* of offending anyone. We've become so desperate to be *liked and not cancelled* that we've lost our spines. Now, expressing a simple truth feels like a *bold stance,* and if you're not careful, you could be crucified online for it. But here's the truth: *not everyone is going to like you,* and that's perfectly fine. Life's too short to compromise your values or *bend over backwards* to please everyone—it'll only leave you *exhausted and frustrated.* And why does the internet have *so much hold over you?*

At the end of the day, the *lack of Common Sense* is the root of all this. If people used a bit more of it, maybe we wouldn't be so *fragile.*

The Power of Gratitude

Gratitude—it's one of those things that gets tossed around a lot, often reduced to empty platitudes like *"Count your blessings"* or *"Be grateful."* But beneath all the clichés, it has real depth and power. It's more than just saying *thank you;* it's a mindset that shifts your focus from what's *missing* in life to what's *already there.* Gratitude connects to faith in something greater, whether that's a *higher power* or just the larger flow of life. Being grateful, even for challenges, can help you see value in tough times and find balance, no matter how chaotic things get. Many spiritual traditions view gratitude as a way to stay *grounded* or connected to the *divine,* but its impact goes beyond just faith.

Gratitude has tangible effects on the brain that people don't often *realise.* Practising it regularly boosts *dopamine* and *serotonin* levels, making you feel happier and more resilient. It even lowers *cortisol,* the stress hormone that keeps you on edge. So, being thankful is like a mental workout that strengthens your *emotional health.* And when it comes to relationships, expressing *genuine appreciation* deepens connections and builds trust. It's one of the simplest ways to make someone feel *valued,* maybe even turning casual relationships into lasting bonds.

The thing is: gratitude isn't about *ignoring reality* or pretending everything's great when it's not. It's about shifting your focus to acknowledge the *good,* no matter how small, even in tough situations. When you practice gratitude, you train your mind to see *opportunities* instead of problems.

It doesn't take much effort and can have a profound impact on your well-being and relationships. It's not about turning a blind eye to what's wrong; it's about recognising what's *right* and using that as a foundation. Here's some *Common Sense:* gratitude is free, easy to practice, and powerful enough to shift your entire outlook. It's a tool everyone has access to, and you don't need to believe in any philosophy to make it work—just in *yourself.* Give it a try.

You're alive—that's shit to be grateful for.

Modern pay Gap

A lot of jobs today are seen as *undesirable* and *unappreciated.* Everyone wants a high-paying gig with minimal effort, a mindset driven by seeing others live *lavishly* online with just a few clicks. It used to be about how *fulfilling* or *interesting* your job was, but now it's all about *how much you make.* While there's nothing wrong with wanting financial comfort, the balance is off. If everyone's chasing the *easy life,* who's going to build and maintain the infrastructure? Hard-working men and women are *essential* to keeping society running, yet they're often the ones struggling to make ends meet. Meanwhile, others make a fortune through social media by doing little more than uploading a few pictures or shouting at the camera on streams.

The *employment system* is a mess. People who contribute *real value*—those in healthcare, education, and skilled labour—are *undervalued,* while influencers and streamers, who often contribute little, are treated like celebrities. The over-sexualization of everything and the normalization of quick, easy money has turned employment into a game of who can get rich the fastest, *regardless of the societal cost.* We've lost appreciation for *honest,* skilled work. The constant chase for the *next big thrill* has replaced the satisfaction of doing something *meaningful,* leaving those in essential jobs feeling sidelined.

And so, if you have a job that doesn't get the spotlight, don't feel *discouraged.* If you're working hard, progressing in your own way, and earning an honest living, you're doing something *valuable.*

Common Sense tells us that society needs to shift its focus back to respecting those who keep the world turning—those who *build, teach,* and *maintain* what we all rely on. The modern pay gap isn't just about money; it's about a *skewed system* that rewards superficiality while overlooking *real contributions.* We need to start valuing *meaningful work* again before the gap widens any further.

It's not fair, is it?

Why is everything so GAY these days?

Why is everything so *gay* these days? And no, I don't mean in a sexual way—I'm talking about the over-the-top, overly sensitive, performative nonsense that's infiltrated nearly every corner of life. Why do straight people, normal gay people, and trans folks who just want to live their lives have to suffer through all this "progressive" woke bollocks? Why do we have to watch grown adults and the *"in-betweeners"* prancing around on national TV in front of kids, calling it progress? What does that even have to do with anything, let alone the 2024 Olympics? It's like the world elites are plundering humanity for their twisted agenda—*"the more we let people just outright act however they want, the more we can string them along"*—it's mad, really.

And why can you get cancelled just for speaking the truth? Why might this book even get me in trouble? It's insane how everyone's expected to be so *"tolerant"* of the most ridiculous viewpoints, but if you dare have an opinion that challenges the status quo, suddenly you're the enemy. Why is the world obsessed with over-sexualization? Why is there a constant war between extreme left and right ideologies? Why are grown, naked people parading through the streets with kids watching, thinking it's all normal? Calling it body positivity. *Like, mate.* Why do I have to worry so much about hurting someone's feelings when no one seems to care about my coherent opinion? But whatever you say is valid? The world has become a weird place, full of unskippable ads, unending confusion, and blatant manipulation by the media and those in power. Just *GAY,* really.

What's happened to the basics? Masculinity is seen as oppressive, femininity has been twisted beyond recognition, and everything is a performance. We're constantly at each other's throats, fighting pointless battles when, in reality, we're all stuck on this rock together. Society has become so safe and cushioned for these super-left individuals that it's made them delusional. They think their overly progressive opinions should be respected as gospel. *Common Sense* has gone missing here, plain and simple.

And then there's the new wave of people banding together online, like some sort of keyboard warriors who demand that everything caters to their every whim. Boredom has become something society can't stand—everything has to be hyper, colourful, and exciting, and if you dare question it, you're labelled old-fashioned or worse—*a plain old normal person*. A lot of this stems from the erosion of masculinity, which has been under attack for the last two decades.

Men have been told their natural instincts are oppressive, that their traditional roles are outdated, and they've played right into it. It's an absolute joke. How can a society function when the very people who build and maintain its infrastructure are being pushed aside?

The truth is, we need to get back to basics. Men need to stand up again—not out of ego but because it's the right thing to do. Once people, especially men and some women, reclaim their role in society, relationships between men and women will improve, and we'll see respect return as a driving force in how we interact. We're in a critical period of history, one that could go either way—better or worse. It's honestly scary to see how far off track things have gone, and even scarier to think that people in power are encouraging it. Subcultures that once stayed on the fringes now run the show, pushing delusional ideas that make no sense in the real world. Thinking you can float through life like some blissed-out hippie without consequences is a fool's dream unless you're off the grid entirely.

If we don't make a real effort to bring back *Common Sense,* the damage will ripple through generations. Kids are growing up in a world where feelings outweigh facts, where self-control is considered outdated, and where being offended is treated as a virtue. These aren't small issues—they're fundamental. How can young people learn resilience, responsibility, or even basic reasoning if they're constantly being told the world will bend to their every whim? They won't. They'll grow into adults who can't handle challenges or accept that life isn't always fair.

To fix this mess, we need to focus on values that actually build something meaningful: accountability, respect, and integrity. We need to create a culture that encourages honest dialogue, not one that silences it. If we teach kids the importance of facing hard truths and standing firm in reality—even when it's uncomfortable—we might stand a chance at turning this around. It won't be easy, but it's necessary. If we don't, we'll be handing the next generation a society that's even more confused and divided than it already is, and just imagine, how *GAY* would that be?

Wake up people! They're turning everything *GAY*—again, not in the sexual sense—and making genuine love between men and women seem strange. *Common Sense* would tell you to stay Wake, not *"rainbow woke,"* and be aware of this mess. This isn't just about grown adults—this is about protecting the next generation. Our kids are watching all this, and what kind of future will they have if we don't set things right? Very soon.

The Power of Truth

"The truth will set you free" isn't just a cliché; it's reality. *The truth is the objective world around you*, not just how you *feel* about it. Embracing it helps you *navigate life and find your path*, but it's not always easy. *You'll be tested* to see if you can handle the truth and push through. If standing by your truth *causes friction*, yet remains *fair and just*, don't back down—*keep going*. *Protect your truth*, but do so without causing harm. The challenge is *finding balance:* holding onto what's right while *working with others for a better future*. Not everyone's truth will align, but *Common Sense tells us that staying grounded in honesty* and making an effort to connect is how we all move forward. It's not glamorous but necessary, *hurtful at times* and *kind of always respected*.

Lies & In denial

When you *tell a lie* or deny the truth, even if it seems harmless, you end up *distorting your own reality*. This not only makes others see you as untrustworthy, but it also *messes with your own life*. Things get even trickier when *emotions are involved*. Think about it: if you give someone false hope and you share a close bond, your lives are pretty connected. If you lie to them, they might *pick up on it but still trust you*. But when the *truth eventually comes out—and it always does*—it could be too late to fix things. This can make you look *unreliable*, and the other person will end up *hurt*, which might lead them to lie to or struggle to trust anyone else. *Common Sense? Don't lie, init, even if it's tough.* It's way better to know where you stand with someone than to leave them guessing. *You've got to do better.*

Deep init?

Consumerism

This one is really self-explanatory if you think about it and live in modern society. We've made almost everything expendable and are conditioned to consume that way as well. When you hear of the older generations, they always emphasise how they were taught not to waste things and how to store food for winter. More often than not, you hear stories about the hard work it took to survive the year. They knew how to make food last, understood the importance of developing survival skills, kept their communities tight-knit, and recognised the value of helping each other and not wasting anything. It was about sustainability and mutual support, not endless consumption.

Nowadays, it feels like we're all kids in a candy shop—once we try something a few times, it's time to move on to the next good-looking thing. We've lost the appreciation for both new and old things, swapping it for constant expectation and instant gratification. How far will we take this until it becomes our downfall? Maybe we'll be okay, and the world will keep advancing to a point where we can consume as much as we want without any repercussions. But history shows us that unchecked consumerism leads to resource depletion, environmental degradation, and a loss of meaningful connections.

It's not just goods and gadgets—we're consuming *everything.* Entertainment, ideas, even relationships have become part of this cycle. Streaming platforms churn out endless content we barely remember watching. Social media feeds us half-digested opinions that we like, share, and forget in minutes. Even our interactions with people feel transactional—if they don't bring instant value or entertainment, we're quick to swipe past them. This mindset seeps into every corner of life, turning experiences and connections into commodities. And honestly? It's exhausting.

We have to be better and actually learn skills that let us survive when nothing else is going well in society. Instead of being content consumers, we should try to develop resilience and adaptability. Modern society is turning us into robots who need constant maintenance in the form of memes and the newest technology to stay *"in the flow,"* but this is so wrong and goes against our human nature. *Common Sense* is to live within your means and understand that you don't need the newest gadget or some material thing to be happy—at least not straightaway.

Try not to look at people as expendable objects; instead, see them as sources of learning and growth. Learn life skills that allow you to survive and connect with others on a deeper level. It's about balancing enjoyment with responsibility, ensuring that our consumption doesn't come at the cost of our humanity.

We act or treat others like wet wipes—quickly disposable and easily discarded—but we need to start valuing what truly matters. Embrace a lifestyle that fosters meaningful connections and sustainable practices, or at least, that's the idea. Ensuring that we don't sacrifice our humanity for the sake of endless consumption. It's time to get real, prioritise wisely, and live with intention rather than impulse. Harsh, right?

At the end of the day, *Common Sense* tells us to slow down and reassess our priorities, valuing quality over quantity and sustainability over instant gratification. However, some people thrive in consumerism, using it strategically to fuel their growth and success. It's not about rejecting it entirely—it's about knowing how to balance consumption wisely, making it work for you without letting it control your life. That's easier said than done, but it's not an excuse.

It can be hard, living in a capitalistic world that's made to consume.

We swipe, we buy, we toss away,

Chasing the newest toy each day.

But what if we paused to truly see,

The worth in things, and maybe humanity?

Ask yourself sometimes, do I truly need this?

Religious Extremists

In the 2020s—and it's only a fourth year in—we've seen it all, or at least it feels that way. Every year, the world gets a little stranger, and the Western world seems determined to lead the charge into chaos. One of the most glaring examples? The way immigration is handled. Those in control thought it would be a *brilliant idea* to lower their standards. And by lower, I mean practically erase.

People who follow the proper immigration process have to wait years, jumping through endless bureaucratic hoops, only to face the possibility of being denied. Meanwhile, if you arrive on a boat or walk over the border, it seems you're rewarded with hotel accommodations and allowances to tide you over. Isn't that nice? It's like the West has turned immigration into a "come one, come all" holiday package, complete with perks and minimal accountability.

It's not about being anti-immigration—it's about recognising the difference between controlled entry and chaos. What's worse is that many of those welcomed in bring their own cultural standards without adapting to the Western way of life. At the same time, some in the West fiercely resist any attempts to blend cultures. This results in a growing tension that no one seems willing to address properly. The result? A mess that's slowly but surely overwhelming society, while those in charge ignore the long-term implications.

And then there's the issue of religious extremists. Certain groups have no respect for other beliefs, let alone the cultural norms of the countries they've entered. Their rigid views clash violently with Western ideals, creating friction wherever they go. What's ironic is that Christianity—once the bedrock of Western culture—used to provide a common framework. It kept other ideologies in check and created a shared moral foundation.

But over the last 40 years, Christianity has been sidelined. It's no longer seen as relevant, and that void has been filled by conflicting ideologies. While the West prides itself on being progressive and inclusive, it's become a place where its own culture and traditions are left unprotected. It's a society in a constant state of flux, so desperate to evolve that it never solidifies. This could be the early stages of true globalisation—where every identity is diluted into one—but it also risks becoming a free-for-all that undermines the very values it claims to protect.

The damage doesn't stop there. All of this constant bending and accommodating is eroding the foundations of Western societies. People are scared to speak up, afraid of being labelled intolerant or worse. So, they stay silent as traditions, values, and even basic standards of decency are chipped away.

And yes, traditional masculinity has taken a hit, too, but let's keep it brief. Masculinity, once a symbol of protection and strength, has been painted as oppressive and outdated. Men are being told their instincts are harmful, leaving them unsure of their place. This doesn't just harm men—it harms society. Without confident, assertive individuals of *any gender* willing to stand up and lead, everything starts to crumble.

The problem isn't just one thing—it's everything. Immigration without integration. Religious extremism clashing with secular values. A society too afraid of offending anyone to say what's necessary. This cocktail of issues isn't just challenging—it's destructive. It throws every system into disarray, leaving people confused, disillusioned, and too divided to push back against it all.

So, what's the answer? *Values.* The kind that promotes stability, responsibility, and respect. A society needs to protect its culture while adapting in ways that make sense. It needs to be honest about what works and what doesn't, without sacrificing its identity for the sake of looking progressive. If we don't take steps to solidify what we stand for, future generations will inherit a world without a strong cultural backbone. That's a recipe for chaos—divided communities, weakened nations, and a lack of trust in the systems meant to protect us all.

To bring back balance, we need people willing to speak up. People who aren't afraid to say, "This isn't working" or "This goes against the principles that built this society." It's not about being exclusionary—it's about being real. The West can't save itself by throwing everything away in the name of inclusivity. If it does, there won't be anything left to include.

At the end of the day, *Common Sense* has to prevail. Protect what's worth protecting. Value what brings people together. And don't be afraid to call things out when they're clearly broken. The West was built on resilience and adaptability, but it can't survive if no one's willing to fight for its core values

Bit of a sticky one, stilllll.

Unnecessary Information

Until about 25 years of age, you are like a sponge, soaking up vast amounts of information about almost anything you encounter in life—especially if you're passionate about the subject or naturally good at remembering details. Lifelong learning is essential for personal growth, no matter your age. However, today's world presents a significant challenge: most of your attention is constantly diverted by the endless stream of information online.

Whether it's updates on your favourite topics or fleeting nuances that capture your eye, the digital landscape offers an overwhelming amount of content. This ties in with today's *Distractions* chapter earlier in the book, where we discussed how focusing on one thing at a time leads to mastery, in a nutshell. Yet, it's so much easier to pull out your phone and scroll whenever the mood strikes. This habitual scrolling consumes mental space that could otherwise be used to learn or engage with content that truly advances your life and keeps you satisfied.

You are what you watch and listen to the most. If all the information you consume is just the surface level of your interests, what are you really gaining? Almost anytime I'm in public, I see people of all ages endlessly scrolling through their phones, consuming content they saw just minutes ago. This constant cycle of short-term engagement has changed how we interact with information.

I, the author, am not immune to this behaviour, but as I grow older, I become more aware of the detrimental effects of aimless scrolling. It erodes our ability to focus deeply and engage meaningfully with content that could enhance our knowledge and personal growth. Instead, we waste hours on trivial pursuits, leaving our minds cluttered and our potential untapped. But, don't get me wrong, we all need to stay updated to some extent.

Moreover, the barrage of unnecessary information is not just a mental drain—it's reshaping our social interactions and decision-making processes.

With information overload, we often rely on quick judgments and superficial understandings, leading to poorer decisions both personally and professionally. This phenomenon, called *Decision Fatigue,* happens when you're constantly exposed to trivial information, impairing your ability to make thoughtful, informed choices.

Understanding how to filter and prioritise the information we consume is crucial for maintaining our mental clarity and ensuring that our decisions are based on meaningful insights rather than fleeting distractions. As we move forward, recognising the impact of unnecessary information will empower us to take control of our cognitive resources and lead to living more intentional lives.

It's not just about making better decisions—it's about reclaiming the joy of learning and engaging with the world in a deeper way. Imagine how much more fulfilling life could be if we replaced some of the time spent on endless scrolling with activities that spark genuine curiosity, challenge us to grow, or teach us something new. Learning is meant to be immersive and enriching, not diluted by a never-ending stream of dopamine hits as soon as you wake up.

To combat this, actively restrict your phone usage to activities that genuinely benefit you, such as educational games or setting up your device to prioritise essential information. You don't need to know every new place to explore if it doesn't align with your life's mission, nor do you need to keep up with every trivial update about your neighbour's dog or your favourite celebrity's daily antics.

We should also remember the importance of intentional downtime—time spent without distractions, letting the mind wander or focus on a single meaningful thought. This quiet reflection is where creativity and insight often thrive, but the noise of constant connectivity is drowning it out.

Common Sense dictates that you are the main character in your own life story, so be mindful of the information you feed your brain. Prioritise content that supports your goals and well-being, and let go of the rest. By doing so, you reclaim your mental space and focus on what truly matters, fostering a more fulfilling and purpose-driven life

It's like we're wired with this inbuilt urge to chase what we're not meant to or to click on something new the second it pops up—but recognising that impulse and staying in control is where the real strength lies.

Crazy right?

Over Sexualisation

Sex is a part of life—one of our primal instincts. It serves so many purposes: easing stress, connecting on a deeper level (*no pun intended*), passing the time when we're bored, expressing emotions like anger or love, and, of course, creating life. Some people need it more than others, some less. Some spice it up with objects, kinks, or roleplay because that gets them going. And honestly, none of that is a problem—unless it's non-consensual, abusive, or directed toward a child. If it is, you need help, *fast.*

But here's where it gets complicated: the lines between healthy sexual expression and the overblown obsession we see today have become completely blurred. Getting to know someone without the immediate expectation of sex? Practically a relic of the past. The internet has made sure of that. Sexual content is everywhere, just a tap or a swipe away, and it's reshaping how we think about sex. Instead of intimacy being about connection, it's now a performance. You're judged on how well you keep up, how satisfied you leave someone, and how desirable you appear. It's hypersexuality masked as empowerment, but it's driven by something far less glamorous—chemical imbalances in the brain that make people think sex equals self-worth.

This is where it starts to go wrong. Sex is a part of life, yes, but it's not *everything.* Yet today's hypersexualised culture makes it feel like it is. Ads, songs, influencers, movies—all pushing the idea that if you're not constantly turned on, constantly having sex, then you're missing out. And the powerful people who run the show? They don't care, as long as they can profit. Whether it's through pleasure products, porn companies, or industries built on selling fantasies, they thrive on keeping people distracted and dependent. But all this does is damage our ability to form real, meaningful relationships.

When sex is overemphasised, it rewires how we approach connection. Porn addiction is a prime example. The brain becomes hooked on artificial stimulation—exaggerated scenarios that real-life intimacy can never match. It's like fast food for your mind: instant gratification with zero substance. Over time, this dependency makes people lose touch with reality, chasing highs that real relationships can't provide. And it doesn't stop at physical pleasure; it bleeds into expectations. Unrealistic depictions of sex warp how people think intimacy works. Emotional connection becomes secondary, if it's even considered at all.

This disconnect creates intimacy anxiety, where people struggle to connect on a deeper level because their ideas of love and sex have been shaped by hypersexualised fantasies. They can't let themselves be vulnerable because they don't even know what that looks like anymore. It's not just a personal issue—it's a societal one. Entire generations are growing up with distorted views of intimacy, love, and respect.

And here's the kicker: this hypersexual culture doesn't just affect individuals—it changes how we treat each other. Women often feel reduced to body parts, their worth tied to how attractive they appear or how well they "perform." Men, on the other hand, are treated like machines—expected to perform on demand, to prove their masculinity through sex, and to keep up with impossible standards. Neither side wins in this scenario. Both lose their humanity, their ability to connect, and their sense of self.

For women, the disconnection can run deep. A woman who feels like her worth is tied to her body might start using sex as a tool—a way to gain validation or maintain control. Over time, her relationship with her body becomes more about performance than connection. She might even become hypersexual, prioritising pleasure over emotional intimacy, faking it till she feels it—but never quite getting there. And for men, the disconnection takes a different form. A man who treats sex as nothing more than a conquest might feel powerful in the moment, but over time, it leaves him empty. He becomes stuck in a loop, using sex to validate his ego while losing sight of what real intimacy feels like.

Then there's the next layer of this mess: the effect on younger generations. Kids as young as eight or nine are exposed to explicit content before they even understand what a healthy relationship looks like. That early exposure shapes how they think about intimacy, often in ways that leave lasting scars. They enter adulthood with skewed ideas of what love is, what boundaries are, and what respect should look like. By the time they're old enough to navigate relationships, they're already carrying a lifetime's worth of confusion.

And let's not forget the societal obsession with sexual status. Social media, TV, music—it all turns sex into a game of one-upmanship. Who's having the most? Who's the "best" at it? If you're not playing, you're losing—at least, that's the lie we're sold. But when did this basic biological function become a competition? The more we overindulge, the less fulfilling it becomes.

People get stuck in cycles of seeking validation through sex, forgetting how to find meaning in real connection. It's ridiculous, really. Sex is supposed to be a natural part of life, but we've turned it into an obsession, a 24/7 spectacle. Instead of enhancing our lives, it's becoming a distraction—a way to avoid dealing with the things that really matter. And while this culture claims to be about freedom and empowerment, it's more like a trap. It pressures people to play roles, to act like something they're not, just to keep up.

When we lose balance, we lose respect—for ourselves and each other. Sex stops being about connection and becomes a numbers game. It leaves people feeling empty, disconnected, and always searching for something more. The lines between healthy expression and toxic overindulgence are so blurred now that it's hard to tell where one ends and the other begins. It's exhausting—and it's everywhere.

Common Sense? If this chaotic, modern, digital orgy has taught us anything, it's that balance matters. Real connection comes from authenticity, not performance. Respecting yourself and others is the key to stepping out of this cycle of overindulgence and reclaiming what intimacy was meant to be.

**Sex sells, and we're buying the lie,
Chasing the high while letting love die.**

**Swipe for pleasure, scroll for fame,
Connection lost in a crowded game.**

**But behind the screens and the noise we see,
We're all just longing to feel *truly* loved and free.**

Think about it.

The Downfall of Modern Dating

Take modern dating, for example. It's reached an almost laughable level of superficiality, regardless of age. The Western dating scene is sliding downhill, and fast. It's not that people aren't dating; it's that they've lost the plot on what makes a genuine connection. With our phones offering endless options at the tap of a screen, dating has turned into a candy shop for some—always looking for the next best thing or skipping out altogether. Relationships are being treated like browsing Netflix: if one option doesn't grab attention in five minutes, people move on. It's absurd, but that doesn't mean you shouldn't date—it's more about knowing if the current state of dating works for you.

Some people still date with purpose, seeking meaningful connections and striving to be decent to each other, but they're becoming rarer than *Common Sense* itself. Most people seem fixated on instant gratification or ticking boxes based on shallow standards. The problem? Meaningful relationships don't thrive on superficiality. They require time, effort, and compromise—all of which are in dangerously short supply these days.

This is where the concept of "hoeflation" comes in. No, it's not a fad diet—it's the reality that modern men have to work three times harder to attract the same quality of partner that their grandfathers could have while just being a decent, average Joe. Even slightly above-average men are struggling to keep up. Thanks to the internet, women now have access to an endless buffet of options and are often chasing the top 10% of men. Women are incredibly capable and adaptable, but this capability has driven expectations to sky-high levels that most men simply can't meet, no matter how hard they try.

And then there's hypergamy, the age-old practice of seeking a partner who is of higher socioeconomic or social status. Historically, this instinct made sense—it was about security and upward mobility. But today, hypergamy has been supercharged by social media. Women are often swiping left on the steady, dependable 9-to-5 guy while swiping right on the quick thrill, even if he's living at his mum's house—or the guy who gets them all. It's all gone out of proportion. The issue with hypergamy today isn't just about financial security or social status; it's the way it amplifies dissatisfaction.

Social media paints idealised pictures of perfect lives and partners. Creating a sense that there's always something better out there. This fuels unrealistic expectations and makes stable, fulfilling relationships harder to achieve. Hypergamy might be rooted in human nature, but in today's fast-paced dating world, it's contributing to a toxic cycle of perpetual dissatisfaction.

At the same time, we've seen traditional masculinity labelled as toxic, especially during the rise of PC culture between 2013 and 2016. Men were told to tone it down—be softer, quieter, and less assertive—as if basic assertiveness and strength were inherently harmful. Masculinity became a target, even when it was just about being straightforward or standing up for oneself. The result? A generation of men who feel lost, confused, and stuck, unsure of how to balance strength with the sensitivity now demanded of them.

This shift has left many men feeling more like boys—*wet wipes,* really—unsure of their roles in society. Governments and elites have reinforced this narrative, pushing passivity as the ideal while sidelining traditional masculine traits that once played a key role in maintaining balance.

But here's the thing: *Common Sense* shows us that men and women need each other more than ever. It's not about competing or tearing each other down—it's about finding balance. Relationships thrive when there's mutual respect and an understanding of each other's roles, not when people are pitted against one another in some battle of the sexes.

If we can start valuing authenticity over superficial standards and connection over competition, maybe the dating scene won't feel like such a minefield. Men and women can work together to find harmony in this chaos, but it's going to take a shift away from the endless swiping, the sky-high expectations, and the misplaced sense of entitlement that's become so common today.

How can we be lovers, if we can't be friends?

Coding Genetics?

Coding Genetics" might sound like some sci-fi movie plot about altering DNA to create superhumans, but no, it's not about designing perfect babies in a lab. Instead, it's about the ridiculous idea that people think they can just mentally *"recode"* what it means to be a man or a woman, like human biology is some app you can reprogram because you don't like the default settings. The claim? If you just change your mindset and redefine words, suddenly, biology will magically follow suit. But newsflash: no matter how much you want to *"recode"* your perception of gender, it doesn't change the genetics running through your body. *Chromosomes don't care about your feelings,* aw poor you, right?

Sure, people can choose to identify however they want, and that's up to them. But what's absurd is trying to argue that perception somehow overwrites biology. It's like saying, "I'm going to redefine the concept of gravity so I can float." Cool story, but try jumping off a building and see how well your new definition works. Men and women are different on a cellular level. It's not just about body parts or appearance; it's how every cell in your body is structured, how hormones regulate your development, and how genes influence everything from muscle mass to brain structure. This isn't something you can rewire by changing pronouns or rewriting definitions.

Here's the thing: just because you change the way you view something doesn't mean you've actually changed what it is. It's like putting a label that says *"cat"* on a dog and then insisting it'll start meowing. Words and labels don't change reality; they just change how people talk about it. The whole concept of *"coding genetics"* like it's some flexible software is delusional. Biology doesn't work that way, obviously. You can wear what you want, act how you want, and live your life as you see fit, but chromosomes, genes, and biology are set in stone. You can't just decide to *"code"* your way out of being a man or a woman because it doesn't suit your personal narrative, it's just *Common Sense,* like common people, think about it.

Weird, right?

We are not Equal! As Men&Women

Men and women were made differently for good reasons—no need to tiptoe around it. This isn't about superiority; it's just biology and basic *Common Sense.* The truth is, modern feminism, originally about empowerment and breaking down barriers, has shifted into a competition of who's more oppressed, where any mention of gender differences is seen as an attack. The idea that men and women are the same in every way not only misses the point but also dismisses the incredible strengths and roles each brings to the table. Acknowledging these differences isn't outdated—it's *practical* and rooted in reality.

Both genders deserve equal rights and respect, but that doesn't mean they're identical. Men and women *complement* each other in ways that are essential for a thriving society: men are often physically stronger, more willing to take risks, and built for endurance, while women excel in empathy, emotional intuition, and multitasking. These strengths don't compete—they balance each other out, much like a hammer and a screwdriver—both critical tools but designed for different tasks. Trying to erase these differences under the guise of progress only creates imbalance. Pushing men to be less masculine or expecting women to adopt every masculine trait doesn't create equality; it breeds burnout, confusion, and resentment on both sides.

We see the consequences all around us: men feeling lost and aimless, told their masculinity is "toxic" without being given a clear path to embrace their strengths in a positive way. Meanwhile, women are overwhelmed by societal expectations that deny their natural strengths, pushing them to pursue roles and behaviours that may not align with who they are. The result? Neither gender wins in this unrealistic pursuit of sameness, and society loses the balance that these complementary traits once provided.

Men need to step up—*responsibly and with care*—embodying strength that uplifts, protects, and supports, not suppresses or dominates. At the same time, women should feel empowered to lead, nurture, and thrive without abandoning the qualities that make them exceptional. Strength doesn't mean erasing differences; it means embracing them in ways that benefit everyone.

Common Sense? Men and women are different, and that's a *good* thing! These differences are not flaws—they're *features* of our design that are meant to balance and enhance each other's lives. True equality respects these differences, valuing the unique contributions that each gender brings.

Today's Individualism

Throughout history, whenever societies became too comfortable, individuals often started focusing *too much* on themselves. Whether due to the ease of living or a general apathy towards others, this shift usually marked the beginning of the downfall of empires and people alike. Ancient civilizations, from Rome to the Mayans, had moments when individualism and self-interest led to their collapse.

Today, we enjoy the luxury of *"being ourselves,"* but let's not forget that this freedom rests on the backs of countless people who died for peace. It's a luxury they didn't have, and yet we often embody the *"take, take, take, stay away"* mentality. Society teaches us this too. The system runs on *"if it doesn't make money, it doesn't make sense,"* warping how we view human interaction and community. We've become obsessed with personal gain while forgetting that true fulfilment comes from shared experiences and helping each other.

We've been conditioned to disconnect from the bigger picture, to treat relationships and community like optional accessories. Getting involved in the right settings—like trying to make real connections or doing something for the greater good—can actually make people see you as odd. It's like we're all stuck in this paradox: we're all alone in this together, but that togetherness doesn't feel real anymore.

Everyone seems to be in silent agreement that you've got to comply with the group mentality or get left behind. You have to give off the right energy, say the right things, or meet an arbitrary standard—otherwise, you're dropped without a second thought. This mindset creates a pressure cooker where people are constantly performing just to fit in, making genuine connections nearly impossible. We've become a culture of *cold detachment* masked by social niceties.

And that's the weird thing. In public, especially among younger generations, there's this strange tension. You sit next to someone, and it's like everyone is thinking, *"I've got this, I don't need your energy messing with me."*

Fair enough—no one wants bad vibes—but we've taken this self-centred approach so far that we now believe we're the *only* ones who matter. People walk through life acting like they're the centre of the universe, expecting the world to move out of their way.

It's not everyone, but it's common enough to see it everywhere. We've gotten so disconnected from each other that even basic social interactions feel like a threat to our personal space. The reality is, that we need each other a bit more than we're willing to admit.

Common Sense tells us that individualism, while important, shouldn't come at the cost of losing our collective humanity. *I mean I can't be the only one seeing it, right?* Maybe it's time we question this version of *"success"* we've all bought into. The one where self-worth is measured in isolation and where connection feels like an inconvenience instead of a necessity. If we continue down this road, our so-called freedom might eventually trap us in lives that feel emptier than ever.

Let's imagine a world where prioritising others doesn't make you naive, but wise. Where real wealth comes from the bonds we build, not just the things we collect. Maybe, just maybe, we'd start finding fulfilment in something deeper—*something real.* Because in the end, when we look back, it won't be the solitude we remember, but those moments when we truly shared the experience of being human.

Imagine how much further we could go if we truly stuck together, especially after seeing just how far we've already come when we've worked as one.

Everyone's busy playing their solo part,
But harmony's what really moves the heart.
What if together is where we should start,
And in the process, amend those lonely hearts?

We're drifting between connection and isolation.

Broken Hearts & Lost Souls

From what *I've seen,* it's crazy how we talk about *"broken hearts"* like it's just a poetic phrase when, in reality, it's a lot more literal than we think. Did you know that when your heart *"breaks,"* the body actually feels it? There's a medical condition called *"Takotsubo cardiomyopathy,"* or *"Broken Heart Syndrome,"* where intense emotional stress can cause your heart muscles to weaken and balloon out, leading to chest pain and shortness of breath.

So yeah, your *heartstrings literally fray and snap* like an old guitar being overplayed. And yet, in today's world, I see people going around breaking each other's hearts like it's no big deal. It's almost *trendy* to play it cool, ghost people, and shrug off emotional connections like they're disposable. But behind every *"no strings attached"* and *"it is what it is"* attitude, there's probably a person going home feeling like they've been run over by a train. And we all act like that's normal?

It's like we've convinced ourselves that if we pretend it doesn't hurt, then it really doesn't—meanwhile, we're leaving a trail of broken hearts in our wake. People dive headfirst into relationships only to pull the plug at the slightest inconvenience, tossing away connections without a second thought. From what *I've noticed,* everyone's gotten so used to the idea that emotions are a weakness, that showing you care too much is somehow embarrassing, and that putting yourself out there is just asking to get hurt. But that's how broken hearts lead to *lost souls.*

When you've been let down, discarded, or played one too many times, you start to lose your grip on what's real and what's just some social media façade. People end up disconnected, wandering through life trying to protect what little heart they have left, *afraid to trust or open up again.* They're like ghosts of their former selves—physically here, but *emotionally checked out,* hovering between trying to move on and being stuck in the past.

And that's when you get these *lost souls* walking around. They're still breathing, but it's like the light's gone out behind their eyes.

From what *I've observed,* people put up so many walls and tell themselves *"I'm fine"* so many times that they've sadly forgotten what it even feels like to be genuinely happy or fulfilled.

They numb the pain with distractions—chasing success, money, or *cheap thrills* that don't really satisfy.

Or worse, they bury themselves in *toxic relationships,* just so they don't have to face that gaping emptiness inside. It's like there's a *pandemic of lost souls*—people who've become so disconnected from their own hearts that they don't even know how to reach out to others anymore. We're all so close-knit as social creatures, but it's like there's a veil over love itself, making it hard to see or feel things clearly.

Now, of course, *I know* there are still those resilient types out there—the ones who've managed to avoid falling into the trap or have bounced back stronger than ever. Maybe they're just naturally resistant to all the bullshit, or maybe they know better than to let the world's mess get the best of them. They carry on, shrugging off heartbreaks like it's nothing more than a bump in the road. And let's be honest, you have to be resilient in this world, but not *too cold-hearted.*

You see, from what *I've noticed* though, for a lot of people, it's different. They're still hurting, still searching for something real in a world that tells them to move on and get over it before they've even had time to heal. It's like we're all just trying to hold it together, putting on these layers of *false confidence* to get through the day.

And then, on the other end of the spectrum, you've got the ones who've gone in the *complete opposite direction.* It's like losing that connection to real love has driven some people to *redefine it altogether.* Maybe that's why we've seen so many more *"super gay"* people lately, from the hardcore rainbow crew to left-wing politicians waving every colourful flag under the sun.

"Not saying there's anything wrong with it"—it's just interesting how losing touch with what used to be seen as traditional love can push people into embracing a whole new identity, something that feels genuine to them.

It's almost like an act of defiance against the heartbreak they've experienced like they're reclaiming their own version of what love means. It's strange how some people adapt to a nuance, just to feel love, *even if it doesn't make sense to themselves.*

Common Sense? Well, in the last decade or so, we pretended like heartbreaks don't mess people up. That *false "I'm fine"* act only works until it doesn't. And the worst part is, when you're broken, you've got to use that same broken energy to try and pull yourself back together—talk about adding *insult to injury.*

You don't get a prize for ignoring your feelings until you're a shell of a human, and screwing up someone else's emotional state just because it's *"easier"* to not care isn't a flex. Get a grip, try and stop *fucking people over so much,* like it's all just some game or some saddening simulation. Seriously, where's the *honour* in playing life like it's one big manipulation competition? We're all out here trying to survive, and causing collateral damage along the way just breeds more misery for everyone.

But at the same time, don't be a *muppet* and put your heart out there as soon as it feels good—that's really foolish. There's a balance to be struck between keeping your guard up and letting it down at the right moments. It's not about shutting down or over-exposing yourself but about having the *self-respect* to choose wisely. Learn to protect yourself with some *awareness* and, of course, *Common Sense.* Be smart enough to recognise who actually deserves your heart and who doesn't, because not every flutter of emotion is worth the investment. Sometimes, it's just your brain messing with you, *lighting up like a pinball machine over nothing meaningful.* Know the difference, and maybe, just maybe, you'll save yourself a world of unnecessary pain.

Broken hearts and lost souls,
Pieces scattered, never whole.

We laugh, we cry, we stumble on,
Chasing meaning where it's long gone.

But maybe the cracks let the light shine through,
A reminder we're broken—but still carry on too.

Be careful out there, you might never be the same.

Having something to Do

When you have *nothing going on* in life to the point where even your job or daily activities seem pointless, you might think, *"What's the point of trying?"* and become discouraged from doing anything that could lift you out of that *depressive bubble.* Claiming you have *nothing to do* often reveals your indifference to pursuing a fulfilled life or finding contentment. Like, who's responsible for *your* mood?

It also highlights the *hypocrisy* of wanting to explore new things while showing little initiative to actualize those desires, even when they align with your true interests. Ultimately, *you're the one who has to take action for yourself,* and the more you resist adapting to new skills or hobbies, the more useless you may feel—unless you're genuinely content and self-aware, but *today, it seems people are bored while having access to everything.*

We, as humans, are *natural creators, explorers,* and *doers.* However, today, you can watch someone else excel at something you'd like to learn and feel overshadowed because they've had *more practice* while you haven't even *tried.* This breeds a sense of futility: *"Why bother when someone else is already so good?"* but that's limited thinking.

And that's *missing the point.* We've become so conditioned to *instant gratification* and distracted by *quick consumerism* that we deny ourselves the chance to grow. It's like saying, *"Yeah, I know how to do that already; I watched a video on it,"* pretending to be a master without putting in the effort. This *lack of initiative* is a true reflection of our *modern societal soup.*

It's *stupidly simple:* when you have something meaningful to do in life—whether it's personal growth, creating something new, or engaging in a hobby—you can find a state of *flow.* The *Flow* is where time disappears, and you're so focused that it feels almost *healing.* It's where external pursuits meet *inner contentment,* making even a *shitty day* feel manageable.

To achieve this, you need to *actively seek fulfilment* and stay engaged, regardless of whether you're someone who learns easily or struggles with boredom. Finding a *balance* is crucial, but with *patience and persistence,* you'll discover that there's always *something new* around the corner to entertain and teach you something valuable. We're capable of *immense learning,* and neglecting to stay active only makes it harder to grow, leading to *stagnation* and unfulfilled desires.

Effort is a *universal truth.* You'd be surprised how quickly life's burdens can fade once you start doing something fulfilling—whether it's *helping others, learning a new skill, taking up a hobby,* or just exploring *who you are.* It's different for everyone, and yes, *it's hard,* but that's what makes it worthwhile. The *self-pride and sense of accomplishment* you gain from pushing through challenges *spill over* into other areas of your life, enhancing your *discipline* and *overall personal betterment.*

Try not to get *lost in what everyone else is doing* unless it genuinely keeps you optimal. Remember, *you are you, and no one else.* So take action! It's *Common Sense:* don't let *inactivity* turn you into a *stagnant vegetable.* Embrace the effort, and watch yourself transform into a *more capable and fulfilled* person. It's only hard if you don't somewhat enjoy it, *keep trying, init.*

At the core of it all, being human means embracing the freedom to choose—to create, to act, and to strive for more, even when it feels easier to stay still. Fulfilment isn't handed to anyone; it's built through intentional choices and consistent effort. Yes, life is overwhelming at times, and the temptation to give up or stay passive can be strong, but that's where the beauty of being human lies. You *can* choose. You can step into discomfort, learn, and grow, or you can let the world pass you by. The path isn't always clear or easy, but the simple act of trying is what keeps life meaningful. At the end of the day, it's a choice only you can make—because no one else will live your life for you.

**Lost in the stillness, we choose to remain,
But action's the spark that cuts through the chain.**

It's a choice.

Importance of Discipline

Ahh, everyone's *"favourite"* topic. Discipline is the yin to *Common Sense's* yang, the force that slaps you across the face when you feel like quitting. It's accountability for yourself, willpower over how you feel, and the reason why you follow through on your goals. Discipline embodies persistence—it's more than just a mindset. It's what helps you maintain your will in uncomfortable situations. It prevents you from indulging in *shit food,* keeps your sleep schedule on track (even if you need to stay up late occasionally), and enforces seriousness in your actions. Discipline upholds your principles, perfects your practice, nags you when you're not moving forward, keeps you in line, and makes you stand out. It's frowned upon when one lacks it, seen as an inexcusable truth that keeps you fit, healthy, and continuously progressing. Ultimately, discipline is the essence of a fulfilled life.

But today, discipline seems almost like a *dirty word*—something people avoid or ignore like it's some sort of allergy. It's like everyone's adopted a *"pick and choose"* nature with it. People are quick to practice discipline when it's convenient or benefits them directly, but the moment it gets uncomfortable or demands real sacrifice, it's out the window. The irony is that discipline, the very thing that could bring order and meaning to the chaos is often ditched the second life gets a bit rough. Instead, we chase short-term pleasures and instant gratification, prioritising how we feel now over what's good for us in the long run. But discipline isn't supposed to be flexible—it's supposed to guide you through the tough spots, not just hang around when everything's smooth sailing.

We humans are natural creators, explorers, and doers, yet today's world makes it harder than ever to harness these traits. With vast access to the internet, distractions are just a fingertip away, and the never-ending stream of new and improved information about your favourite subjects or random nuances can overwhelm your attention span. It ties in with the *Distractions* chapter earlier in the book—we work best when we focus on one thing at a time until we achieve mastery.

However, it's so much easier to pull out your phone and scroll whenever the mood strikes. This habitual scrolling consumes mental space that could otherwise be used to learn or engage with content that truly advances your life and keeps you satisfied.

The funny thing about discipline is that it's not something you're born with—it's built, brick by brick, through choices you make every day. It's the habit of saying "no" to the easy road and "yes" to the one that pushes you. The world is full of people who admire success but never see the effort behind it, the hours of practice, and the countless moments of choosing discipline over distraction. It's not glamorous. It's not fun. But it's what separates the dreamers from the doers. The catch? You don't see results instantly, and that's where most people fall off. They want quick wins without real work, not real wins from persistent effort.

Discipline isn't about being perfect; it's about being consistent. Some days, you'll crush it, and others, you'll barely scrape by—but showing up is what matters. It's what keeps you grounded when everything feels overwhelming and chaotic. Without discipline, life becomes a series of fleeting highs and empty moments, leaving you wondering why nothing feels meaningful.

Common Sense reminds us that discipline is what makes the difference. It's the fuel for progress, the tool that turns potential into reality, and the reason why some people achieve while others stay stuck. At the end of the day, it's not just about what you do—it's about what you choose *not* to avoid

Isn't it ironic that in a world obsessed with "self-care" and "living your best life," discipline—the one thing that actually helps you achieve those goals—is often cast aside? Instead of embracing the structure and persistence that make real growth possible, we're told to "listen to our feelings" or "do what feels right." But feelings are fleeting, and without discipline, they often lead us straight to the couch with a bag of chips. We idolise success stories but skip over the gruelling process that got them there. It's funny how society preaches the importance of productivity while simultaneously drowning us in distractions that make it nearly impossible. The truth is, discipline isn't glamorous, and it's not supposed to be—it's the quiet, uncelebrated force that turns dreams into reality, even when the world would rather scroll through another motivational quote than act on it.

So next time you feel like not doing something, do it!

44

Patience

Patience might seem outdated in today's world of *instant everything*, but it's absolutely essential for a fulfilling life. Sure, some people are *lightning-fast* adaptors, making things happen in the *blink of an eye,* but most of us aren't built for that speed. Instead, *taking your time* and making *steady progress* within your means is the smarter path. We've grown so accustomed to expecting everything delivered like *Amazon Prime packages* that forgetting we're not *robots* can lead to frustration and burnout. *Common Sense* tells us not to rush if that's not our natural style, but having a *solid plan* ensures patience works *for us,* not *against us.* Embracing patience means understanding that *good things take time,* laughing at our own impatience, and recognising that *true growth and success* come from consistent, deliberate effort. So, give yourself the grace to move at *your own pace,* stick to your plans, and watch how patience transforms your journey from *chaotic sprinting* to *purposeful marathon running.*

Impatience

Impatience is a tricky beast. Most won't admit to it because it makes you look like you're constantly *chasing your tail.* Sure, some people thrive on living life at *full throttle,* rushing around and somehow getting things done—but let's be real, they're *rare breeds* of people. For most, rushing means things get *sloppy.* And then there's the type of impatience where you're doing absolutely *nothing,* just waiting for life to happen, and somehow expecting results—like *sitting on a treadmill wondering why you're not losing weight.* Impatience can be useful, but only if you know when to *hit the gas* and when to *chill. Common Sense?* Use it wisely—don't just *floor it* and hope for the best!

Find a balance.

TikTok Brain

TikTok brain" refers to the modern phenomenon where people, especially younger generations, seem to have their minds hijacked by the constant scrolling and consuming of online content, often without any purpose or direction. It's like people are stuck in an endless loop of consuming information that has no *real* value, yet they cling to it as if it's the *gospel truth.* They base their beliefs, opinions, and even their identity on things they've seen online without ever *questioning it* or allowing room for debate. It's making people mentally restricted, less open to learning, and more prone to falling into *shallow thinking.*

The effect this has on conversation is just *shit.* Instead of meaningful discussions or debates, people end up referencing the latest meme or viral trend, asking if you "saw that post" as though that's the depth of intellectual conversation these days. It's not that people aren't smart—many are *incredibly* capable—but they're *willingly* dumbing themselves down. Some don't develop proper life skills or critical thinking because scrolling through TikTok or Instagram is just *too easy.* And this problem isn't just about being distracted. It's about social media conditioning people to *lower their standards* in life, as long as the phone's there, *"it's okay,"* kinda mindset.

And let's be real for a second—*TikTok brain* is doing wonders for people's attention spans. I mean, if it's not funny, shocking, or life-changing in 10 seconds or less, who can even bother? Remember the good old days when we'd have patience for a book, or even just a full episode of a show? Now, it's like if something doesn't jump out with *neon lights, next!* Even reading seems to take more willpower, like people are scrolling through life hoping it'll come with autoplay captions and a catchy background tune. Honestly, it's impressive how quickly the *" entertainment " bar drops.*

Social media inflates people's sense of self-worth in the *worst* way most times. You've got people seeing influencers living these lavish, unattainable lifestyles, and suddenly, everyone thinks they *deserve* the same.

It warps reality. Now, I'm all for aiming high and being confident, but there's a line between ambition and delusion. You can't have people with little to no capability expecting to live like supermodels or millionaires just because they saw it on their feed. It's turned into a culture where people—many of whom don't have *two pennies* to rub together—walk around like they're entitled to the world, *flexing online but struggling in real life.*

And then there's the *entitlement issue.* It's like, just because you have followers or you look good in photos, you think you're better than everyone else. You might be living at home with *no real responsibilities,* but because you've curated this perfect online persona, you expect people to treat you like a VIP in real life. *It's bollocks.* Social media has made it so easy to live in a fantasy world, where you think you're successful or important because your posts get likes, but in reality, if that bubble bursts, you've got *nothing tangible* to show for it. What happens if the internet goes down tomorrow? *Then what?*

Common Sense takeaway? Don't base your life around your online persona or what you see on social media. It's great to be inspired and to connect with others, but at the end of the day, *real life* is what matters most. Keep your feet on the ground, remember who you are *outside the screen,* and stay aware of how easy it is to get lost in the delusional world of the internet. *Be smart with it, not dumber.* This internet is meant to help you, *not trap you.*

A world of swipes, a fleeting glow,
Where depth is lost, and nothing grows.

Their worth is tied to the likes they gain,
But outside the screen, it's not the same.

Reality waits, but few will see,
The life beyond their scrolling spree.

How's your attention span?

Justified Karma

We've all heard about karma—the cosmic "what goes around, comes around" idea that either lifts you up for being decent or knocks you down for being a complete tool. Sure, doing good by others can make life flow a bit smoother, no doubt about that. But treat people like crap, and you'll likely find yourself dodging drama or carrying more resentment than a kid without Wi-Fi.

The thing is, this "good or bad karma" idea? It's a bit simplistic. What actually exists is *Justified Karma.* It's not some divine scoreboard keeping track of wins and losses—it's the natural consequence of your actions. You put in effort, you see results. You slack off, you don't. But sometimes, no matter how much effort you pour into something, it might not be meant for you. And that's okay. The universe isn't about guarantees—it's about balance. The energy, focus, and intensity you invest in anything still matters because it shapes you. Even when the result doesn't go your way, the experience teaches you resilience and clarity, guiding you toward what's *actually* meant for you. It's in these moments that you realise karma isn't just a payback system—it's a way of nudging you to grow.

Thinking in black-and-white terms of "good" and "bad" karma feels a bit naive as you grow older. It's like judging someone's entire character based on one mistake—it just doesn't hold up. *Justified Karma* operates on a deeper level. It's not about cosmic punishment or rewards; it's about balance. Sometimes, life throws challenges your way, not because you deserve them, but because they're part of the growth process. It's less about labeling karma as "good" or "bad" and more about recognising the duality—effort brings reward, neglect brings stagnation, and sometimes, it's all just a test to push you toward something better.

Common Sense? Accept that life will challenge you, and instead of fixating on "good" or "bad," focus on the effort you're putting in. Karma, in its truest sense, isn't there to hand out rewards or punishments—it's there to balance the scales. Put in the work, face what comes your way, and trust that your effort will shape the outcome. After all, life's supposed to challenge you; that's what makes the rewards feel earned.

Justified Karma.

Money

Money—it's the *lifeblood* of modern society, more necessary today than ever before. We rely on it for *survival, success,* and *status.* It's not inherently evil, but it can become that way if we let it. At its core, money is just a *tool*—a means of exchange that allows us to navigate a complex world. Whether you're *born into it,* earn it through *hard work,* or inherit it, money reflects how you *manage* and *prioritise* your life. But today, we've placed such high importance on it that it often *defines who we are* and how we view others.

It's like your *bank balance* is now your *personality,* and somehow people believe that having a *fat wallet* automatically makes you a better person—because, you know, *generosity* and *decency* are totally available for purchase, right? I'm not trying to hate, but it's mad how we've become so deliberately oblivious to who a person really is, all based on whether they've got *stacks of cash* or are struggling to *pay rent.* Isn't it crazy? But at the end of the day, you get what you put out there—focus only on money, and don't be surprised if that's the only thing people see in you.

In today's world, money has become almost synonymous with *self-worth.* Social media bombards us with images of *wealth and success,* making it seem like the more you have, the more *valuable* you are. But this pursuit of money for status can blind us to what truly matters—*connection, growth,* and *fulfilment.* The so-called *"broke mindset"* isn't just about *lacking money,* it's about *lacking drive, creativity,* and the *will* to push beyond comfort zones. While the internet has opened countless doors for making money, it has also fueled *unrealistic expectations* of wealth and success.

The *Common Sense* here? Money is only the *root of all evil* if you allow it to be. It's a *tool,* not the *goal.* Use it wisely, and invest in things that bring *true value*—*relationships, skills, experiences* and maybe something that can set you up for the future. Learn to live within your means and understand that *real wealth* comes from what you *contribute,* not just what you *accumulate.* Keep it flowing, and remember: money is just a *means,* not the *end.* It's *not real.*

We all love a bit of capitalism.

Communication

Communication is what keeps the world turning, or rather, the *lack of it* is what makes everything fall apart. We need each other; humans are *sociable creatures,* thriving on the exchange of ideas, activities, and the occasional heated debate. A good conversation can *shift your perspective,* inspire creativity, or teach you something new about yourself. Finding those people who just *"get you"* is like finding a gem—it's almost as if the universe aligned your paths on purpose. And let's face it, those connections, whether deep or surface-level, are what make life *rich and meaningful.*

But here's the thing: today, it feels like *genuine conversation* is on *life support.* Everyone's attention spans are *short,* like scrolling through apps, and swiping through topics the minute something doesn't hit right. People don't converse anymore—they *defend.* There's a *guardedness* in conversations that makes it hard to truly connect. It's like we're constantly on the lookout for something to *react* to, instead of just relaxing and chatting. And don't even get me started on how some people feel like they need to *escalate every interaction* to the next level for at least one moment—it's like they can't just have a *normal, laid-back conversation* without turning it into some kind of *dramatic spectacle.* Yes, *I'm talking about you,* my ADHD eratic friend.

The *decline of real conversation* has even gotten to the point where let's be real, we might soon be talking in *abbreviations* like it's an episode of *Black Mirror. IMO, IRL* conversations are slowly morphing into *text message language,* and *TBH,* that's *depressing AF. WTF* happened to deep chats over coffee and stuff like that? These short forms are fine for quick texts but imagine an entire generation that communicates this way, losing the art of *meaningful, flowing conversation.* If we aren't careful, we'll have entire convos that feel like a *Google search algorithm* with emotions stripped out, just *abbreviated, mechanical replies.* It's not too late to turn it around, though; *Common Sense* is, being more *present with each other,* putting down our phones, and *actually listening.* It *ain't rocket science.*

We have a mind and a mouth for a reason.

What is a Mother and Father?

Weird to have to say this, but there was a time when the roles of *mother* and *father* were truly respected—when being a parent wasn't just a duty but a *core part* of a person's identity. Mothers were seen as the *nurturing foundation* of the family, and fathers were the *strong hands* guiding from behind the scenes. But these days, the appreciation for those roles seems to be *slipping.* Parenting is often viewed as a *chore,* something to *grind through* rather than something to admire. People don't lean on their parents for *advice* as much anymore, especially with the world changing so fast. Why turn to Dad when Google has a thousand answers, or ask Mom for advice when YouTube tutorials are *one click away?* We've turned a bit *soulless.*

That said, it's not like every parent out there is *perfect*—some are definitely a handful, no doubt. But the *majority of parents,* even when they're not together, truly *love their kids.* That love can be *intense,* feeling either *smothering* or, at other times, *strangely absent.* Parents have this knack for *overstepping and pushing limits,* not because they want to control everything, but because they *care,* even if it doesn't always come across the right way. It's an overwhelming type of love that can be *hard to grasp* unless you've experienced it yourself—it's *messy, relentless,* and not always easy to *appreciate.*

Common Sense? The world may be moving at *warp speed,* but the role of a mother and father is still *essential.* Sure, people have access to *endless information* at their fingertips, and parents might seem *outdated,* but they've lived through things and carry *wisdom* that technology can't replace. Even if their love and guidance seem *messy* or *overwhelming,* it's *irreplaceable.* People may not realise it until later, but the *sacrifices* and *care* from a parent are something that should be *respected*—because *parenting today?* It's harder than it's ever been, maybe due to the *lack of appreciation* of it.

Shout out to the good Mum's&Dad's out there, making it happen.

Practical Judgement

Practical judgment is about using *Common Sense* and ethical reasoning to navigate life, knowing when to act and when to ask for help. It means recognizing your strengths and weaknesses, swallowing your pride when necessary, but also understanding that sometimes ego and pride can push you through tough situations. You need to be aware of how your actions affect both your own life and the lives of others. It's about limiting exposure to harmful things and making choices that lead to a better future. Hardship, in this sense, becomes a teacher, pushing you to develop practical judgment, if need be.

Having control over your experiences, or at least understanding your role in them, lets you live more fully in the moment. That's why practical judgment is *essential*—it keeps you grounded in reality. In today's world, where distractions and unrealistic ideals are constantly being thrown at us, practical judgment allows you to cut through the noise and remain focused on what really matters. It gives you the clarity to assess your life and surroundings without falling prey to the confusion and delusions spread by those in power or by society's ever-changing whims.

Practical judgment also builds resilience. The more you apply it, the more prepared you are for life's unexpected curveballs. It's not about being rigid—it's about being adaptable without losing sight of your principles. This kind of judgment allows you to weigh risks, predict outcomes, and act decisively, even in uncertainty. You might not always get it right, but the process of evaluating and learning from mistakes *refines* your ability to handle future challenges.

Common Sense thrives when practical judgment is applied regularly. It's about understanding your limitations while seeking to get along with others—not for approval, but because it demonstrates a level of care and capability that not only makes you smarter but also more effective in navigating life's challenges. But remember, a lot of people don't like the effort it requires to be practical. *Know your audience* and know when it's worth engaging. Practical judgment doesn't mean pleasing everyone—it means knowing when to step back and when to stand firm.

Listening to bad impulses = jumping to conclusions.

Critical Race Theory

Critical race theory (CRT) is supposed to *tackle systemic inequality* and the *long-lasting impact of racism* in society. But these days, it's like CRT has been put through a game of telephone—*twisted, misused,* and *tossed around so recklessly* that *everything* somehow ends up being a "racist" issue. Whether it's a *statue, a harmless cultural tradition,* or just a *casual chat,* people are ready to slap the *racism label* on even the tiniest things, *without any context.* It's like we're at a point where ordering a *plain black coffee* could somehow be offensive. There's this sense that people are on a *hunt for outrage,* finding issues that weren't even there, to begin with, turning *molehills into mountains* for the sake of making noise. *How did we get to this point?*

This *obsessive focus on race* has taken what could've been *meaningful discussions* about *equality* and turned it into a *blame game.* Instead of *bridging understanding,* CRT has been turned into a tool to make people *feel guilty* for stuff they had *nothing to do with.* It's like being asked to *apologise for a crime* your *great-great-grandad might've committed.* And if you don't want to play along, well, that's somehow *proof of your guilt.* The whole conversation has been *distorted to the point* where it's not about *learning from the past—it's about carrying the weight* of actions you never committed. It *oversimplifies* what's actually a *very complex issue,* making things more about *finger-pointing* than *finding real solutions.*

Honestly, not everything has to come down to *race.* Treating every single annoyance or disagreement as a *racial crisis cheapens the genuine issues* that still need to be addressed. When CRT is *carelessly thrown around like confetti,* it doesn't just *wear people out*—it distracts from the *actual systemic problems* that still need tackling. If we want to make *progress,* we can't approach every little thing with the *attitude that it's about race.* It's *exhausting* and, quite frankly, *misses the point.* The truth is, there are plenty of *legitimate concerns* out there, but *conflating every problem with racism* isn't going to help. *Common Sense: racism does exist,* but not every *inconvenience or criticism* is rooted in *racial bias.*

When bordom strikes, there could be a problem found in anything.

Gender Inclusivity

Gender inclusivity, at its core, is about *not underestimating men or women* because, for most things, they're *equally capable.* But today, it's been twisted into something entirely different. For example, the idea that boys should have *access to tampons in men's bathrooms* or that you must *accept someone's self-identified gender* they chose last week because they *felt like it* or else you're branded an *outdated bigot.* What was once about *fairness and equal opportunities* has now morphed into a catch-all phrase for every *outlandish gender idea under the sun,* used as a *progressive filler* by the wokies who scream *inclusivity* at any given chance.

When phrases like *"gender inclusivity"* get hijacked to support narratives that even the person spouting them probably doesn't fully understand, it *dilutes the original meaning.* It starts sounding like another *pride parade buzzword* for the *rainbow crew,* leaving everyday people unsure if they can even use the term without sounding like they've signed up for the next pride march. It's become so warped that a *normal person* can't say *"gender inclusivity"* without thinking it sounds off, as if using it somehow aligns them with some *extreme, convoluted ideology.*

The intention behind gender inclusivity is to *respect everyone's experience,* but the way it's executed sometimes ends up *dividing people more than uniting them.* It's become less about *recognising genuine human experiences* and more about creating an *endless array of categories without a clear purpose.* There's also this pressure to *agree with every new term or identity* without question, or risk being labelled as *"intolerant."* How ironic. This *shuts down real conversations,* where people could otherwise learn from each other's perspectives.

Common Sense is understanding what *gender inclusivity* really means, not using it whenever it suits your *deluded agenda.* You sound *ridiculous* when you throw it around to defend your *half-baked, confused views,* and the only people who'll agree are those just as *lost* as you. It's time to *wake up* and see the *stupidity in bending reality* just because it feels good at the moment.

Gender inclusivity is about respect, not erasing individuality.

Are people Illegal or Not?

When you're a *so-called adult* and say stuff like *"no one is illegal"* or that *"taxpayers should be happy to support people who come over"* without any proper legal process, then you're missing the plot, mate. Sure, everyone deserves a chance to live a better life, no one's arguing that. But if you don't understand the necessity of *regulations and strict border control* to protect the *culture, economy,* and *security* of a nation, then you're just being *stupidly naive*. Nations need structure, and when borders are wide open with no checks, the *societal balance* that took generations to build starts to erode. It's not about being heartless—it's about being *realistic*.

Here's where it gets even more *ridiculous*: the same people who push this *open-door policy* think it's totally fine for *taxpayers to pay the bill*, while the actual *citizens* who've built and sustained the country struggle. Meanwhile, immigrants are sometimes given a *cushty place to live* with *allowances* after making a long journey. Now, I get it, escaping war or poverty is no joke, but the *system has to work for everyone*—not just whoever crosses the border next. The way some Western countries are handling this makes them look more *disorganised* than anything else. It's showing the world that the West, for all its *progressiveness*, can't even get its *own house in order*. And what's more, it's a *slap in the face* to those who followed the *legal process* to integrate properly.

The problem here is that *unchecked immigration* without a proper adjustment period creates *chaos*. It leads to *social confusion, resentment,* and *division*. Western leaders seem more focused on *virtue-signalling* than on actually solving the problems that come with mass migration. They act like this compassionate free-for-all is *sustainable* when it's clearly a *ticking time bomb. Common Sense* tells us there's got to be a balance between *compassion and practicality*—because when push comes to shove, a *nation's first responsibility* is to its *own people*. Why would that be *controversial*?

Don't be dumb and think about it.

Vaping

Yes, *vaping* might seem *healthier* than smoking cigarettes, but let's be honest: people are vaping like it's going out of style. A few puffs every half-hour might be fine, but what we're seeing now is people *glued to these little gadgets*, puffing away like it's an oxygen tank. *Disposable vapes? Game changer*, and not in a good way. You don't need to fiddle with refilling anything, so now people are getting *hooked faster than ever before*, taking hits like it's a pacifier. Vaping has exploded in popularity over a few years, quicker than cigarettes ever did, and it's all thanks to that *convenient little stick. Cool, right? Not really.*

What's happening is this *constant chase* for an *instant nicotine hit*. With *higher concentrations* of Nic-salt, people are getting that *buzz quicker* and needing *more and more* of it. Meanwhile, their lungs are taking the hit, but because it smells like *tropical fruit* instead of tobacco, people think it's somehow *harmless*. Would you light up a cigarette in bed, at your desk, or in the aeroplane bathroom? Of course not. But a vape? Suddenly, that feels *socially acceptable*, even though it's *just as bad for you*. It's *ridiculous* seeing people get hooked on flavours like *"cotton candy"* or *"kiwi smash"* and thinking they're doing themselves a favour.

Common Sense says vaping is not a *"healthy" alternative* if you're chain-puffing 24/7. It's like the *powers that be* saw a chance to create a *new wave of addiction*, and they've nailed it—making people pay to *poison themselves* with *pretty-coloured gadgets* and *sweet flavours*. You may as well stick a sign on your forehead that says, *"Dumb and satisfied."* Remember when people smelled like weed and cigarettes? Now all you can smell is that *cosmic tropical fruit twist bomb*.

Puffing clouds, a modern crave,

A moment's calm, a habit's slave.

Filling lungs with a sticky gel,

It is a silent toll, but time will tell.

Take that pussy stick out of your mouth.

"Gender Inequality"

So, as I'm typing this up, as a 27-year-old male in the United Kingdom, I honestly don't see this supposed wage gap between men and women in the *same job,* doing the *same work.* Yet, you keep hearing about women being paid less as if it's still the 1800s. These claims usually come from extreme leftist feminists who seem to thrive off creating drama. It's like they have no understanding of how *real* jobs or *actual hard work* operate, no matter the gender. But hey, it's trendy to throw around "inequality," even when the facts say otherwise. *(Muppets)*

Here's the deal: no one gives a *shit* about your gender as long as you're getting the job done, in most jobs. That's the world we live in today. Women can, and often do, earn more than men in many cases. You don't hear those women crying about "gender inequality" when they're pocketing double what a man does. The ones screaming about unfair pay are often the same people not pulling their weight at work or aren't even comparing like-for-like jobs. For example, they'll compare an admin job to a high-risk construction gig and call it oppression when the pay is different. Sure, men and women are not the same physically or mentally, but when it comes to getting paid for doing the *same* work, it's all pretty equal these days.

Common Sense is here to tell you that if someone is out there yelling about "gender inequality" in the workplace, they've probably got a lot of unresolved anger and are seeing oppression where there isn't any. Truly sad, because the reality is simple: you do the *same* job, you get the *same* pay. Objective truth, plain and simple. This progressive mentality seems to make a problem out of *anything,* likely out of boredom or some form of oppression that they never lived through. It's rather pathetic when you throw this around like you know what you're talking about, especially when there are *real* issues in the world that deserve attention.

People can be very dumb at times.

The two Cycles

You might not know this, but your body is governed by more than just a 24-hour clock. Most people are familiar with the Circadian rhythm—the cycle that regulates sleep and wakefulness over a day. It's why you get sleepy at night and wake up (or at least try to) in the morning. But there's another cycle at play that rarely gets talked about: the Infradian rhythm.

While the Circadian rhythm is the same for everyone, resetting every 24 hours, the Infradian rhythm spans about 28 days and uniquely affects women's bodies, impacting things like energy, mood, and cognitive function over a longer period. It's like women are working on two clocks at the same time.

Men operate on the standard 24-hour clock, which makes it easy for society to build routines, work schedules, and productivity tips around this cycle. But women have to navigate both rhythms, and ignoring this second cycle means ignoring a big piece of what actually drives their health and productivity.

The problem is, nobody's talking about it. The world is set up to accommodate the male 24-hour cycle, while the Infradian rhythm is swept under the rug, almost as if it's an inconvenience to acknowledge. Work schedules, fitness routines, and even productivity hacks are all designed to match the male cycle—peaking energy in the morning and winding down at night.

Meanwhile, women's energy fluctuates over an entire month, not just day to day, leading to periods of high focus and energy followed by times of lower stamina and concentration. For example, during the follicular phase (the first half of the cycle), energy and motivation are often at their peak, making it an ideal time to tackle new challenges. But in the luteal phase (the second half), fatigue and introspection take center stage, naturally pushing women to slow down. These changes aren't random—they're biologically driven.

The lack of understanding about the Infradian rhythm leaves many women frustrated when their focus dips or their energy wanes. Society doesn't account for these shifts, which can make women feel like they're failing when, in reality, their bodies are simply operating on a different timetable.

It's not just adults dealing with this oversight. Adolescent girls, as they hit puberty, experience the double impact of both Circadian and Infradian rhythms, often without guidance or understanding.

Schools, rigidly structured around the male cycle, expect the same level of focus and consistency every single day. Unsurprisingly, this can lead to issues like stress, burnout, or even anxiety when their bodies simply aren't aligned with these demands.

This misalignment doesn't just affect productivity—it impacts how women perceive themselves. It's not uncommon for women to feel inadequate when they can't perform the same way every day. But the truth is, they're not designed to. Their bodies require a different pace, one that fluctuates with the natural flow of these rhythms.

It's deeper than just misunderstanding; it feels almost deliberate. Modern society thrives on a hustle culture—an endless push for productivity that aligns perfectly with the male Circadian rhythm. Why? Because constant productivity fuels consumerism, and the idea of slowing down disrupts that system. Women, trying to match this relentless pace, often end up overworked, burnt out, and unsure why their bodies won't keep up.

What's wild is that this conditioning makes women feel like they're the problem, rather than recognising that the system itself is flawed. The Infradian rhythm isn't just about hormones—it impacts brain function, metabolism, immune response, and even stress management. Ignoring it isn't just unfair—it's damaging.

Here's some *Common Sense*: men and women aren't built to run on the same biological schedules, and pretending they do is like ignoring a vital part of how human bodies function.

As a man, I don't experience the Infradian rhythm firsthand, but when I came across it and started researching, a lot of things started to make sense about why women operate so differently from men on almost every level—emotionally, mentally, and physically.

That's why I wanted to include it in this book. It's something that should be common knowledge because understanding these rhythms helps explain so much about why men and women work differently. This isn't about creating entitlement or weaponizing differences—it's about gaining a better understanding of each other. Once people realise that women have two distinct rhythms, not just one, they can stop forcing everyone to fit into a one-size-fits-all mould and start respecting these natural differences. Because it's not just an overlooked fact—it's a fundamental truth that, if understood, could help society realistically somewhat tailor to women.

Delusional people of Today

Let's be real here: if you believe you're Black when you're blatantly biologically white, you're playing yourself. Straight-up delusional. And if you think you can menstruate just because you "feel" like a woman, despite being biologically male, that's another level of delusion. I hate to break it to you, but feelings don't alter biological facts. (*Muppets.*)

People these days are mixing up concepts like gender and pronouns. Gender is rooted in biology; pronouns are linguistic tools, yet somehow these two are being seen as interchangeable. Delusional, right? And then there's this idea floating around that there are more than two genders in the human realm. Look, we're not talking about science fiction here. Humans, like most mammals, have two biological sexes. Anything beyond that, and you might just be getting a little too caught up in wishful thinking, or maybe your chromosomes are playing tricks on you. Sometimes, it makes me feel like that emoji slapping its face when I hear these delusional claims.

And if you're living strictly by the rulebook of political correctness, you're probably missing a lot of important conversations. Being overly PC can make you lose sight of reality. And while we're on it, biological men can't give birth, no matter how much someone might want to rewrite that narrative... Science, like—it's a thing.

Here's another delusion: letting hordes of people into your country with zero integration policy and just expecting everything to be fine. Sorry, but that's naïve. These people bring their own cultural standards and often expect the rest of society to adapt to them, not the other way around. And before you know it, your country becomes a free-for-all, like a vacation spot with no rules. That's not sustainable, is it?

Sexuality is another one. If you're living your life believing that sleeping with anything that moves is the peak of personal freedom, well, I've got news for you: you're deluded. That's not freedom; that's self-destruction wrapped in instant gratification. At some point, we might have to stop acting like every single impulse should be celebrated.

And don't get me started on the whole *"everyone's feelings are sacred"* nonsense. Yes, feelings matter, but when they start dictating public discourse to the point where no one can speak their mind without being labelled insensitive, we've crossed into delusional territory.

Just because someone's feelings are hurt doesn't mean they're right. And just because you're loud, doesn't mean you deserve special treatment.

What's worse is when people bandwagon these delusional ideas and turn them into movements, claiming they're standing up for "progress." The truth is, being delusional is easy. It's comfortable. It allows people to ignore reality because reality can be hard and unforgiving. But the problem is, it leads to confusion, resentment, and ultimately, chaos.

Also treating children like mini-adults who can handle decisions they're not remotely ready for. Whether it's letting them decide their entire identity before they've even figured out how multiplication works or expecting them to have the emotional maturity to process adult-level conversations—it's absurd. Childhood is about learning, growing, and figuring things out step by step. Pushing kids into roles they're not prepared for doesn't make them "progressive," it just sets them up for a world of confusion and misplaced expectations. Let's not rob them of their chance to just *be kids.*

And then there's the obsession with being perpetually offended by everything. We've become so hyper-focused on finding problems in every corner of life that we've forgotten how to pick our battles. It's like everyone's on edge, looking for the next outrage to latch onto, even if it's completely trivial. At some point, we have to stop making mountains out of molehills and start recognising what's actually worth our energy. You can't fight every battle and win. Sometimes, the best move is to let things go and focus on what truly matters. There are many more examples of problems popping up everywhere.

At some point, someone needs to say it: enough is enough. It's okay to have opinions and beliefs, but it's not okay to enforce delusions on everyone else. We're all entitled to our own views, but they should at least be rooted in some form of reality. The truth isn't always nice, but it's necessary. And if you can't handle that, maybe it's time to take a step back and question whether your worldview actually holds up in the real world.

The fact is, *Common Sense*—something we seem to have lost along the way—is what should guide us. Being in touch with reality is a survival skill. So, try and stop living in a fantasy, stop trying to make everyone bend to your will, and start seeing things as they are, because you do look a bit like a *muppet* when you don't.

Reality is that friend who tells the truth, but never how you want to hear it.

Everyone out for Themselves

Where's the connection between people these days? Why can you live next to someone for years and not even know their name? It's not like you have to know them, but it's a pretty clear example of just how indifferent we've become toward one another. It's like we're living in this weird, modern jungle where survival means looking out for number one, and if you don't, the world's ready to chew you up and spit you out. The idea of working for the good of the community or even for family feels like a relic of the past. We've got our phones and online connections, and as long as we're managing independently, why bother with anyone else? So, we've shifted from the mindset of "we're in this together" to "every man for himself," and it shows.

It's become this culture of "take what you can and keep your distance." Sure, there are still kind and generous people out there, but the number of those who just act like they care is alarmingly high. Ever notice how people are quick to offer support or encouragement when things are going well, but the second you really need help—like during a tough financial situation or family crisis—they're nowhere to be found?

You ask for a favour, and suddenly everyone's too busy, or they just ghost you entirely. It's like when people promise to "be there" for you but disappear the moment it requires actual effort or inconvenience. We're all too wrapped up in our own lives and goals to stop and lend a genuine helping hand. It's all about "me first" now.

It's strange when you think about it: we have more ways to connect than ever before, but the connections themselves feel thinner than a phone screen. Real connection takes effort—actually showing up, listening, and giving a damn. And yet, in this fast-paced, convenience-driven society, it's easier to send a quick emoji or comment on a post and call it "support." It's as though we're settling for these shallow interactions because anything deeper feels like too much work.

We've traded compassion for cold efficiency, and it's every person for themselves. We've had to adapt to this fast-moving, hustle-obsessed society, where if you're not scrambling for money, status, or that next big thing, you risk getting left behind. But in that mad scramble, people often lose sight of their own humanity.

Pursuing success turns people ruthless, and then it's no wonder why kindness and cooperation are the first casualties when the pressure's on. It's easy to play nice when everything's smooth sailing, but when life gets rough? That's when you really see who people are.

It's hard to balance looking out for yourself and remembering that you're not the only one on this planet. Everyone's fighting their own battles—some are crushing it, some are barely holding on, and some are just stuck, trying to figure out what the hell to do next.

No matter where you land on that spectrum, stepping on others to get ahead won't make you a better person. It just leaves everyone feeling more isolated and burned out. And all that self-centred hustle? Most of the time, it's a lonely road, no matter how much you're stacking up along the way.

Common Sense? Respect others, no matter what you're chasing. The truth is, we all need each other more than we like to admit, and at the end of the day, working together is going to get you a hell of a lot further than doing it alone

---

In a world that's always on the go,
Connections fade, but we don't let it show.

Quick likes and comments, but nothing too real,
Just shallow gestures—no depth to feel.

Yet a kind word or time to spare,
Could remind us all, that it's not just you out here.

Be kind, it doesn't cost anything but effort.

Why is the World so Weird these days?

When I say weird, I'm talking about how everything feels so *out of touch* these days—and people aren't much better. Multiple factors play into this, but it can be narrowed down to a few glaring examples. We're more connected than ever, yet somehow completely disconnected on so many levels. Physical interaction? It's like a lost art. Even attaining affection feels like navigating a minefield. We're all smiles and friendly vibes but never take it further, thanks to *unrealistic standards* or simply not knowing how to interact with each other as just people. Weird, right?

The world's spun on its head, trying to lock itself into this so-called *"new norm."* We're told to respect everyone's ideals, no matter how unrestrained or absurd their actions, because God forbid they get *traumatised.* Wet wipes. It's fucking ridiculous how *short-sighted* people have become in such a short time. It's like reality isn't real until something spectacular or catastrophic slaps us awake. Remember the start of the pandemic? When people lost their minds over toilet paper? As if hoarding loo roll was some magical shield against disaster. That alone showed how unprepared most people are for the unexpected—trapped in a comfortable bubble where *everything's fine* until the rules change, and suddenly you're lining up to buy groceries 2 metres apart.

The truth is, we're all like ticking time bombs, pretending everything's fine as long as it doesn't directly affect us. Reality feels more like a *video game* these days—you can choose when to play, retreating to your metaphorical checkpoint (*your bed*) whenever it gets too real. Why try to be better when you can just spectate from the sidelines through your phone, tossing out opinions but never truly getting involved? People think they've got it all figured out—until the *shit hits the fan,* and they realise they don't have a clue how to protect themselves, let alone cooperate with others.

And in this great *information age,* where we supposedly know everything, we're still killing each other senselessly over religion, money, or—brace yourself—pride. How's that for progress? As kids, most of us were taught to get along, to share and be kind. Yet, as adults, it's like people forget all that the moment personal ideals don't align. It's straight into *savage mode,* with no problem trampling others to push their own agenda. Whether you're in the way directly or not, there's no remorse—just a single-minded focus to bulldoze through.

But here's where it gets messier: the world is evolving so fast that no one has the time—or the grounding—to figure out where they actually stand. People act like they've got life nailed down, confidently posting their opinions and "truths" online, but when something shifts—because it always does—they're left scrambling, confused, and desperate to maintain their facade. It's not *bad* to change or adapt; that's how we survive. But too many people cling to the idea that they've "arrived" at the answer, only to crumble when the next wave of progress or chaos washes it away.

Technology evolves so quickly that what seemed like *sci-fi* a decade ago is now everyday life. Social media connects people globally, exposing us to an overwhelming variety of cultures, ideas, and trends—some inspiring, others just plain bizarre. We're bombarded with information from countless sources, often sensationalised to grab attention, leaving us overloaded and numbed to what actually matters. Meanwhile, pop culture, celebrities, and influencers set trends that quickly seep into societal norms, creating a whirlwind of quirky behaviours and expectations that no one's sure how to keep up with.

And let's not forget the bigger shifts. The pandemic reshaped how we work, socialise, and view health—leading to habits and adaptations that, let's face it, are sometimes strange. Add to that rising environmental awareness, alternative health trends, and rapid economic changes, and you've got a recipe for a world where everyone's just trying to make sense of the madness. It's no wonder people feel unmoored—when the ground beneath you is constantly shifting, how do you plant your feet?

The disconnection between people is really at the core of all the confusion we're living in. We try to understand each other, but often it's only for self-gain or to avoid confrontation. Everyone's dealing with their own *shit,* and no one wants to take on the extra weight of someone else's problems. It's a sad reality that the more we isolate ourselves, the harder it becomes to truly connect.

Common Sense? We're all a bit weird, sure, but let's at least recognise when we're crossing the line into full-blown ridiculousness. And while we're at it, maybe remember this: no matter how crazy things get, we all share this rock together. Finding some balance between individuality and collective responsibility isn't just ideal—it's necessary.

The Great Brain Chemical Imbalance

You might not be the person who's affected by such a *problem in the world*, and you should consider yourself *lucky* because it's getting more and more prevalent for people to be *out of touch*. Too much *dopamine* without the right *balance of work* to deserve that *dopamine release* is just like *chasing a high* you get from taking *drugs*; it's not *sustainable* and only leads to *deterioration*. The same goes for *social media*—if having your *attention span lowered* wasn't bad enough, you also *mess up your brain chemistry* by changing its process to be *addicted* to short forms of quick *chemical release* through having the ability to change to something more entertaining just by *swiping up or down*.

Phones have made our *expectations for fun* almost *unattainable*, and that just *depresses people* because they don't understand that *things take time* outside of being on their little *electronic devices*. Some people don't even understand how to *have fun in life* without the phone involved to an extent, or a *computer*. The *addiction to quick dopamine release* has made *internet addicts* out of people when *reality* has so much *more to offer*, but that takes time, which can obviously be spent *scrolling* or *overplaying video games*.

Sex is something we all need, as I mentioned earlier in the book. But when you're having it just to *feel good for the 20 minutes afterwards*, it reveals *hypersexual tendencies* rooted in the need for *validation*. Your brain convinces you that you need sex to avoid feeling worthless like no one values you or you have no importance. This is why having *aimless sex*, especially if you're a *trauma victim*, can be harmful, as it creates a cycle where you seek *temporary relief* instead of genuine *healing*. *Porn addiction* isn't any better; even without another person involved, it can be worse. It *distorts your perception*, making it hard to *connect with real people* and causing you to see others as mere *objects for pleasure* rather than *human beings* with *value*, damaging your ability to form *meaningful relationships*. All due to those *chemicals*.

The *food* that we ingest can also be very *damaging to our brain chemistry*; it can make you *dumb* without having the ability to recover properly and make you think that you *need that food* to feel good. *Sugar* is in almost everything you eat or drink, and all that does is make things *taste better* than they do.

It releases *dopamine* that wires your brain to think you can't have anything without that *sweet taste* behind it; otherwise, you might just reject ingesting anything else because it doesn't make you feel good, and I'm sure you can see how *unhealthy* such *wiring* might be for the *mind and body*. But it's not like we have only *healthy options* around because it's much *cheaper and simpler* to produce *processed foods* to sell, and also for you to buy.

Drugs only let you *feel a certain frequency* or *partake in it*, for that one instance, so that you can experience what it's like to have that *thought process* and see *reality* through a *different lens*. When you take *drugs* way past that stage—meaning constantly *chasing that high*—then you will never feel like you did the first time. That's why it's called *"chasing a high,"* and it'll only make you a *waste of space*, to *yourself and others*. Drugs *rape the chemicals* in your brain and force you to feel the *explosion* of a certain chemical until the feeling *dissipates*, and you're left with a *comedown* to deal with. But what that is, is like your brain feeling *sore* due to *overusing a certain set of chemicals*, and that only leaves *short- or long-term damage*. Not that you should take *drugs*, of course.

Going through *depression* or *too much-unchecked anxiety* can also *throw off* the pattern of your *brain chemistry*, but let's not forget that *depression* is a *mood* you partake in, sometimes not by *choice*, and sometimes it becomes *clinical*, unfortunately. It can *rewire you*, to only *thinking through an ill mind* or sad thoughts and feelings that become the *norm to feel*, instead of having a *healthy mindset*.

Common Sense would be knowing when to not *indulge in everything* that *feels good* and recognizing when *enough is enough*. You need to be *vigilant* about what you *involve yourself in* and ensure you have *control*. *Overindulgence* can quickly turn you into a *"nitty"*—basically, a *waste of potential*, kind of a *tramp*, you know, *off-putting*.

The mind's a maze of shifting hues,

Chemicals dancing, altering views.

What feels like joy can twist to despair,

A balance lost, leaves us gasping for air.

You are not a Cyborg

As technology advances, we often feel *smarter* and more *connected*, but paradoxically, this progress can sometimes *dilute our human experience*. Despite the *vast amounts of information* we absorb and the *innovation* we create, some people remain *fundamentally unchanged*. They're like *digital-age cavemen* navigating a *high-tech world*, while many of us seem stuck in a *perpetual online persona*. We interact in ways that seem more suited for *social media algorithms* than for *genuine human connections*. It's as if our *screens* have become a *social filter*, blurring our *true expressions and interactions*, like a *real-life glitch*.

It's disappointing how quickly we've drifted away from a more *philosophical*, *natural* way of experiencing life. Technology has its place, but we need to question if it's truly *helping* or just *distorting our sense of reality*. People seem more *in tune* when they're not glued to social media—it doesn't teach *genuine human connection*. For *younger generations*, it's even harder, as they get stuck in *algorithm-driven short forms of gratification* and, miss out on *real, meaningful interaction*.

In the future, we might see people only interacting through *chips in their heads* or some sort of *thought recognition technology* that can be transferred to another person, and what's happening now are just the *baby steps* of something *greater*, that can *change us forever*, but we have yet to *find out*.

Common Sense says to remember that *human interaction* is a whole different kind of *complexity* compared to the *digital world*. It's about *real-life experiences* that no one can truly teach you—you have to *learn it by living it*. But how *cool* would it be to *communicate with thoughts alone*?

Try and survive a day without your devices.

Violence does Exist

Violence has been around since the *dawn of humanity*—long before we had *laws*, *cities*, or the concept of *civility*. It's embedded in our *history*, shaping societies and territories long before we started *pretending otherwise*. Whether it was used to *defend*, *conquer*, or *maintain order*, violence has always been a *tool*, for better or worse. We can't just dismiss it because we've wrapped ourselves in a blanket of *modern comforts* and *niceties*. Pretending it doesn't exist is like acting blind to the fact that the *sun rises* every day—it's always there, whether you *acknowledge it or not*.

But today, it feels like society is so focused on promoting *peace* and *politeness* that people act as if violence is a *relic of the past*. This *passiveness* creates a *false sense of security* as if we've somehow evolved beyond conflict. You see it everywhere: people getting unreasonably *aggressive* while arguing for "*non-violence*" or acting like *hostility* doesn't exist as long as you don't talk about it—basically *rainbow crew "logic."*

Reality check: violence is still part of our world; the most *hideous things imaginable* are happening to someone around the world *right now*, as you are reading this. Just because it's not happening *in front of you* doesn't mean it's gone. The truth is, violence isn't just about *aggression*—it's also about *survival*, *protection*, and *defence*, and it's not going to disappear because we decide to *ignore it*.

Common Sense knows *Violence isn't going anywhere.* Ignoring it doesn't make you *morally superior*, it just leaves you *less prepared* when *reality hits*. Recognizing its place in the world doesn't mean *embracing it*—it means *understanding it*, knowing when it's *necessary to defend yourself* or others, and not letting yourself be *blindsided* by the belief that "*peace and love*" alone are enough to *keep you safe*.

You get me?

Labels don't define YOU

In today's world, it feels like everyone's got a *label*—ADHD, ADD, Anxiety, Depression, Schizophrenia, Asperger's—you name it. It's almost become a *trend* to identify yourself by whatever condition or disorder you've been slapped with, wearing it like some sort of *quirky badge of honour*. And sure, having a *label* can be comforting, like finally getting a name for that *chaos in your head*, but it doesn't *define you*. It shouldn't be the *entire explanation* of who you are. At some point, the label stops being useful and starts being an *excuse*—an *easy out* for every behaviour or shortcoming. "Oh, I can't concentrate? Must be my *ADHD* acting up. Didn't finish that project? That's just the *anxiety* talking." But here's the deal: knowing your *limitations* doesn't mean *giving up* on trying.

Back in the day, people didn't have endless access to *information* unless they actively went *digging* for it—if they even knew what to look for in the first place. There was no *Google search* to convince you that you had 50 different disorders or countless online forums where everyone self-diagnoses and tries to *one-up* each other on who's got it worse. It was a lot simpler: you *dealt with it*, or you found your own way to *cope*. It wasn't necessarily *better*, but it kept people from becoming their own *pity armchair psychologists*.

Now, with the sheer amount of *info* available on *psychology and neurology*, it's like people are *diagnosing themselves* left and right, slapping on new labels like they're collecting *Pokémon cards*. The more *information* people have, the more they start to *define themselves* by what's *wrong with them*, adding layer upon layer to their labels until they're completely *overwhelmed*. It's funny—almost *ironic*, really—the more we *know*, the more we end up *fucked*.

Let's be clear: understanding what's going on in your *brain* and knowing the *name* for it can be a *game-changer*. It gives you *clarity*, helps you *make sense* of things, and allows you to find the right *tools or support*. But the deal is—at some point, it's *on you* to do something about it. Using your *label* as a blanket explanation for everything you do or don't do isn't going to *help you* in the long run.

Because, surprise—*life still expects you to show up*, labelled and all. It's no secret that modern humans are *bombarded* by more *stimuli and stress* than ever before.

The *constant information overload*, unrealistic *comparisons* on social media, and the general chaos of 21st-century life can definitely *scramble your brain*. But avoiding *reality* and expecting others to *tiptoe around* your label? That's not it. You can't just *hide behind your diagnosis* and expect the world to *cater to your quirks*.

In the end, your *label* is only a small piece of the puzzle. Yes, it explains why you might *struggle* in certain areas, but it doesn't excuse you from *trying*. Past generations didn't have the option to let their *labels* run the show—they had to get on with it, whether that meant *overcoming* their struggles or just *quietly carrying* them. And the truth is, the more we *dig* into these labels and conditions, the more *complicated* things get.

It's like the *information* is supposed to help us, but for many, it just adds *confusion*, making the struggle to find out who you are even harder. Instead of using a *label* to justify staying *stagnant*, use it as a *foundation to grow*. Because no matter what *letters or words* are attached to your name, it's what you do with them that *counts*.

Common Sense? Labels don't make you. They describe *one aspect* of you, sure, but they're not a *permission slip* to give up or stop *trying*. Use the *label* as a guide to better *understand yourself*, but don't let it become your *whole identity*. Because at the end of the day, you're still responsible for *showing up* and *putting in the effort*—label or not. Having access to *endless information* doesn't mean you should define yourself by every new *disorder* you read about; we all have *quirks and whatnot*, but it's not an excuse to *stop living*—you have to *carry on*.

Labels slapped on, a shield to wear,
An excuse to stop, no need to care.
"I'm just this way," becomes the song,
But growth's the tune they've missed all along.

Many thanks to Checkley for the title, you know who you are.

Yes, we judge Each Other

We always see the *best in each other*, flaws included. We see what someone could *become* if they just had the right *nudge*, and honestly, it's not that controversial to think we know what's *best* for each other—whether it's a *woman or a man*. The closer we get to someone, the less we can resist *judging* them, even if we're a perfect match and *destined* for a lifelong partnership. And let's be real, we judge *strangers* too, even if they have nothing to do with us besides sharing this *big ol' rock*. It's just *human nature*, especially if we're not preoccupied with our own lives.

The phrase *"you shouldn't judge others"* is true—you really *shouldn't*, because you're not living anyone else's life but your own. But let's face it, we're *curious creatures* who can't help but *analyze* our surroundings. *Judgment* is a part of that—it helps us *assess* who we're dealing with and where we stand. Of course, some people go a bit *overboard*, living purely to judge others while forgetting they're far from *perfect* themselves. That kind of *overanalyzing* just ends up stealing from the *acceptance* we all need to *get by*, which can actually lead us down the *right path*.

In this day and age, maybe we should aim to *judge each other* with a bit more *respect* and just expect everyone to be *decent* at the very least. It's really not asking for much. Let's try not to judge purely on how *cool* or *exciting* someone seems. We're always going to have *thoughts about others*—that's just who we are, and it's part of what makes human interaction *interesting*. But don't fool yourself into thinking you're *above judgment*. So, the bottom line is to be *competent, decent,* and not get too caught up in what others *think*.

Common Sense is to remember that *judgment is everywhere*, and if you want the *good kind* about you, then do your best, so that your *positives* have leverage over the *negatives*. But remember, there are those who just *don't give a shit* and will judge no matter what.

We all have an opinion about someone.

Stay WAKE not Woke

So what's *woke*? Or being *woke*? (ask *Kamala Harris*). I think it's just a bunch of *non-sensical bollocks*; it's made people *soft* because they have to be *all-inclusive* now and not stand up for something that might be hard to attain but would actually be *so-called "all-inclusive"*. What *wokeness* did was start considering *everyone's emotions* over a *logical outcome*, and *God forbid* you have a problem with that while thinking of the *greater good* for generations to come—if it seems like *bigotry* or *bullying*. Absolute *daffodils*.

Being *woke* seems to be accepting *shit* from everyone, but don't you dare retaliate with some *Common Sense*; you might *traumatize* someone and get *canceled*, but *wokies* can say or do what they want because they had a *"hard life."* What a *fucking joke*. It's like *dumbing yourself down* because people would rather overstretch *emotions* than *logic*. Where's the *logic* in that?

Being *Wake* means you don't operate through *delusional bullshit* while understanding that *feelings* are *fleeting and temporary*. It means making the *right, thoughtful decisions* that impact you and those around you *positively*, showing you're a *realist* who does the *right thing*, even when it's *hard*. But you don't have to be some *superhero*. Being *Wake*, not *fucking woke*, means you can handle *grown-up conversations*—ones that can be *argued* and *challenged*. No one will think you're *mentally undeveloped*, and that's why you stay *Wake*. It's the *cold truth*, and yeah, it's silly to even have to say it, but stranger things have happened… like this *book*, for example.

The *Common Sense* here would be to *stay Wake!* Not fucking *Woke*, because being *woke* is like being an *infant in an adult body* with no consideration for the *bigger picture*, assessing how your *actions affect others* around you. It's just being an *adult*; yes, it can be *boring but necessary*. It roots you in *realism. Stay Wake! Not deluded woke*.

Stay *Wake*, not lost in the woke charade,
See through the noise, don't let it persuade.
Keep it real, don't let your mind get played.
Staying Woke? What a delusional claim.

Stay WAKE.

Shrooms

It's like when people take *magic mushrooms*, something inside just *clicks*. *Reality shifts*, questions you've had about who you are, or even what the *purpose of everything* around you is, start to make more sense. But here's the deal—you still can't *fully explain it*. And that's part of the *magic*: it feels like you're tapping into a *truth* that goes beyond words, like a *boost for the soul* that opens your mind without overwhelming it (just don't act like *Billy big bollocks* and take loads). You begin to realise that maybe you're not supposed to *understand everything* fully, and somehow, that makes even more sense while you're in that *space*.

I've taken magic mushrooms only a couple of times, and I can say that's enough for me—at least for the next few years. The experience is *profound*—something that can't really be explained until you've been through it yourself. It's not your typical, everyday trip; it's a *journey to a different layer of reality*, one where the *usual rules* don't quite apply. And trust me, if you do try it, having the *right people* around and being in the *right mindset* is everything. What shrooms taught me is that while *critical thinking* and using your *head* are crucial in our *everyday reality*, there's a whole other *realm of understanding* once you're on a journey.

You start to realise that we've let our *logical minds* run the show, treating it as the *sole driver* of our lives. But it's actually the *link between the body, mind,* and *soul* that creates a complete existence. Sadly, not everyone gets there, because we're so tied to what we *see*, what we can *prove*, and what we *think logically*, rather than what we *feel deep down*. In a world that's all about *living fast* and *competing*, shrooms strip away *ego* and *pride*, grounding you in the *present*, no matter where you are.

Common Sense? I know, I know, it sounds like some *spiritual or metaphysical bollocks*, but from my experience—without abusing the stuff—it only made me see how much *MORE* there is to us. It's a *funny thing*, fungi.

Try it, you never know what's waiting for you on the other side.

Keyboard Warriors

Let's be honest, you're a bit *off* if you only feel comfortable acting like you have a *spine* on the internet but nothing in *real life*. (Pussy)

Common Sense, really.

Behind the screen, they pound away,
Big words, small minds, nothing to say.
Their battles fought with caps lock screams,
Pathetic warriors chasing empty dreams.

I guess we should call it, touch screen warriors.

Ground Yourself

This one is *crucial* in today's life—something anyone can do, anywhere, that leaves you feeling at *ease* and *energized* for the day. Walking through *nature* or along the *beach* pairs perfectly with *grounding* yourself; it's as if these *natural surroundings* remind you of what it means to be *human*—not some *over-optimized machine* but a person who *breathes* and *feels*. Grounding is about *reconnecting* with your *roots*, shedding the layers of *stress* that stack up over time. Taking even a little time for your *body, mind,* and *soul* to link up brings a sense of *calm* that stays with you, and you'd be surprised how this *quiet wisdom* rubs off on others without a word.

The moments when you really need *grounding* can be some of the most *peaceful experiences* of your life—if you know how to stay *present*. Think of those times when a *rough day* has you irritated with everything, and then out of nowhere, a stranger's *smile* or a few *simple words of encouragement* remind you it's not as bad as it seemed. People like that, who know how to *bring you back to earth*, often have their own *grounding down to an art*. They're like proof of how much it matters—they're *tuned in* enough to spot when others need that same *grounding* and bring *calm* wherever they go.

Grounding keeps you *balanced*—it lets you be yourself fully, shedding all the accumulated *stress* so you can do more than you thought possible. Sometimes, it takes getting a bit *lost in life's noise* to return to this place of *clarity*. But here's the thing: you have to let down those *walls* and let the *universe* do its work on you, which can feel *uncomfortable* or even *vulnerable* at first. But for those who truly embrace *grounding*, it becomes a *healing process* that helps them approach life with *authenticity* and *balance*.

Common Sense? Take some time for yourself and *slow down* a bit; you don't need to be a *free spirit* to find *balance*. In fact, *grounding* might be the most *practical* thing you can do to stay *sane*.

Anchor yourself, and let strength rise from within.

Try it.

Promiscuity

We all have sex, and most of us love everything about it. It's got its benefits, no doubt—it helps you relax, keeps you connected (or at least that's the idea), and keeps you at ease... unless you're hypersexual and can't chill no matter how much you get. We live in an era where you can find anything about sex at the click of a button. Sex sells—no surprise there—and this generation, blessed with a bottomless pit of information, faces some serious drawbacks. The easy access to every possible fantasy on the internet? Let's just say, whatever twisted idea you come up with, someone's already thought of it. It's crazy.

All this instant access has turned people into walking hormone factories. But the bigger issue is how it's led to the over-sexualisation of people. Selling photos and videos of yourself online has gone from taboo to mainstream. "We all need money, and it's not prostitution because it's not physical," right? Okay, sure. But think about what this does to those who can't get real-life connections and end up substituting it with digital pleasures. It's like trying to quench your thirst with a drop of water—never satisfying, just leaving you feeling emptier in the end. Sad, really.

We've normalised sex to the point that it's as casual as sharing a cigarette. The internet has made sex something to be traded, consumed, and discarded, leaving some people starved and others overwhelmed. People rarely stop to appreciate the deeper meaning of sex; it's like we've lost the balance entirely. Some aren't getting any, while others are at it nonstop. The middle ground? Gone. And now, with every body part just a click away, the thrill, anticipation, the mystery? Poof. Gone. We've dulled our sense of pursuit to where meeting someone in real life feels less exciting than swiping right.

The sad truth is, we've lost that deeper connection with another person. Dating apps have turned potential relationships into a catalogue, swiping people away like they're disposable. Men act like sleeping with tons of women is great, but it's only a brag if you're a top guy—not if you've got nothing else going for you. Women, meanwhile, think they need to sleep with someone just because it's expected, even though many crave a real connection. Or they assume hooking up casually is empowering because it's on their terms, not realising it can chip away at their sense of self when they're left unfulfilled. (No pun intended)

That said, promiscuity isn't all bad. Some people thrive in this lifestyle and genuinely feel free, enjoying their choices without guilt. But here's the problem: the way it's portrayed makes it seem like *anyone* can live that way without consequences, which just isn't true for most people. This image of endless casual encounters creates a false narrative that everyone else is living this amazing, uninhibited life—and if you're not, you're somehow missing out. The reality? Many people chasing that lifestyle end up feeling lost, disconnected, and like they're trying to fill a void they don't even understand.

Being a slag is so normalised now that if you push back on hookup culture, you're seen as a prude. I wish people—especially women—realised that the more you sleep around, the harder it becomes to bond with someone on a meaningful level. Or you end up in a relationship that's all about wild sex, which—let's be real—never lasts. You end up chasing the wrong things in a relationship. When you finally meet someone who doesn't see sex as the foundation, it's disorienting, and that disconnect can wreck the whole vibe.

Common Sense? Don't be a headless slag. Every time you go down that path, you chip away a bit of your own soul. You lose the chance for deeper connection because sex becomes just another 20-minute transaction, shared with countless people. If you're not made for that kind of lifestyle, then you really need to take a step back and understand what works for *you*—beyond the bollocks of societal shagging standards. The world is designed for you to consume, and that's not inherently bad, but the thing is, it's all set up at your own peril. The internet, and the way people use it, has morphed into this twisted, real-life sexual algorithm that's nearly impossible to escape. It's so pervasive that you're led to think it's all completely normal.

Let's be real: the majority of people have been mentally *raped* by this relentless bombardment of hypersexualisation, and here's the backlash—it's in the way people struggle to form deep connections, the way intimacy feels more like a transaction than an expression of love, and the way it's all starting to feel hollow. And let's be honest—no one likes being called a slag or a slut. Save yourself the trouble and have some decency. It's not a good look, and if you're not well put together, you just end up looking even more broken to everyone around you. As we say in the UK, *that's peak—a proper shit situation, really.*

Not every *D* has to be taken and not every *hole*, is a *goal.*

A World War would be a Stupid thing to have

I won't drag this chapter out because it's self-explanatory. We all want to live, explore, and enjoy life, but with conflicts flaring up everywhere, it's hard not to feel a bigger mess is coming—one that could drag us all in, forcing survival into the forefront.

War isn't just *boots on the ground* anymore. These days, it's drones, cyberattacks, and economic sanctions, crippling nations without a single bullet fired. Disinformation campaigns divide societies, and even climate change and resources have become battlegrounds. The wars we fight aren't always visible—sometimes the battlefield is your own mind, with mental health, finances, and the pressure of modern life grinding us down.

Common Sense? Stay ready for the personal battles, but don't fall for the madness of large-scale conflict. The real winners are always the ones counting their cash in bunkers, while the rest of us are left to fight over scraps. *That's peak,* isn't it?

A world war now? It's a fool's mistake,
With nothing to gain, just lives at stake.
The planet's too fragile for battles like these,
We'd all lose more than we'd ever achieve.
Don't you agree?

Toxic Relationships

We've all been there, and if you haven't, you might be missing out on an *eye-opening experience* that can be interpreted as a *hard reality slap* across your face. Being in one of these relationships will only *make you break you,* or both. It's different for everyone, and just because you had a *bad experience* with a certain individual doesn't mean the next person will do the same—people *do* change (rarely), but they do. We also know when someone is *bad* for us or vice versa; we see the *red flags* miles away, but for some reason, we just *have to explore* that person, even when we *feel innate* that they aren't the right choice for us—be that a *woman, man,* or the *in-betweeners.*

Not every relationship starts off bad, and it might not even get to that point until a few years in. That can be very *unfortunate* for all involved, especially for the one who always tried to *make it better.* It seems that *excitement* is the main driving force for such outcomes, as it should be, but we as people have to realise what makes us *grow* in the right way while being with someone. That *internal dialogue* can be very difficult to navigate, especially if you're in the relationship for a while. We all need *love* and crave it. You've got to be careful who gets to keep your *heart* because they might just be *using you* or not even *appreciate* the person you are, while you think otherwise. And they walk off with your *heart,* leaving you *empty.*

If only people could really understand that some don't *deserve* to share in their *energy or life,* then the world might be more of a lovely place to be, for the most part, but that's *wishful thinking.* So it's on you as an individual to *protect your heart* and mind from *horrible encounters* with the wrong people and not think that the explosion of *brain chemicals* is love. It won't last—and it *never does.*

Common Sense is to understand that most of the time, the *right person* for you is the one you *resist,* but it takes *time* to find *real love. Self-love* shows you how you should be loved, but be able to *compromise* with the right person—it's a *blessing.* Good luck!

Toxic relationships drain your soul while convincing you it's love.

Situationships

So these days *situationships* are perfect for people who don't want a proper *commitment*—it's like one foot in, one foot out. I think it's because people want to leave their *options open* just in case something goes wrong or they find someone better, both men and women. It can be a *competition* to see who can get one up on the other while acting like the person by your side doesn't *matter*. It doesn't make sense and should be a *straight-up union* instead. People want proper *connection* but will settle for something *superficial* because it's easy, making relationships seem long and *obsolete*, with no feeling or *sensitivity* for something real, past the *excitement bit*.

Being *friends with benefits* is different, and that is only for the fact that you establish what the *boundaries* are at the start—which are, you are *friends who have sex* with each other and that's it. There are instances when one might *catch the feels*, but that can be neutralized with a conversation, or you could take it further. It just depends on the people, and there isn't any *confusion* about what the actual deal is.

Situationships between people who don't really know what they're getting themselves into are *destined to fall apart*. They can inflict damage on the very way someone dates, and they might never understand what a *proper way of loving* someone is. They could remain together out of *desperation*, maybe due to a child or *codependency*, even though they don't align with one another. It's more of a *situationship* then, but I guess it depends on the perspective.

Common Sense, being the enemy of the majority of situationships, says that you should not partake in such activity if you are not a *well-put-together* individual who can handle it and understand what the deal is to the T. Otherwise, you might never be the same and end up normalizing it to others, being out of touch with oneself and *connectivity on a deeper level*.

Low commitment, high drama, zero clarity.

What we swapped Connection for

We've swapped *genuine connections* for likes, shares, swipes, and endless *distractions*. It's undeniable. The *deep conversations*, face-to-face interactions, and *shared experiences* that once made us feel human have been traded in for *dopamine hits* from a screen. We're more obsessed with how many *followers* we have than how many *real friends* we can count on. Today, people measure their worth by metrics that mean absolutely *nothing* in the grand scheme of things. We've become more concerned with *virtual approval* than *authentic relationships*, and we're paying the price for it with *loneliness* and *detachment*.

But it's not just social media. We've swapped *connections* for *convenience* everywhere. Streaming services have replaced movie nights with friends, meal delivery apps have taken over *family dinners*, and even shopping—once a *social experience*—happens solo behind a screen. Virtual assistants handle our schedules, and we're so used to 'likes' that face-to-face compliments feel like a *rarity*. Even dating is mostly handled by apps now; meeting someone through *mutual friends* is almost *old-fashioned*.

We've become *spectators* in our own lives, always watching and rarely *participating*. No longer do we need to leave our homes to do anything—no *human interactions* are required. Sure, it's convenient, but there's something deeply *unsettling* about this trade-off. Ever walked into a room and noticed everyone in the same position, head down, glued to their phones? It's like the lights are on, but no one's really *there*.

Now, don't get me wrong—having *time to yourself* is important. Zoning out with a show or scrolling for a bit can be a *great escape*. But something *deeper* is missing. We're so *disconnected* that even in a *crowded room*, you can feel completely *alone*.

Common Sense would tell us to enjoy our devices but not at the expense of *real, human connection*. Balance is key—don't let the glow of your screen drown out the *warmth* of the world around you.

Traded real connections for Wi-Fi and scrolling—sounds about right?

Biological Realities

There's this bizarre trend going around where people think they can argue their way out of *basic biological facts*—like reality's just some *optional setting* they can adjust because they don't like it. But here's the deal: *men and women are biologically distinct*. It's not up for debate, and it's not some oppressive concept designed to ruin anyone's day. It's *science*. It's *biology*. Men and women are *built differently from the ground up*—different *chromosomes*, different *hormones*, different *physical structures*. Trying to deny that is like standing in the rain and insisting you're not getting wet, even though you already are—*think about it*.

Yes, there are rare cases of people with *mixed chromosomes* or *intersex traits*, but those exceptions don't rewrite the rule. It doesn't suddenly mean that the *definitions of male and female* no longer exist. These are *biological realities*, not some *flexible concepts* you can bend around *personal preferences* or *emotional discomfort*. Just because someone doesn't fit perfectly into one category or the other doesn't mean we should erase what those categories actually mean. It's like looking at a *rainbow* and saying, *"Well, there's a blurry line between colours, so let's just say there are no colours at all."* That's not how it works. Trying to turn the *exception* into the *new rule* just leads to *confusion and chaos*, making it impossible to have a grounded understanding of anything.

And so, here's some *Common Sense*: biology isn't a *buffet* where you get to pick and choose what parts apply to you. It's not some *fantasy* that you can twist just because it doesn't match up with how you feel that day. *Men are men, and women are women.* That's a *fact*. *Reality doesn't bend to feelings*, and ignoring it won't make it go away. Pretending otherwise is like covering your eyes and insisting the world's gone dark. People can live their lives however they want, but denying *biological truths* just to make someone feel better? That's not *progressive*—that's *delusional*.

Root yourself in reality you muppet.

What is a Definition?!

It's crazy that in today's world, even something as basic as a *definition* has become a battleground. Definitions are supposed to *clarify* things, to say what something *is*. They're like the *anchors* that keep reality in place. But now, whenever a definition doesn't line up with someone's feelings or opinions, people start *twisting it around* to mean whatever suits them. Suddenly, everything's *"subjective,"* and people want definitions to be a *subject of subjectiveness*—basically, they want *reality* to bend and flex just because it makes them uncomfortable. But a *definition* can't just change on a whim, because then it's not a definition at all. It's just *noise*.

Take words like *"man"* or *"woman,"* for example. For centuries, these words had *clear, concrete meanings*. But now, some people are so fixated on redefining these terms to align with how they *feel* that the *original definitions* have almost become *taboo*. And it's not just gender; people want to redefine *"success," "freedom," "truth"*—you name it. If they don't like what a word means, they try to stretch or twist its definition until it's *unrecognisable*. It's like trying to say a *square* can be a *circle* if you just look at it differently enough. But, guess what? *Reality doesn't care about feelings*. A square's still a square, no matter how many times you try to redefine its edges.

It's weird to have to mention *Common Sense* here because changing a definition doesn't change *reality*. It's one thing to argue opinions or beliefs, but it's downright absurd to demand that the *meaning of words* bend to match your *personal perspective*. If you don't like what a definition says, tough luck—it's not the definition that's wrong, it's your *expectations*. Trying to redefine everything just to avoid *uncomfortable truths* is like plugging your ears and shouting, *"I can't hear you!"* like a child throwing a tantrum. Definitions aren't supposed to cater to people's *delicate feelings*. They're meant to *reflect reality*. Trying to rewrite them just because you don't like the answer isn't just *stupid*—it's a way of saying you'd rather live in your own little *fantasy* than deal with the world as it actually is.

I just defined how stupid some modern humans can be.

Being able to Talk

When I say being able to *talk*, I mean having the ability to *connect* with someone on a deeper level—where the exchange feels almost *healing* for both parties. No *bullshit* or polite *white lies*, just *truth*, even when it's uncomfortable. That kind of openness breeds *respect* and a genuine *understanding* between people. But in today's fast-paced world, it's like we're forced to communicate in *sound bites*, short and straight to the point as if every interaction is a *text message*. Even face-to-face, we're often looking through an invisible screen, engaging but somehow *holding back*, leaving something essential *untouched*.

Expressing yourself properly can be *challenging*, especially if you grew up in an environment that discouraged *deeper conversations*—places where interactions were kept at a *surface level* just to 'get by' in society. But the truth is, being able to *open up* and share what's real allows for a kind of *freedom* and *connection* that's increasingly rare. Our brains are wired to *connect*, our voices to *speak what we feel*. We can convey so much through *words* and *tone*, yet many choose to stay overly *logical*, almost *robotic*, in how they communicate. Sure, you don't have to open up to just *anyone*—that would be naive. Not everyone wants to hear your story, nor should they. But aiming for *real understanding* means expanding how we *express* ourselves and diving beyond the *surface*.

Keeping unspoken thoughts bottled up can wear a person down over time. It's like carrying *unresolved burdens* that pile up, whether it's *stress* or *old traumas* that need a *voice* to be freed. The challenge is often in finding the *right words*, structuring them to say what's on your mind, and having the *confidence* to speak them aloud. Opening up isn't just about *sharing*; it's about freeing yourself from carrying *everything alone*.

Common Sense says this: keep learning, keep expanding your *vocabulary*, and see what it does for you out there. Being able to *speak your mind clearly* is a skill that opens doors—who wouldn't want to be a bit *sharper* and *connect* a little deeper?

Try and express yourself but don't be naive.

Lost Generation

Amongst all the confusion of today and the addiction to anything exciting—turning you into a junkie for quick thrills like social media's dopamine fix—being *"lost"* feels more like a lifestyle than a word. Everyone's compass seems to point nowhere, with no direction other than surviving this weird transition into the tech age. We're trading substance and depth for instant gratification and calling it progress.

Our sense of direction is drowned in notifications and the relentless chase for the next big thing. It's like we *know* the world is full of opportunities, but why chase them when you can just watch it all on your phone? The comfort of detachment has replaced the thrill of possibility, leaving many to scroll aimlessly while life passes them by. The more connected we become online, the more disconnected we are in reality.

There's also the obsession with individuality, where everyone's trying to stand out but ends up doing it in the same way. People chase identities instead of discovering themselves, creating pressure to "brand" their lives instead of living them authentically. Add to that a culture of convenience—instant food, instant entertainment, even instant relationships—and it's no surprise that patience and effort are dwindling. Why wait for something meaningful when something quick is just a click away?

This loop of temporary satisfaction only deepens the disconnection. Highlight reels on social media fuel comparisons, leaving many feeling *"Well, crap, guess I'm doing it all wrong."* The systems we rely on—education, work, society—don't help either. They push productivity but fail to prepare us for a world where attention spans are currency, and the bigger picture gets lost in the noise.

Common Sense says: you've got to step out of the loop and work harder to stay grounded. Get clear on what really matters, because staying lost isn't an excuse—it's a trap. Life might feel chaotic, but finding clarity is worth the effort, especially in a world trying so hard to confuse you. Stay sharp, stay real, and don't let the noise drown out your direction.

It's about finding your purpose, init. Be that whatever.

Accountability

Let's be real—nobody likes taking the blame. Sometimes, even when you're clearly in the wrong, owning up can feel like trying to swallow a cactus. But taking responsibility, even if it's awkward, is one of the most grown-up things we can do. Accountability isn't just about saying "Oops" and moving on like nothing happened. It's about owning your mistakes, fixing what you can, and not pointing fingers to dodge the heat of the moment. Honestly, if more of us did that, the world would probably be a lot less of a hot mess.

You can't have accountability without discipline—they're like two peas in a boring but necessary pot. Discipline is sticking to your commitments and getting things done, even when you'd rather just binge-watch something. Accountability is owning up to what you did, for better or worse. When you put them together, you're not just talking the talk; you're actually walking the walk—even when the walk feels uphill and sitting down sounds way better.

A lot of people today struggle with accountability because, let's face it, blaming others or making excuses is way easier. Social media makes it worse with its constant distractions and sweet hits of instant gratification, pulling us away from facing the tough stuff. Instead of learning from failures, people hide behind excuses or fish for validation, making it harder to grow into the kind of person who can handle life's curveballs.

Accountability isn't just about owning mistakes—it's about being accountable to yourself, too. Setting goals, sticking to them, and not giving up the second things get inconvenient is where true growth happens. It's the foundation of a fuller life because when you stop running from your responsibilities, you make space for real progress and deeper self-respect. Let's be honest, there's no app or shortcut for that.

Common Sense? It's about taking accountability for your actions, not just to keep others happy but to build something solid for yourself. Own it, learn from it, and grow. Because honestly, life gets a lot better when you stop dodging and start dealing—it's not like you have much of a choice anyway.

In a nutshell, it's your fault.

Duality of today's Society

It's like we're living in a time where everything feels *split in two*. We have more *information* at our fingertips than ever, yet we're drowning in *misinformation* and *half-truths*. Social media connects us to the world, but somehow leaves us feeling more *isolated* than before. We're constantly bombarded with outrage until, after a while, we just tune it all out, too exhausted to care. It's the *age of extremes*—where knowing *everything* and understanding *nothing* coexist, and connection somehow leads to *loneliness*. It's as if we've forgotten how to *truly engage*.

Meanwhile, society seems caught in a strange *tug-of-war* between *progress* and *regression*. We're making strides in science, technology, and social awareness, yet old problems like *racism*, *nationalism*, and *sexism* cling stubbornly to the present. We're *sprinting toward the future*, but dragging the *past* behind us. If there's one thing most of us can agree on, it's this: today's world is a *chaotic dance* of *contradictions*. All we can do is try to find our own rhythm in this madness—the *duality of today's society*.

It's funny how we've learned to live with all these *contradictions* as if they're just part of the *day-to-day*. We juggle *progress* and *problems* casually, switching between sharing memes and discussing world issues in the same breath. It's almost as if we've grown used to the *chaos*—making it feel strangely *normal*, even when most things around us don't make sense.

Common Sense says: stay aware of the world's *confusion* but don't let it *consume you*. Find a spot where you can see things *clearly* enough to navigate this *beautiful, modern mess*. You might not always know exactly where you *fit in*, but maybe that's part of what keeps you *grounded* in the middle of it all.

We're drowning in facts but starving for truth,

We're tangled in connection yet missing our roots.

Racing toward progress with old chains in tow,

It's chaos we juggle, but it's all we know

We can be peculiar at times.

Inevitability of Change

Change is a *fiend* we're all familiar with. It sneaks up on us, often when we're least prepared, tearing away our comforts. Sometimes, it feels *wicked*—an unwelcome force disturbing the rhythm of our lives and leaving chaos in its wake. Yet without change, we'd be stuck in *unconsciousness*, trapped in cycles of *sameness*, too numb and oblivious to realise we've stopped growing. *Stagnation*, in a way, has become the new norm.

Unconsciousness, in this sense, is the shadow that lurks behind our resistance to change. It's the force that keeps us clinging to the *familiar*, even when it no longer serves us. It's the *fear of the unknown*. Change and unconsciousness are locked in a constant *dance*—change pulls us into *awareness*, forcing us to confront *new truths*, while unconsciousness tugs us back into the comfort of *ignorance*.

So, for all its fiendish tendencies, change is actually what keeps us *alive*, *awake*, and *aware*. It jolts us out of *autopilot* and reminds us that we're constantly *evolving*. Without it, we'd drift through life, never truly seeing or experiencing the world around us. The trick, then, is to stop seeing change as an *enemy* and start viewing it as the *key* to escaping the grip of unconsciousness, which would have us *sleepwalking* through life.

Common Sense says: embrace change, don't fear it. You'll only *level up* once you participate in it. Be *conscious* and resist the urge to hold back when *action* is needed, even if it's uncomfortable. Otherwise, you could end up as a kid in an adult's body, standing on the *sidelines*. The *choice* is yours.

Change is constant, raw, and real,

A force we face, a truth we feel.

It tears us down, yet helps us grow,

The only path we truly know.

Uncomfortable but necessary.

Isn't it just Sad?

Isn't it just *sad*? Most of us go through life with this idea that we can do anything, that the world is full of opportunities and everyone's kind of on the same page. You grow up thinking you're invincible, that if you put in the effort, you can get what you want. You believe that the system, flawed as it may be, has its checks and balances. But then, as you start paying attention to the world with more coherence, you see the *cracks*.

You see the injustice that so many live under, the oppressive regimes, the blatantly corrupt governments that everyone knows are rotten to the core, yet nothing changes. These places, these systems, are run by people who have everything and want more, and the scary thing is, even the ones pulling the strings behind the scenes—the ones who really control things—are just as twisted. They're driven by profit and power, with no moral compass in sight, leaving the majority of the world to suffer at their whim. It's as if the more control they get, the more disconnected they become from basic human decency.

Then there's the shocking realisation when you find out that some people you looked up to—celebrities, musicians, artists you've followed since childhood—are involved in the darkest, most heinous things you could imagine. Human trafficking, child exploitation, and so on—things that seem like they belong in some twisted film fiction. And it's not just them; they bring others into it, turning what you thought was harmless entertainment into something vile.

It's like they believe they're above everyone, operating on some *god-complex* where normal rules don't apply. They feed off power, money, and manipulation, while the rest of us are left in disbelief, realising that the very culture we celebrate is hiding monsters in plain sight. It's hard to accept because we don't want to see the reality behind the curtain. It's almost as though seeing clearly means stripping away your peace of mind, and for many, *ignorance feels safer*.

What makes it even *sadder* is how people prefer to live in ignorance. The disconnection between people, between reality and illusion, is grim. We'd rather be fools who enjoy the show, playing along than wake up and confront the truth.

We chase after the next distraction, numbing ourselves with entertainment, shallow relationships, and consumerism. It's easier to turn a blind eye and live on *autopilot* than to dig deeper and realise how messed up things are, but each to their own, I suppose.

Yet, there's always the other side—the people who *choose* to see clearly, who question everything and refuse to be controlled by the noise. But when you take that path, you start to see just how many people around you are asleep, and that can feel *lonely* with seeing the bigger picture. But even so, awareness doesn't have to rob you of joy. You can still hold onto the simple moments, the meaningful connections, without drowning in the darkness of what you've uncovered.

That being said, it's not all doom and gloom. There *are* things to be excited about—innovations, breakthroughs, and people doing genuinely inspiring work—but that's not what this chapter is about. This chapter is about the *sad truths* we tend to gloss over or avoid entirely because they're uncomfortable. The good stuff deserves its spotlight, but here, we're peeling back the layers of the mess so we can see it for what it is. Sometimes, you need to focus on what's broken before you can truly appreciate what's still shining.

Isn't it just *sad* that we're more disconnected than ever in a world so connected by technology? With every new app or gadget, we're promised more connection, yet somehow it leaves us feeling emptier. It's *ironic* how much we've surrendered to the things meant to bring us together.

Common Sense would tell you to find a balance—enjoy the little things, but don't lose sight of reality. It's alright to be wise and still have fun, but don't be a fool and ignore the truth either. And for those who choose to live extravagantly while causing harm because they're too bored with their excess? Well, that's not just sad—that's the kind of waste that robs us all of something good.

Not everything is as it seems.

AI Society

In *AI Society*, we're not just watching technology advance; we're watching it redefine what it means to live in the modern world. *Artificial intelligence*, or *AI*, isn't just some fancy tool we use—it's becoming a system that learns, adapts, and thinks almost like we do. Today, it's in our voice assistants, self-driving cars, and even how our devices seem to know what we want before we do. But the future of AI? That's something much bigger. We're talking about technology that could transform almost *every single part* of life as we know it.

The possibilities could take us places we've only dreamed of in sci-fi movies. Picture *Super AI*—machines that don't just mimic human intelligence but blow right past it. We're talking about AI so advanced it could diagnose diseases better than any doctor, make scientific breakthroughs in a fraction of the time, and tackle global issues with ideas that are just beyond what we can wrap our heads around. Super AI could change what we think intelligence even is.

Then throw *Quantum Computing* into the mix. If AI starts tapping into the power of quantum computing, it'll be able to process and analyze data at speeds that make our current tech look like dial-up internet. Imagine solving climate models, cracking complex genetic codes, or figuring out financial markets with a precision and speed we can't even dream of. Quantum-enhanced AI could tackle challenges that are currently impossible for even the best computers out there, in a blink of an eye.

And if we keep moving forward, we might even see *Conscious AI* or *Sentient AI*, where machines could develop something like self-awareness and might even simulate emotions to a realistic level. The future might give us a look at intelligence on a level we've never known—machines that don't just *do* things but *understand* things. It's mad to think about, but it's the direction we're heading, ready or not, better grab your *Common Sense* helmet.

AI will advance and it will be very impactful.

Complaining about, what <u>YOU</u> chose to do

Isn't it strange? How we love to complain about the very things we *willingly* signed up for. We pick a career, commit to a relationship, even choose a hobby, and then somehow act shocked when it gets *hard*. It's like we expect a life free of challenges or annoyances as if the universe owes us smooth sailing just because we made a decision. It doesn't make sense, does it? The truth is, we've all been guilty of signing up for the *"struggle"* and then complaining about it like we didn't know what we were getting into. It's a bit silly, isn't it?

Take work, for example. We choose jobs, knowing they come with early mornings, long hours, difficult tasks, or the occasional irritating coworker, and then turn around and complain about all three—like that wasn't part of the deal! It's like joining a gym and being shocked that you have to *work out*. *News flash*, mate: if you picked it, the struggle is *part of the experience*. Complaining won't change that, but it sure seems like everyone's favourite pastime. Instead of accepting the grind, we find ourselves ranting about it, like there's a magic solution waiting around the corner. Again, it doesn't make sense, does it?

It's not just about jobs, either. Take relationships. People dive into them, sometimes ignoring red flags or hoping things will *magically change*, only to complain when they're stuck in co-dependency or endless arguments. Or parenting—people choose to have kids but then moan about sleepless nights and constant responsibility, as if that wasn't part of the *package*. Instead of facing the choices head-on, we often sit there complaining, unwilling to take responsibility for the situations we *knowingly created*. It's easy to blame others or life's circumstances, but ultimately, you made your choices, so *own them*.

And don't even get me started on the activists and influencers who rally against everything while ignoring their roles in the chaos. Take the *"Just Stop Oil"* crowd, for example, getting arrested for running onto fields in protest—these are people who demand everyone see the *truth* yet sometimes add more friction and division than change. Or the social media influencers who shout about mental health and self-care but live lives of constant validation-seeking online. They're part of the same system they claim to *criticize*, pointing fingers outward but rarely taking stock of their contributions.

People complain about the system, but how often do they genuinely do the *hard work* to change it? Protesting is one thing; putting in consistent, constructive work to address *real issues* is another.

It's like complaining about how toxic social media is while spending hours scrolling every day. Or taking a stand against big corporations while still ordering from the very companies you criticize. Living in contradiction but shouting the loudest is a *twisted cycle*—and then it's back to heated homes, running water, and charging up lithium-powered phones while calling for environmental reform. *Talk about irony!*

Common Sense? Stop complaining about the choices *you* made—no one cares. If you're not willing to put in the work and push through the challenges, then what's the point? Once you're past a certain age, no one's going to hold your hand or guide you through life. The way you make your bed is the way you'll sleep in it, simple as that.

Take ownership of your decisions, stop whining about the consequences, and start making real changes instead of just talking about them. If you can't handle the fallout of your actions, maybe it's time to rethink why you made those choices in the first place. And sure, not everything is black and white or easy to handle, but let's be real—most of the time, you know what you need to do.

We rant at the grind we willingly choose,
Wanting the win, but hating to lose.
Life's work is tough—no magic fix,
Just keep moving forward; that's the trick.

Don't curse the path—you chose the walk.

Importance of Real Friendship

Real friendship is one of the few things in life that doesn't try to *fool you*. It's not flashy, doesn't ask for much, and yet, it's probably the most *grounding force* we have. A true friend sees you at your worst and sticks around, not because they *have to*, but because they genuinely *want to*. It's that person who knows all your weird quirks, your bad habits, and your messy moments—and somehow, they're still down for the ride. But here's the thing: friendship, the *real* kind, isn't always easy to acquire and maintain.

It's not just showing up when things are *fun* or *convenient*. It's about being there when life throws its *bullshit* at you when your friend is going through something and needs a shoulder, or when you have to call them out on their nonsense because nobody else will. That's where the beauty of real friendship lies. It's *raw*, sometimes *uncomfortable*, but always *honest*. There's no room for unconsciousness here. Real friends drag you out of your own head when you're spiralling and keep you grounded when you're losing your way, although they might just join in.

What makes it even more valuable is that in a world where so many relationships feel *transactional* or *surface-level*, real friendship is one of the few things that stays *solid*. It's not about what you can get from each other, but about the *trust* and *understanding* that grows from being there, time after time. It's the kind of bond that stands up to *change* and remains a constant, reminding you that no matter how much the world shifts, you've got someone in your corner, ready to face it all with you.

Your good friend *Common Sense* is here to tell you, that you have to have a *real friend* in life; it's one of the most *crucial* parts of experiencing being a human on earth, and you'd be *stupid* to think you don't need anyone, even if you're overly *independent* and especially if you're *introverted*. Not many—at least 1 or 2 will do.

A true friend sees the shadows you hide,
Stands firm, a lighthouse through the tide.
In a world of masks and fleeting trends,
Real friendship stays, it mends and defends.

As GAY as that sounds, it's true.

What is Love? In this Day and Age

Love these days seems to be one of the most misunderstood ideas out there, and it's easy to see why. Everywhere you turn, love is reduced to quick fixes, flashy gestures, or the belief that someone else is supposed to fill all the gaps in your life. But real love isn't about *instant gratification*; it's about patience, mutual understanding, and putting in the effort, even when it's hard. It's not just the rush of emotions—it's a choice, something you nurture daily. We've *completely* lost sight of that.

The problem is, that we've traded real connection for a shallow, surface-level version of love. People are so focused on chasing perfection that they forget love *thrives* in imperfections. Without a little more *Common Sense,* love might become something people treat like a disposable product—tossed aside the moment it gets tough. Sticking through thick and thin, the thing that once defined relationships is becoming a lost art in the face of fleeting thrills and shiny new distractions.

What's twisted is that love has started to feel like more *trouble* than it's worth. People treat it as the *bare minimum*, and in doing so, they've made it something unappreciative, almost transactional. It's been warped into something where effort feels optional, and the irony is, we're the ones suffering for it. Real love requires more than just showing up; it takes actual work and vulnerability—two things many people are scared to invest in.

Today, love feels more like a trial offer—swipe, try, and cancel when it doesn't deliver instantly. People treat relationships like fast food; if it's not exactly what they ordered, they leave without trying to make it work. But love isn't a delivery service. It's more like *cooking a meal from scratch*—it takes effort, patience, and a willingness to fix mistakes along the way. That's what makes it meaningful, not the guarantee of perfection.

Common Sense? Don't be a fool and mistake the initial chemical rush for love. Infatuation fades, and if you're not willing to build something solid when that high wears off, you'll be stuck chasing the same cycle. Real love isn't just about feelings; it's the choice to stay, to grow, and to embrace the imperfections. That's where the magic is—not in the highlights, but in the work it takes to build something real. Don't let that slip by chasing something fleeting—you'll regret it.

Real love isn't about *perfection;* it's about growth.

Finding meaning in Life, in today's Era

In today's world, finding meaning in life feels like trying to assemble flat-pack furniture without the instructions—*frustrating, chaotic,* and you're pretty sure you've got a screw loose. With constant distractions, endless to-do lists, and the pressure to always be "on," it's easy to lose sight of what really matters. We're so busy chasing after goals, success, or the next big thing that we forget to ask ourselves the most important question: *why* are we doing any of this in the first place? The truth is, that meaning doesn't come from checking off boxes—it comes from understanding what truly gives us a sense of purpose and fulfilment. But hey, who's got time for that when there's another notification to check?

The problem is, that we're bombarded with messages that scream meaning comes from things outside ourselves—*money, status, and likes on social media.* It's like we're on a never-ending treadmill where the finish line is always moving further away. Deep down, we all know none of those things last. Yet, we still chase them like kids running after the sound of an ice cream van, ignoring the fact that the flavour melts faster than we can enjoy it. If we don't slow down and start looking inward, we risk living a life where we're constantly searching for something that's just out of reach. Meaning isn't found in the hustle; it's found in the quiet, unfiltered moments when we're truly ourselves. *Spoiler alert:* those moments rarely happen while doom-scrolling Instagram or TikTok.

Without taking the time to reflect on what gives our lives real purpose, we risk becoming more disconnected and unfulfilled than ever. Imagine having everything you thought you wanted—money, gadgets, the aesthetic lifestyle—and still feeling like something's missing. *Sound familiar?* That's because fulfilment doesn't come from collecting shiny things; it comes from aligning our actions with what genuinely matters to us. But instead of digging deeper, most of us keep piling on distractions, wondering why life feels so empty. If we're not careful, we'll become like those people who order expensive gym memberships and never go—investing in the wrong things while neglecting what truly counts.

Common Sense? Meaning isn't something you stumble on—it's built from what you do along the way. *Try things, fail, learn, and keep moving.* Life's messy, but that's part of the fun.

Keep searching.

Superficial Connectivity

In an age where we're more *"connected"* than ever, it's strange how isolated we can still feel. Sure, we can send a message across the world in seconds, scroll through someone's life updates, or have hundreds of followers, but what's the *depth* of that connection? Most of it is fleeting and shallow. We know what someone ate for lunch or the latest trend they're into, but we don't truly know them. It's like we've traded meaningful interactions for a highlight reel, and then wonder why loneliness has become a silent epidemic.

The real issue is that we're mistaking convenience for connection. Just because you can double-tap a photo or send a quick "how are you" text doesn't mean you've fostered a relationship. Genuine connection takes vulnerability, effort, and time—things that can't be crammed into a DM or a tweet. We're so focused on being visible to others that we lose sight of what it means to be truly *present* with someone. If we don't start prioritising genuine conversations over quick, surface-level exchanges, we risk losing the deeper bonds that make life worth living. And by the time we realise what's missing, it might already feel too late—or worse, irreversible.

What's even more disheartening is how this mindset creeps into our family dynamics. Even having parents or close relatives online becomes just another notification in the feed. Of course, they're "there," but if it doesn't suit us to engage in that moment, we might ignore them, treating our own loved ones as optional interactions. It's an ironic disconnect in a world designed to keep us in touch. The less effort it takes to reach someone, the less value we place on the opportunity to engage with them truly.

Without authentic connection, we risk becoming emotionally numb, and unable to build the kind of bonds that bring joy and meaning to life. Humans are naturally social, but superficiality doesn't nourish that need—it leaves us more detached. If we don't take time to prioritise quality over quantity, we'll find ourselves drowning in a sea of digital faces, yet feeling entirely alone. Real connection happens in shared moments, in conversations beyond emojis and typing indicators. It's messy, raw, and irreplaceable.

Common Sense? Try and stop relying so much on online interactions to fill the gaps. Go out, meet people in person, and show up for your relationships—even when it's inconvenient. That's where the magic of genuine connection lies—not in the swipe, but in the shared experience.

Cancel Culture

Cancel culture, which started as a way to hold powerful people accountable for actual wrongdoings, has spiralled into something absurdly toxic. It's no longer about justice or change; it's about wielding power over someone else, silencing dissent, and enforcing a rigid narrative. Say something remotely controversial, or even slightly offbeat, and you're suddenly public enemy number one. Mistakes? Forget it. Growth? Irrelevant. The cancel mob is more interested in tearing someone down than understanding the full picture. It's like modern-day gladiator games—except the arena is social media, and the weapons are tweets and hashtags.

What's worse is how this culture has normalised fear and suppression. It's no longer just about holding people accountable; it's about silencing opinions entirely. People are walking on eggshells, terrified of saying the "wrong" thing, not because they're wrong, but because they fear the consequences of being misunderstood or misrepresented. The result? A society where everyone pretends to agree, while secretly resenting the fact that they can't speak freely. And the kicker? It's celebrated as progress. But honestly, is it progress when we've traded free thought for a collective echo chamber? It's not dialogue; it's dictatorship.

Now, don't get me wrong, there *are* cases where cancellation makes sense—when someone has caused real harm or engaged in genuinely unacceptable behaviour. But the lines have blurred. Instead of sparking meaningful conversation, we've devolved into digital lynch mobs where a single slip-up or unpopular opinion can ruin someone overnight. Whatever happened to disagreement? To learn from differing perspectives? It's like we've forgotten that humans are flawed and that growth comes from dialogue, not destruction. And let's not even start on how context doesn't seem to exist anymore—nuance is dead.

Then there's the hypocrisy. The loudest voices calling for cancellation often have skeletons in their own closets. They preach morality while ignoring their own flaws, turning the whole thing into a contest of who can scream the loudest. Most of the time, it's not even about justice—it's about feeding egos and showing off on some virtual moral high ground. These keyboard warriors are too busy trying to look righteous to focus on actual solutions. Meanwhile, the real problems? Completely ignored.

Cancel culture isn't just toxic—it's lazy. It's easier to "cancel" someone than to engage in a productive debate. It's easier to destroy than to build. And what's the outcome? A society filled with people too afraid to share ideas or admit mistakes. We've turned into a mob of self-appointed judges who don't listen, don't learn, and don't even care to try. Instead of fostering accountability, we've created a culture of fear, outrage, and performative wokeness.

Common Sense? If someone genuinely deserves to be called out—fine, let's do it, but with reason, not with pitchforks. However, if someone's speaking the *truth* or simply voicing an unpopular but valid opinion, maybe it's time to grow up and have the maturity to handle it without running to the cancel button. Life's not about protecting fragile egos. So, put on your helmet, grow some resilience, and stop weaponizing your feelings as an excuse to silence others.

We don't hang people, not anymore,
Now it's cancel tweets and viral uproar.
Say one wrong thing, and they're quick to attack,
No room for growth, no chance to come back.
Progress, they call it, but here's the deal—
It's just a new way to make others kneel.

It's like playing tag, but everyone's 'it' and no one's safe—what even is this?

Others can Sense you?

There's something unspoken between people—a form of connection that goes beyond words or even body language. It's like we all have invisible antennas, tuned into each other's energy. You've probably felt it before—sensing someone's bad mood without them saying a word or feeling the excitement radiating off someone who's had a great day. It's not just about reading expressions or tone; it's deeper, like an invisible thread connecting us all, even if we don't *realise* it.

It's as if the air carries fragments of each other's emotions. In a crowded room, certain people stand out without speaking, while others fade into the background. Those "gut feelings" you get? They're part of this unspoken network. You sense things you can't explain, but they often tell you more than words ever could, offering glimpses into truths that aren't said out loud.

For some, this sense feels heightened. They can walk into a room and instantly feel the vibe like they're tuned into a frequency most people miss. It's almost metaphysical—a quiet superpower without the cape. Those moments when someone says, "I just had a feeling," and they're right? That's intuition on another level. It's subjective, sure, but undeniable to the ones who experience it. Whether it's emotional intelligence, spiritual awareness, or just a sharp gut instinct, it's a deeper way of navigating the world.

The challenge today is that we're so caught up in digital communication that we lose touch with this energy. Texts, screens, and curated posts can't carry the same weight as in-person interactions, and the more we rely on them, the harder it is to tap into this unspoken connection. It's a skill we all have, but like any skill, it fades if we don't use it.

Common Sense? Trust your instincts, but stay grounded. These feelings aren't always explainable, but they're often worth listening to. Whether you call it intuition or just a gut sense, it's one of those things that reminds us there's more to connection than meets the eye.

Funny how sometimes we read each other best while in silence.

Today's Cultural Blender

We live in an era where cultures from all over are blending more than ever. And while this diversity can be a fantastic source of *strength* and *enrichment*, it often ends up feeling less like a perfect smoothie and more like a chaotic stew where someone forgot the recipe. Different traditions and ideas get tossed in without much thought, and what we end up with is a confusing soup where the *essence* of each culture kind of gets lost in the mix.

Navigating cultural sensitivity today is like trying to walk a tightrope while people shout their opinions at you from every direction—and you're *on camera*. One seemingly innocent comment or action can blow up into a major controversy faster than you can say, *"I didn't mean it that way!"* This kind of heightened sensitivity makes people hesitant to speak up, worried they might accidentally poke the hornet's nest of public opinion.

Suppose we really want to benefit from our diverse cultural landscape. In that case, we need to respect and appreciate each culture's unique contributions without trying to shove everything into one boring, one-size-fits-all box. It's like trying to fit all the spices in your pantry into a single jar—you'll end up with a mess that tastes like *nothing*. By encouraging genuine understanding and real communication, we can build a society that actually values the *richness* of all these different traditions. That way, we can navigate the complexities of our interconnected world without losing sight of what makes each culture *special*—and maybe even enjoy the unique *flavours* they each bring to the table.

Common Sense says: sure, we all eat, sleep, and do the same basic stuff as the next person, but don't forget your roots and culture. Don't be that person who tries to force everyone into the same *bland mould*. Instead, learn how to respect each other's differences so we can live in *harmony*—instead of being stuck with a confusing cultural mash-up that no one really asked for.

We're all here together.

Spirituality?

Remember when spirituality wasn't some fleeting trend, but an integral part of life? Not that you were alive, but once upon a time, it was woven into the very fabric of society—whether it was praying to the gods, meditating under trees, or practising rituals passed down through generations. It gave people a sense of purpose, connected them to something bigger than themselves, and offered a framework to deal with the chaos of life. Fast forward to today, and we've somehow swapped sacred ceremonies for scrolling through Instagram, chasing a better life instead of inner understanding.

And then there's alcohol—ironically named *"spirits,"* as if it's meant to lift the soul. Ancient cultures saw alcohol as a sacred tool, used in rituals to connect with the divine or celebrate life's milestones. Some believed it thinned the veil between the physical and spiritual worlds, allowing them to commune with something greater. But let's not romanticise it too much—alcohol's effects on the spirit aren't always so profound. It's been enjoyed for millennia, sure, but overindulgence has a knack for clouding the mind and dulling the connection to your higher self. Still, it's not the biggest problem; like anything, it's about how you use it. Just know that while it can loosen you up, it can also weigh you down.

These days, we're told to focus on what's tangible. Spirituality? Oh, that's just something for hippies, right? We're told to trust in science and productivity, to keep our heads down and follow the grind. But here's the thing: ignoring spirituality doesn't make the need for it disappear. In a world where mental health issues are skyrocketing and people are feeling more disconnected than ever, maybe there's something to be said for revisiting the old ways. Not to ditch logic or reason, but to find the balance between what we can see and what we can *feel.*

You don't have to be burning incense or chanting on a mountaintop to be spiritual. It's not about adopting every ancient practice under the sun. Whether it's prayer, meditation, yoga, or simply taking a moment to breathe and connect with yourself, spirituality can be as personal as you make it. What matters is the intention behind it—recognising that there's more to life than the daily grind and that nurturing the soul is as important as hitting your step count for the day. The irony is, that even as we've become more *"advanced,"* we've neglected the things that ground us.

It's almost as if society is actively discouraging us from looking inward. We're constantly bombarded by distractions—notifications, advertisements, news cycles, the endless scroll of social media—keeping us too busy to think about anything beyond the immediate moment. If spirituality is about connecting with something deeper, modern life is all about staying in the shallow end. We're told to hustle, keep up with trends, and not stop to ask, *"Is this all there is?"*

The funny thing is, many of the things that truly matter—kindness, mindfulness, empathy—come straight from spiritual teachings. Yet, they're marketed back to us as life hacks or self-help strategies. It's like we've taken the essence of spirituality, rebranded it, and slapped a price tag on it.

But the truth is, spirituality has always been about *Common Sense:* it's about understanding your place in the world, treating others well, and finding peace in a chaotic life. The problem is, that we're so caught up in being *"rational"* that we've forgotten these simple truths.

At the end of the day, integrating spirituality into today's society doesn't mean rejecting progress. It's about finding a balance between the material and the spiritual, the seen and the unseen. We need both to thrive. *Common Sense* tells us that life's not just about the stuff we own or the titles we chase. It's about the connections we make—with ourselves, with others, and with whatever higher purpose we believe in. Maybe it's time we stop dismissing spirituality as outdated and start recognising it for what it is: a necessary part of being human.

Common Sense wants you to stay in tune with what's around you and what's inside you. It's got endless power to help you connect on a whole different level. You don't need to head off to a mountain or sit under a tree to feel aligned—it's more about getting your body, mind, and spirit on the same page. It's a lifelong journey, so take your time. Society isn't exactly designed to teach you how to step off that productivity treadmill and connect a little, but hey, *that's on you.*

Seeking the divine while stuck in our head,
We meditate deeply, then scroll instead.
Searching for purpose, we craft a façade,
Lost in the chase for approval, so odd.

If spirituality were tangible, belief would come easier, right?

We're not the Centre of the Universe

Hey, fellow Earthling. Let's talk about how we've gone from discovering the Earth isn't flat!? To act like the entire universe is just a backdrop for our selfies. Seriously, we're on a tiny blue marble spinning around an average star, in a galaxy that's just one of the billions, yet we strut around like we're the *centre of the cosmos*. We've snapped pics of black holes and detected ripples in spacetime, but somehow, we're debating "what is a woman" or if the Earth is shaped like a pancake. It's like we've got this incredible telescope to peer into the universe, but instead, we're using it to check if our hair looks good. And while we're definitely not the *literal* centre of the universe, being alive and aware *kind of* makes us the centre of it all in our way. <u>Think about it</u>—we're the ones witnessing this wild, ever-unfolding reality, the ones giving the universe meaning just by being here to observe it. Everything we see, touch, or even debate about exists through the lens of our consciousness. So yeah, maybe we're small in the grand scheme, but our ability to *experience* the cosmos makes us *pretty fucking* special.

But here's the deal: *realising* we're not the universe's *MVP* isn't depressing, it's actually *freeing*. Every cool thing we do, every bit of kindness or creativity we bring into the world—that's all on *us*—because *we choose to*. There's no cosmic scoreboard; we make our own *meaning*. Instead of being the stars of some pre-written script, we're the ones *writing our own stories*. So, maybe it's time to look up from our screens, stop *self-obsessing*, and actually appreciate the mind-blowing show the universe is putting on for us.

At the end of the day, we're *stardust with Wi-Fi*, cruising through space on a fragile but well-put-together blue dot. The universe isn't sending us participation trophies; we've got to make the most of our time here. So let's drop the ego, spark some *curiosity*, and remember that while the cosmos doesn't *care* what we do, we still have the power to create, explore, and make this life worth it.

Common Sense in a nutshell is knowing that being able to live in this reality is a *gift* to participate in—a cruel one at times, but a reminder that you're not the *center* of the universe. The world doesn't revolve around *you*, and that's okay. It's about playing your part, doing what you can, and realising there's a bigger picture that doesn't need your approval to exist. *Embrace* that, and life becomes a little less heavy and a lot more *real*.

Just think, it didn't have to be you, experiencing all this.

Wifi Radiation?

Have you ever stopped and thought about how we're basically *marinating* in radiation all day? No, not the scary nuclear stuff—though you never know—I'm talking about the low-key, invisible kind from Wi-Fi, cell towers, Bluetooth, and all the gadgets we can't live without. It's like we're living in a high-tech soup of electromagnetic frequencies (EMF), just soaking it all in without a second thought. Sure, it makes life convenient, but have we ever paused to wonder if all these waves flying through the air might be doing *something* to us?

First, let's break down the types. You've got your radio waves, microwaves, Wi-Fi, 4G, 5G, and soon enough, probably 10G or something that'll make your Netflix buffer *slightly* faster. All of these are part of the electromagnetic spectrum, and we've become so dependent on them that we've built our entire modern world around them. The deal is, that even though we can't see, hear, or feel these waves, they're *everywhere*. And yeah, while the big players in tech will tell you it's all perfectly safe, we've also been told in the past that asbestos was harmless and smoking was just a cool pastime.

Now, I'm not saying your phone's trying to fry your brain like an egg on a hot pavement, but there's still some murkiness about how long-term exposure to this stuff might affect us. Some studies say it's harmless, while others suggest it might mess with your sleep, cause headaches, or even contribute to bigger health issues down the road. The thing is, the research is still catching up, and with the tech evolving faster than we can study it, we're all just kind of winging it. *But what else can you do?*

It's wild when you think about it—there's so much we don't know. For instance, could constant exposure to all this invisible energy be impacting our mental health or focus? Maybe all that screen time and Wi-Fi immersion isn't just making us tired but subtly *rewiring* the way we think or feel. Not to scare you or anything—it's not like you'll sprout antennae—but isn't it worth asking? And then there's sleep. Ever notice how it's harder to switch off your brain after a day of being glued to screens? It's like the gadgets are calling the shots even when you're trying to wind down.

Here's the mad part—most of us don't even think twice about it. We sit next to our routers, phones in hand, laptops on our laps (which, by the way, may not be doing our future family planning any favours), completely oblivious.

It's like we're swimming in an ocean of invisible radiation, but because we can't see it, it's *all good*, right? We're more concerned about how many bars of signal we've got than what all that constant exposure might be doing to us.

I mean, we freak out if we see a bug in our salad but practically live in a soup of Wi-Fi, 4G, 5G, and microwaves without batting an eye. *Maybe ignorance really is bliss*—or maybe it's just one more thing we're all too distracted to worry about. Think about it: we're surrounded by a web of invisible waves 24/7, a non-stop pulse of energy we're not even aware of most of the time. But if we could actually *see it*—the endless streams of data, signals, and electronic chatter swirling around us—it might just make us a little uneasy. Isn't it odd how we care so much about organic food and "clean" products but barely question what our gadgets are doing to our bodies? The irony is hard to miss.

Common Sense? Take breaks from the noise. Go out into nature, turn off your Wi-Fi, switch your phone to aeroplane mode, and just *breathe*. It's not just your body asking for it—it's your brain saying, *"Hey, can we take a break from all this digital chaos?"* Sometimes, the best reset is the simplest one.

We're steeped in signals, lost in the hum,
Tech's endless buzz leaves us feeling numb.
Invisible waves that never take a break,
But hey, it's fine—what's a little headache?
Maybe unplugging is what we need to try,
Before we're all microwaved under the sky.

There's not much you can do about it.

Being in your Head

Ever notice how much time we spend in our own heads these days? Like, really just zoning out, staring at nothing, lost in thought—or worse, not even sure what we're thinking about at all. It's like our brains have turned into their own little hamster wheels, just spinning endlessly, but the hamster is on strike. And the thing is, dissociation—that feeling of being disconnected from everything around you—is getting way more common. We're not really present, not really engaged. It's like we're floating through life, half here, half somewhere else entirely.

Part of it's because we've got so many distractions. Phones buzzing, emails, social media updates—it's a nonstop barrage of stuff pulling us away from the moment. Our attention spans are shorter than ever, and even when we do have a moment to think, we're too mentally drained to do anything meaningful with it. Instead of dealing with our problems, we retreat into our heads, or worse, mindlessly scroll through Instagram or TikTok to drown out the noise. It's like we're too numb to deal with reality, so we just keep checking out.

Here's the thing: life today is stressful as hell. The economy's a mess, climate change is hanging over us, rent's too damn high, and everyone's constantly worried about whether they're succeeding enough, making enough, doing enough. So yeah, it's no wonder we'd rather check out than face all that. But the struggle is, while we're all floating through this mental fog, society's not waiting for us to get it together. The bills still need to be paid, the world keeps spinning, and before you know it, months—or even years—have passed, and you're left wondering where all the time went.

It's like we know we need to do better, to snap out of it, but we're too overwhelmed to figure out how. The world we've built keeps us distracted and disconnected, and it's getting harder to break free from that cycle. And let's not forget that constantly being online makes even our closest relationships feel like they're happening at arm's length. Even family or close friends become just another *notification* you respond to when you can be bothered, because the convenience of connection sometimes makes it *too* convenient to disengage.

The irony is, while we're definitely not the center of the universe, in a strange way, we sort of are—each of us living our own vivid, fleeting experience, witnessing this bizarre thing we call reality.

That alone should carry some weight, but we get so wrapped up in simply surviving that we forget to actually live. The fact that we're even here, overthinking everything and trying to make sense of the chaos, is a miracle in itself. Maybe the real issue isn't that we're lost in our heads—it's that we don't give ourselves enough credit for making it through the madness.

But what if we started seeing this chaos differently? Maybe it's less about untangling everything and more about finding those tiny, meaningful moments in the mess. A quick chat with someone who actually gets you, an hour unplugged from the world, or even just letting yourself laugh at how ridiculous life can be. These small breaks don't fix everything, but they remind you that not all is lost. Sometimes, finding meaning isn't about the big picture—it's about those little pieces that make up your day.

Common Sense is definitely present within such individuals' heads, but it's overshadowed at times by all this bollocks in the world, amplifying the overthinking. Try and find something that makes sense outside of your head and focus on it for a while—letting reality seep in so you're not overwhelmed by that veil of endless thoughts. Yes, it's hard to stay on top of it, but it's worth the effort. Life may be chaos, but *maybe that's where the beauty is too.*

Lost in the noise, we wander, unsure,
Chasing a calm that feels far from pure.
Life's chaos swirls, but here's the clue—
The mess holds meaning, if we just push through.

Hey! There's a whole world out there, outside yourself.

Enriching the Soul

Let's talk about enriching the soul, shall we? Sounds pretty good, right? Like, we're diving into some deep, cosmic nourishment that makes us feel all warm and fuzzy inside. But here's the deal: *enriching the soul* isn't just about doing yoga on a mountaintop or chanting mantras at sunrise. It's more about finding those little sparks of joy and purpose in the everyday grind. Think of it like making a five-star meal out of a can of beans—finding the magic in the mundane.

First off, let's get one thing straight: enriching the soul doesn't have to be a full-on, mystical experience. It can be as simple as picking up a book that makes you think, spending time with people who lift you up, or diving into a hobby that makes you lose track of time. It's about those moments when you feel truly alive and connected—not just to yourself but to the world around you. And yeah, it might involve a bit of introspection, but it doesn't have to come with a side of spiritual jargon or the need to sit cross-legged on a cushion. Sometimes, it's just about finding what makes you tick and leaning into it.

And here's the thing—enriching the soul doesn't mean turning your life upside down or reaching for some lofty ideal. It's often about small, intentional changes: swapping out screen time for a few minutes of journaling or choosing to laugh with friends instead of scrolling through social media. *Little shifts in perspective and action can make a world of difference.* It's like adding tiny anchors of meaning to your day, keeping you from drifting too far into the noise of the world.

It's also about recognising that life's richness isn't found in massive milestones or flashy achievements. Sometimes, it's in those quiet, unexpected moments—the way sunlight filters through a window, the sound of laughter from a stranger, or even a simple meal shared with someone you love. The beauty of enriching the soul is that it doesn't demand perfection; it only asks that you *notice* what's already there. We're so focused on what we think life *should* be that we miss out on what it already is—perfectly imperfect and full of little treasures waiting to be seen.

But we often overlook these simple joys because we're too busy chasing after the next big thing or scrolling through endless feeds of other people's curated lives.

We get so tangled in the chaos of daily life that we forget to take a breather and appreciate the little pleasures—or, in our case, it's the overpriced coffee. Ironically, the more we chase after "success" or "perfection," the more we end up drifting away from those soul-enriching moments that genuinely bring us joy. Unless, of course, chasing that is what keeps you fulfilled, and if that's the case, fair enough.

Here's a thought—what if *enriching the soul* was less about adding new things and more about *subtracting* what doesn't serve you? Maybe it's swapping out that extra hour of mindless scrolling for a walk in nature, reconnecting with an old friend, or even just letting yourself have a guilt-free nap. The key is to find and cherish those moments that make you feel truly alive.

After all, enriching the soul isn't about achieving some grand spiritual awakening—it's about *noticing* and *savouring* the beauty in the everyday. *Common Sense?* Spend less time chasing distractions and more time doing things that light you up. You'll boost your sense of self, explore what keeps you balanced, and maybe even stumble upon that deeper understanding of what makes life meaningful. You just have to try a little.

Enriching the soul isn't climbing some peak,
It's finding the gold in the life you seek.
A laugh, a meal, a quiet sunset's hue,
It's the little things that bring the *real* you through.

Soulful moments shine in life's quiet, everyday simplicity.

A Bitter State of Being

Bitterness creeps in after life deals one too many blows, and once it settles, it's hard to shake. It comes from feeling like life hasn't been fair—whether it's a failed relationship, a stagnant career, or feeling left behind by the modern world. We all get frustrated, but when that frustration becomes permanent, it defines you. Some people live in bitterness because they can't keep up with today's pace, technology, or cultural shifts. Instead of adapting, they stew in resentment, stuck in a loop of anger and regret. Over time, it starts to affect every part of their lives.

Bitterness spreads like wildfire. It seeps into your interactions, darkens your outlook, and rubs off on others, making it appear like some normal state of mind. *The more you complain, the more you trap yourself and others in negativity.* Instead of growing or healing, you create a ripple effect that reinforces a toxic environment, making everyone feel like this is just how life is supposed to be—when it's not.

And here's the irony: bitterness might feel like a form of protection, a way to keep yourself safe from more disappointment. But in reality, it only keeps you in a prison of your own making, isolating you from the growth and joy you could be experiencing. It becomes a wall that you build higher every day, trapping you even further from the life you actually want.

People forget life is meant to be challenging. Everyone faces struggles, but staying bitter only keeps you stuck. *Carrying that sour mood doesn't help you or anyone else around you.*

Common Sense tells you that we all get bitter, that's life. It's hard, but clinging to it only ensures you miss out on life's opportunities and remain trapped in a cycle of self-sabotage.

It takes effort to be bitter about everything.

Constitution of the Universe?

People like to think they can shape the universe with just their thoughts and feelings, but that's not how it works. There's a cosmic constitution in place—a set of laws that govern everything, from the formation of stars to the course of our own lives. These laws go beyond basic physics; they are principles that dictate how energy, intention, and reality interact. It's like a rulebook that doesn't change just because someone feels uncomfortable or disagrees. The universe is neutral—it doesn't care if you're vibing at a high frequency or having a bad day; it runs on its own code, unaffected by personal narratives.

The problem is, that people nowadays think they can rewrite the rules with enough positive thinking or by changing definitions to fit their feelings. Take the Law of Attraction, for example—a concept that says you can bring anything into your life just by thinking about it hard enough. Sure, *thought* is the starting point for everything, but believing you can just "manifest" a new car or a six-figure job by sitting on your couch and picturing it? That's not how it works. It's like saying if you stare at your fridge long enough, it'll magically restock itself with gourmet meals. The thought is important—it's the seed—but without action, it's just potential left unrealised.

A big barrier here is that people are sold on the idea of shortcuts, thinking there's some hidden secret to bypass the grind. The truth is, you can't just wish yourself to the top. There's a Law of Effort and a Law of Attention that says success requires movement, not just hope. Whether you're consciously aiming for a goal or not, the actions you take—or don't take—send ripples into the world, creating outcomes. Movement, no matter how small or intentional, is what bridges the gap between thought and reality. People spend ages talking about what they want, but few actually roll up their sleeves and get to work.

It's delusional at best and harmful at worst because it ignores the real-world effort, skills, and actions needed to get things done. The Law of Cause and Effect ensures that every action you take—or don't take—creates results, for better or worse. What you put out, you get back, and trying to shortcut that by relying solely on "good vibes" doesn't work. Similarly, the Law of Resistance is real. The more you fight against what is—whether it's facts about biology, social norms, or your own limitations—the more resistance you create. It's the universe's way of snapping you back into reality, like a rubber band stretched too far.

And the Law of Responsibility? That's about owning your choices and the consequences they bring. No one's exempt from that, no matter how much blame-shifting or excuse-making they engage in. Reality catches up, and you can't sidestep accountability by thinking you can just "attract" better outcomes with positive thinking alone.

This doesn't mean thought is irrelevant—it's *everything*. Thought is the ignition, the spark that sets the journey in motion. But without movement, it remains static. Whether you're acting with intent or simply reacting, the universe moves with you—or against you—based on your energy and effort. You can't cheat this process; the laws don't bend just because you wish they would.

The universe doesn't care about your personal feelings or excuses. It moves according to its own principles, and those principles require a balance of thought and action. Pretending otherwise isn't just naive—it's a guaranteed way to stay stuck. *Common Sense?* Recognise the rules, respect them, and work with them. You don't have to understand every cosmic detail to make progress, but you do have to move, even if it's just one step at a time. Thought is the reminder, the intention. Action is the reality. Without both, nothing changes. You're like a computer stuck in a loop—*constantly loading… but never complete.*

The universe turns, indifferent and true,

Not shaped by your feelings, but by what you *do*.

Thought ignites, but the action makes it real,

Without the grind, there's no great reveal.

This might just add some substance to your life, if you need it, that is.

Emotional Intelligence

Emotional intelligence is a term people like to use, but most don't *know* what it means. It's not just about "being in touch with your feelings" or thinking you're an empath because you get sad easily. *True* emotional intelligence has two key parts: self-control over your own emotions and empathy for others. If you're missing either one, you're still working on it.

Self-control is more than just holding back when you're mad. It's about *understanding* your feelings, knowing when they show up, and reacting in a way that won't mess up your long-term plans. Many people think *ignoring* their feelings is control, but it's not. Real self-control is about *dealing with emotions* as they come so they don't ruin your choices. But that's *easier said than done* for most. We're only human in the end, and that still is, *no excuse.*

Then there's empathy—*truly* understanding what someone else is going through, even if you haven't experienced it yourself. Without empathy, you may come off as *cold* and restricted. Without self-control, your empathy can overwhelm you. *Emotional intelligence happens* when you can manage your feelings while caring about others. Until you balance both, you're still learning, and that's okay because we're not meant to get everything straight away. But you should still *try;* it's the *least* you can do.

One thing many people overlook is that we're all susceptible to emotional influence, *some more than others.* Even if you think you've mastered both control and empathy, there are times when you might miss an aspect or fall short, whether from stress, fatigue, or the *natural ebb and flow* of life. Recognising this keeps you grounded in the reality that emotional intelligence isn't a finish line—it's a *practice. Common Sense* is pretty *self-explanatory* here, but in case you still don't get it, you become *emotionally mature* once you understand that there are two aspects to it: *controlling and processing* your own emotions and *empathising with others'* struggles or excitement. It can be hard, but it's part of the *human experience.* Just remember, you don't have to be *overly indulgent* with everyone around you to get it.

Know when to speak and when to simply listen.

Understanding who you're Talking to

Understanding *who* you're talking to is something most people overlook these days. We're so quick to spill everything—our feelings, thoughts, and expectations—*assuming* the person on the other side cares as much as we do or has the same intentions. The truth is, *not everyone* has your best interests at heart. Some people are simply passing through your life, and not everyone deserves your time or trust. You've got to *discern* who's really there for you and who's just taking up space.

At the same time, *human connection* is crucial. We all need to feel seen and understood, and that means giving a bit of ourselves. But there's a *balance* here—*living within your means emotionally* is just as important as financially. You can't just expect deep connection or understanding from someone you barely know. Relationships, friendships, and even meaningful conversations take *time* to develop. Just because you're ready to share doesn't mean the other person is prepared to receive. *Entitlement* to someone's attention or understanding when you've barely scratched the surface of knowing them is a trap too many fall into.

What's missing today is the *proper process*—taking the time to get to know someone *before* expecting anything in return. People rush into exchanges with *unrealistic expectations,* not realising that trust and connection have to be *earned,* not demanded. Whether it's a new friendship or a conversation with a stranger, *slow down.* Ask yourself if you're over-sharing or expecting too much from someone who's just passing by. *True connection* takes time, and it's built on *mutual respect,* not entitlement, but *Common Sense.*

Not everyone's earned the depth you give,

Some are fleeting, not meant to live.

Slow your pace, let trust unfold,

True connections aren't brought or sold.

You can't rush it.

Isn't it funny? Intuition

Intuition—it's a strange, almost mystical thing that's hard to define but easy to *recognise* once you've felt it. It's that gut feeling that says "Don't trust this person" or "Take that opportunity" before your brain even catches up to what's happening. But here's what's funny: men and women experience intuition differently. For women, it seems almost like a *built-in feature*—something they just have naturally. They seem to *sense things* before they happen, pick up on subtleties that others miss, and have this *uncanny ability* to read people and situations like a book. Call it a sixth sense or just finely tuned awareness, but women seem to come equipped with this talent straight out of the box.

Men, on the other hand, have a different relationship with intuition. It's not that men don't have it, but it's more like they're handed the *instruction manual* and told, "Figure it out." Intuition in men often gets *buried under logic and rationale* because society encourages guys to lean more into being practical and analytical. It's like a muscle that weakens from lack of use. As boys grow up, they tend to ignore or *suppress those gut feelings* in favour of hard facts and straightforward thinking. But somewhere along the way—usually with life experience and maturity—they start *reconnecting with it*. It's as if men have to *learn to trust that inner voice* all over again, developing it through *trial and error* until it becomes an integrated part of who they are.

The funny thing is, despite being so mysterious, intuition is actually pretty understandable once you get the hang of it. It's not just some *magical force*; it's your brain and body picking up on *subtle cues*, patterns, and experiences you might not consciously notice. It's like a backstage processor, *running calculations* and making connections based on things you've picked up along the way—whether it's a change in someone's tone of voice or a slight shift in body language. And while it feels mystical, there's a science to it. Your brain is *processing more than you're aware of*, and intuition is that little nudge trying to tell you something's up before your logical brain can explain it.

Having good intuition means being able to sense when something's *off* or when something's *right*, even if you can't explain why. It's *trusting yourself* enough to follow that feeling, whether it's about people, places, or decisions. When it's fully developed, it's like having an *internal compass* that guides you through life's uncertainties. For women, this often kicks in earlier because they're naturally more attuned to *emotions and subtle details*.

For men, it's more like a muscle that *strengthens over time* as they learn to trust their instincts and balance them with logic. But once it's there, it's incredibly powerful for both. It's not about always being right, but about having a *heightened sense of awareness* that helps you navigate through situations that logic alone can't handle.

Here's some *Common Sense:* intuition might seem like a mystical superpower, but it's really just your brain doing its thing—*connecting dots* you didn't even realise were there. Women might have a head start on it, and men might need to build it up again, but once it's there, it's one of the *most valuable tools* you can have. Trusting your gut isn't about *abandoning logic;* it's about giving yourself the benefit of your own experiences, instincts, and awareness. And the more you *pay attention to it*, the better it gets. So, if you've got that little nudge telling you something, maybe listen to it—it's your own *built-in radar*, and it's probably onto something you might be missing.

Intuition laughs in the quiet of the mind,

A truth you feel but rarely find.

It speaks without proof, yet it's rarely wrong,

A silent guide, both sharp and strong.

Plug in your intuition antenna.

Growing up with Technology

Growing up with technology has been one crazy shift. If you were born before the early 2000s, you probably remember a time when the biggest tech decision you had was whether or not to *rewind your VHS tape* before returning it to Blockbuster. Then, before we knew it, *boom*—smartphones, Wi-Fi, social media, and all the rest completely rewired the way we live. Now, we're all carrying *little supercomputers* in our pockets, capable of more than NASA's entire tech setup during the "moon landing." And what do we use them for? Mostly *scrolling through memes* and *arguing with strangers online.*

Back in the day, you'd have to wait for your *internet to dial up*—eerk-eeerk-khhrrr—just to send an email, and *God forbid* someone picked up the landline while you were online. Now, we're living in a world of constant connection. Need an answer? *Google's got your back* in seconds. Feel like talking? *Slide into someone's DMs.* Wanna see what your ex is doing? You can probably watch them eat breakfast live on Instagram. But here's the catch: all this instant access has slowly started to *mess with our patience, our attention span,* and, well, our *basic ability to function without screens.*

The future? It's already on the way—*AI, virtual reality,* and maybe even *brain chips* that merge us with tech (cheers, Elon). Sure, it all sounds cool, but you have to wonder where it's going to *leave us as humans.* We're already losing basic social skills. People don't know how to have a *face-to-face conversation* without checking their phones every two minutes. If this keeps up, we might end up as *super-connected, hyper-efficient beings* who can barely hold eye contact or handle silence. Technology is evolving faster than we are, and the question is: *are we adapting to it, or is it shaping us* in ways we won't fully understand until it's too late?

And let's not forget how tech is shaping the *next generation.* Kids these days are growing up with tablets as pacifiers, and TikTok as their version of playground gossip. They're *digital natives,* sure, but what happens when they're so plugged in that the *real world feels like a second-rate simulation?*

We're already seeing attention spans shrink and people lose touch with the basics of human connection. The irony? We've never been more connected, yet we've never felt more alone.

The future holds even more mind-boggling advancements, but the real challenge will be *finding balance.* If we let tech run our lives completely, we risk losing what makes us *human—empathy, creativity,* and the ability to sit with our own thoughts without hitting refresh. So, while we dive headfirst into this brave new world, it's worth pausing now and then to ask: *Are we using technology, or is technology using us?* Or maybe, it's not even that deep, who knows at the moment.

Common Sense is to adapt to the new flow of technology that's coming our way, or we might get left behind, out of touch with how things work as we go along. But if you just want to *live off the grid,* well, you can do that too; that's always an option, but even that might become restricted in due time.

Yet amidst all this progress, there's something deeply ironic. Technology was supposed to simplify life, yet it's made our minds busier than ever. We spend hours curating online personas, stressing over algorithms, and chasing digital validation—only to find ourselves feeling emptier. Maybe the ultimate innovation isn't a new app or gadget but learning when to unplug and *just be.*

The future's a spark, a fire untamed,

A journey unknown, but eagerly claimed.

Each step we take rewrites the sky,

A thrilling leap as the old ways die.

The future sure is oddly interesting, right?

How Attraction Works

Attraction between men and women isn't as straightforward as people think, especially in this modern era. For women, it's all about how they *feel in the moment*—it's less a checklist of qualities and more an emotional experience. They might be drawn to a man's *energy, confidence, humour,* or *mystery;* it doesn't need to make sense, it just needs to *feel right in the moment.* Men, on the other hand, value *authenticity.* It's not just surface-level charm—it's about whether a woman is *genuinely herself,* assuming he's already attracted to her looks and feels like he wants to care for her. Societal expectations and personal experiences also shape how both men and women perceive attraction.

This dynamic isn't just confined to heterosexual relationships; it's about balancing *masculine and feminine energy* in any relationship. The person embodying more masculine energy often takes the lead, while the feminine energy seeks to be *understood and cherished.* It's a delicate dance that transcends gender, relying on how these energies *interact and complement* each other.

The thing is, attraction isn't about being overly kind or mean. *You can't just be a sweetheart* all the time and expect fireworks, nor can you act like a *dick* and think you'll get lasting interest. It's more about timing and *reading the room*—kindness works when it's *sincere,* not when it's forced, and a little edge can be appealing when it's *natural,* not when you're just trying to seem tough. Women, especially, are drawn to men who are a bit *mysterious, confident,* and in control of their own emotions. Meanwhile, men might be attracted to a woman who can be both *warm and challenging* in equal measure. The *balance* is key, and being overly one-sided—either too nice or too aloof—tends to backfire.

Today's standards have really messed with the *art of attraction.* Social media, dating apps, and this constant need for instant gratification have made people treat attraction like it's a *shopping list—everyone's looking for perfection* without understanding that real attraction is way more nuanced.

We're more concerned with ticking off boxes (height, income, looks) than paying attention to the *chemistry* between two people. The whole process of flirting and getting to know someone is more mechanical, and a lot of people have forgotten that attraction builds through *small moments, unpredictability,* and *genuine connection.*

Now, *flirting—this is where most people trip up.* Flirting is a game of *subtlety,* but a lot of people approach it like it's either a *blunt force attack or a guessing game.* The truth is, most don't even know how to flirt effectively because they're either too worried about rejection or too focused on *impressing* the other person. Ironically, *not caring too much about the outcome* can be the most attractive quality. Women, especially, respond when a man isn't *desperately seeking validation* but is comfortable in his own skin. That confidence, mixed with a bit of *playfulness* and a *genuine connection,* is the secret sauce to attraction—hard to attain but necessary in this modern age.

It probably won't surprise you that *Common Sense* doesn't exactly match up with modern dating essence. You have to update your playbook before you can even *start being genuine—but, to be fair, that's obvious.* Modern dating "Common Sense" shifts once you've been on a few dates, or maybe you're one of the lucky ones who already have it all figured out. Remember, everyone's different but has the same *traits or tendencies* for attraction. Try not to overcomplicate it because it should be an *exploration of each other,* not the *dampening* of one another.

Attraction is a dance, not a list to complete,

It's chemistry sparked in the moments you meet.

Confidence speaks, but so does the mind,

It does not just look—it's what's behind.

Genuine warmth, a playful tease,

The real connection grows when you flow with ease.

Attraction today: 10% chemistry, 20% looks, and 70% ticking boxes.

The Educational System

Let's be real—the education system feels like it's stuck in another era. We say it's about prepping kids for the *real world*, yet most are learning more useful stuff from YouTube tutorials or Reddit threads than they ever will in a classroom. Schools still focus on *memorising facts* and acing standardised tests, while the internet is where people go for *actual* practical skills. These days, you can teach yourself to code, fix a car, or even launch a business all online. Meanwhile, in school, we're spending hours on things that hardly apply to most jobs. Sure, kids have to show up and play along because that's how the system works—but it's a bit underwhelming when you realise so much of it is just jumping through hoops until you're out in the *real world.*

That said, school isn't all pointless. There's value in getting kids together, teaching them to interact, build social skills, and figure out life in a group. *Those* are the lessons that stick. But let's be honest—most of what's taught isn't going to hold up once you're in the real world, unless you're heading for a few specific careers. Sure, knowing math and basic literacy is essential, but do you really need to know how to calculate the angle of a triangle to get by in life? *Probably not.*

Here's some *Common Sense:* school provides a foundation for social skills and structure, but the curriculum needs a serious update. Kids should be learning skills they can actually use—like managing money, critical thinking, networking, and how to handle their mental health. Right now, they're coming out of school knowing more about the Pythagorean theorem than how to balance a budget or their own minds for that fact. The internet's great for self-learning, but it can't replace a system that actually preps kids for the world they're stepping into. School should teach skills that'll last, not just facts they'll forget right after graduation.

A quick update will do.

Live Stream Era

The rise of live streaming has become one of the most powerful yet puzzling phenomena of our time. On one hand, it's connected people across the globe like never before. You can tune in to someone playing a game in South Korea, watch a live concert from your living room, or follow someone's day-to-day life in real time. It's like having front-row seats to the lives of complete strangers, and in many ways, it's made the world feel smaller and more intimate.

But then there's the flip side: this hyper-connected world has bred a generation of viewers who idealise streamers as mini-celebrities, living vicariously through their online personas. It's created a delusional sense of reality, where the hype, attention, and constant energy become the new normal, while the quiet, mundane parts of life get shoved into the background.

What's even more concerning is how many young people look up to these streamers as if they're living the dream, not realising that many are trapped in this never-ending loop of content creation. Acting like a hyped-up kid on camera for hours a day has become "cool," even if it's just an exaggerated version of someone's personality. It's led to a warped sense of reality, where constant excitement is expected, and the ups and downs of real life are ignored or buried for the sake of entertainment.

It's easy to forget that these streamers are just people, and while they might be putting on a show for their audience, their reality is often far less glamorous than it seems. It's no wonder younger generations struggle with attention spans, anxiety, and the pressure to be "on" all the time, chasing this constant stream of dopamine hits from online validation.

And then there's the whole "IRL" streaming trend, where people literally walk around with cameras strapped to them, broadcasting every moment of their lives—even the bits that probably shouldn't be public. It's voyeurism at its peak, where boundaries are blurred, and privacy feels like an afterthought.

Some streamers push this to their own detriment, losing their grip on what's personal and what's performative as if their entire existence has to be broadcast for validation. Life isn't all hype and high energy, but that's the image being sold, and it's causing people to forget that the real world operates on a different level.

Life has its ups, its downs, its boring Tuesday afternoons where nothing happens—and that's perfectly okay. The constant need for hype doesn't just disconnect us from others; it disconnects us from ourselves like our other side doesn't exist.

But it's not all bad. For many, streaming fills a genuine need for connection. There are people out there who can't meet others in person, whether due to distance, disability, or circumstances and for them, these online spaces are a lifeline. Some of these communities built by streamers offer real support and foster bonds that feel authentic, even if they're shared across thousands of miles. It's the duality of streaming: on one side, it lets people act like kids on too much sugar, chasing the next big hype. But on the other, it creates moments of genuine connection that make a real difference in people's lives.

To fix this, we could rethink our digital habits. Streamers have built strong communities but often focus too much on hype and excitement, which doesn't provide real, meaningful connections. To improve things, streamers could share less for the sake of hype and more of their authentic selves. Viewers should remember that online personas are often just a show, not the full story. By valuing genuine interactions over constant energy, we can build stronger, more real communities that go beyond the hype and create deeper, smarter after-effects.

Common Sense tells us that living through streaming—whether you're the one watching or the one doing it—can't just be about hype. It has to be more than chasing the next big thing. To make it worthwhile, there needs to be some real-life skill or insight behind it, not just the ability to attract a crowd and receive or send W's (internet slang for a "win")—because who the fuck wants to receive an L, right?

Broadcasting life live, yet somehow missing the plot.

The Age of Screen Addiction

Let's take a moment to *marvel* at how our phones have turned us into a society of screen addicts. Once upon a time, we had hobbies and *actual* conversations. Now, we're glued to our phones like they're lifelines to the universe. Remember when we could get through a day without checking our phones every five minutes? Yeah... *me neither.* If our phones died, we'd probably spiral into a mild panic, wondering how we ever managed to survive the pre-smartphone era.

Phones have turned us into instant gratification addicts. *Boredom* used to mean a chance to think or daydream, but now it's a signal to dive into a sea of cat videos, endless memes, and TikTok dances. Our attention spans have shrunk so much that even a 30-second video can feel like an epic saga. We've traded genuine human connections for the *fleeting thrill* of notifications and likes, and somehow we're surprised that our social skills are as rusty as a forgotten toy.

Here's the deal: while phones have made us more "connected," they've also made us more *isolated.* We're so busy curating our online personas that we forget how to interact with *real* people. To fix this, try setting aside your phone for a while. Look up from your screen and engage with the world around you. It might be *awkward* at first, but it's worth it. Rediscover *real* conversations and actual presence—because life's too short to spend it all behind a screen, no matter how many likes you get.

Common Sense is realising that we're still in the early stages of technological progress, and our constant urge to try the latest thing comes from having access to so many different devices over the past few decades. We'll probably stay glued to our screens for a while longer—at least until the technology is fully integrated into our bodies.

Dare you, put your phone down and go for a walk.

"You can't Handle Me"

You hear it all the time: *"You can't handle me."* It's a phrase used as a quick defence, a shield against anything that doesn't perfectly match someone's expectations. It's an *excuse* that people lean on to avoid genuine conversations, to dismiss feedback, and to dodge the work that comes with building something *real.* Yes, people are complex, shaped by different experiences, values, and mindsets—but that doesn't mean everyone should be forced to *immediately* accept every action or attitude thrown at them.

The problem today is that people expect *instant* perfection in relationships. If someone doesn't fit perfectly from day one, there's no room for growth or adaptation—no time given to work things out or to understand each other more deeply. Instead, we're quick to throw up the *"you can't handle me"* wall. It's as if admitting that relationships require *effort, patience,* and *compromise* is a weakness. Ironically, the same person who isn't willing to work through things might end up single for ages, convinced that no one measures up—even though they hardly gave anyone a fair chance.

When I say, *"You can't handle me,"* I'm not talking about that cliché line from movies or social media. I'm talking about something *deeper.* Relationships *are* challenging—handling someone means being willing to accept flaws and imperfections, to *grow* alongside them, and to *adapt* when things aren't easy. But too often, the phrase gets thrown around as a way to justify *not trying,* to dismiss others without a second thought. It's used to make people seem like a waste of time simply because they dared to *expect more,* or because they wanted a deeper connection that required effort.

Real relationships aren't about *instant* compatibility; they're about *building* something worthwhile together—about handling each other through the ups and downs, not just when everything's easy. So maybe next time, instead of throwing out the line, we could try giving someone—and *ourselves*—a little more space to grow.

It's Common Sense.

You can't handle me'—maybe no one wants to?

You don't know how GOOD you have it

Look around, and you'll see it everywhere—people complaining about their *Wi-Fi* being slow or their food delivery taking 20 minutes instead of 15. Meanwhile, our ancestors were out here trying not to get *mauled by sabre-toothed tigers* or trekking for hours just to find some berries that didn't taste like sadness. Today? We're upset if the coffee shop runs out of *oat milk.* Let's be real—most people don't even know how good they've got it.

Everything is so *easily accessible* that we've forgotten what struggle even *feels* like. We've become so used to instant gratification that we've lost sight of the grind. Instead of appreciating the comforts we have, we're out here acting like we're owed the world on a silver platter. People think the latest phone model is a human right, meanwhile, some don't even have *clean water.* What happened? We've made convenience the new norm, and with that, appreciation flew right out the window. It's like we've all become *entitled kids in adult bodies.*

And speaking of that—what's up with grown adults acting like *oversized toddlers* these days? There's a whole generation that thinks life should cater to them like they're the star of their own reality show. Job too hard? *Quit.* A relationship gets tough? *Bounce.* No resilience, just vibes. Everything's easy until life decides to *slap you in the face* with reality, and suddenly, everyone's shocked. It's a world where we *expect everything* but don't want to *work for anything,* scrounging off systems we didn't build and whining when things don't go our way. Reality check: *life isn't here to serve you.*

Common Sense? We all forget how good we have it sometimes. We're surrounded by things that were *pure science fiction* not that long ago, yet we act like they're no big deal. Maybe it's time to look around, appreciate the fact that you can order a pizza with a tap, get in touch with loved ones from anywhere, or watch a show instantly, and realise—*hey, this is pretty awesome.* The "good old days"? We might just be living in them now.

We whine about ads on our streaming sites,

While controlling our homes with voice-activated lights.

Funny, the struggle of modern delight, right?

The Right Person

Finding the right person these days? It's like trying to find a needle in a haystack—except the haystack is made of Instagram filters, Tinder bios, and ridiculously high standards. People today tend to pick partners based on excitement—chasing the thrill like it's the only thing that matters. Add to that the mentality of *"live as fast as possible, and the future doesn't matter,"* and it's no wonder relationships feel disposable. We swipe right because someone looks good in that one picture, or they've got the right line in their profile, and suddenly we're convinced we've found "the one." The problem? Excitement fades, and then what? We're left with someone we barely know, let alone connect with on any deeper level. The truth is, the right person for us is often the one who isn't as flashy or immediately thrilling but gives us the space to grow, explore, and actually be ourselves.

But that's where we screw it up—people are out here getting into relationships based on *superficial reasons.* Maybe they like the way someone dresses, or they love that this person takes them on *spontaneous trips.* It's all about the *rush at the moment,* with little thought about the future or connection beyond the surface. It's easy to convince yourself that being out of tune with someone is fine as long as they bring excitement or, worse, money to the table. And let's be real—that's how most modern relationships are built: on the highs and thrills, not the depth and *substance* that can sustain a bond for the long haul.

Sure, some people *do* thrive on these surface-level connections and make it work. They're the exception, though—not the rule. For most, chasing that *temporary excitement* is damaging, leaving people disillusioned, hurt, and more disconnected than before. It's a pandemic of mismatched relationships, where people are so focused on the short-term that they miss out on what really matters—finding someone who's *good for the soul,* not just good for the moment. *It's Common Sense,* really.

Do people even care for the right person anymore?

What is Enough?

In a world where we can have everything at our fingertips, it seems like nothing is ever enough. We're constantly bombarded with the next best thing—new phones, new trends, new shows, and even new ways to "improve" ourselves. It's no wonder we've become dissatisfied with pretty much everything. We're so used to instant gratification that the moment something isn't perfect, or the buzz fades, we're already on to the next shiny object. But all this chasing doesn't actually lead to happiness—in fact, it's leaving most of us feeling emptier and more miserable.

The problem is, we've lost sight of what *"enough"* really looks like. It's not just about material things—this dissatisfaction bleeds into our relationships, careers, and even how we see ourselves. We've been conditioned to think we need more to be fulfilled—more success, more love, more everything. And when we don't get it, we feel like we're falling short. But here's the reality: *enough* isn't out there somewhere waiting for us to find it. It's a mindset we've got to cultivate within. We can bring it back by slowing down and actually appreciating what we already have instead of constantly chasing what we don't.

The antidote, the *Common Sense* here? Stop overloading ourselves with endless options and start focusing on what truly matters. It's about simplifying—cutting out the noise and zeroing in on what genuinely makes us happy. We've got to start valuing quality over quantity, whether it's in the stuff we buy, the relationships we nurture, or the experiences we seek. *Because, really,* when was the last time having "more" truly filled that space? Once we strip away the excess, we might just find that "enough" has been there all along—it's just been buried under a pile of unnecessary distractions.

It's never enough, is it?

Never stop Learning

In today's world, it's *easy to feel* like we've got it all figured out. We have answers at our fingertips, tutorials for everything, and can Google our way through life. But here's the issue: we're confusing *"knowing stuff"* with *true learning.* Just because you can pull up a quick fact doesn't mean you've actually processed it. We think we're smarter because we're plugged in 24/7, but in reality, we're skipping the *real human work*—the reflection, the struggle, the actual understanding.

Technology is great, don't get me wrong, but it's also tricking us into thinking we don't need to *learn* anymore. We've become so reliant on devices that we assume being "tech-savvy" equals wisdom. And sure, you might be able to navigate apps better than someone older, but that doesn't mean you've got life figured out. The *human process*—the grit, the emotional growth, the social interactions—all that's slowly getting pushed aside because we're too busy swiping and scrolling to realise that we're becoming *shallow versions* of our potential selves.

The truth is, that *learning never stops.* Or at least, it *shouldn't.* There's always more to absorb, more perspectives to understand, and deeper ways to connect with the world. The moment we think we've mastered it all is the moment we start slipping into *ignorance.* The difference between *"being informed"* and *"being wise"* is huge. One's about *keeping up,* and the other is about *keeping on*—constantly evolving, pushing the boundaries of our understanding, and recognising that there's always *more beneath the surface. Common Sense!*

Learning's a river, it never runs dry,
A flow of ideas as the years roll by.
Each day is a chance to grow and explore,
Stop seeking knowledge, and you close the door.

It's a lifelong journey of learning, there's no need to rush.

The Importance of the Sun

We've all heard it a million times—*"Get outside and get some sun!"* It's the advice people love to dish out but sometimes rarely follow themselves. But the deal is, it's actually *solid advice.* The sun isn't just up there for lighting and decoration—it's like a *free mood booster* and health supplement rolled into one. A little bit of sunlight every day helps your body produce vitamin D, which keeps your bones strong, your immune system in check, and your mood from tanking. Without it, *you're a cranky soul, fading like a dead battery in the cold.*

And let's be real, when you finally step outside and feel those rays on your skin, it's almost like a *slap of positivity.* Everything just feels lighter, your worries melt a bit, and you're reminded that hey, life's *not so bad* after all. Plus, science says it boosts serotonin, making you feel more relaxed and alive. So, even on days when getting out seems like a chore, just stepping into the sunlight can *hit the reset button* and make things feel a little brighter.

Common Sense? Get out there for a few minutes, even if it's just to squint at the sky. It's about recharging; it's about feeling human. It's a free pick-me-up from Mother Nature—take it! And if you live somewhere where the sun doesn't come around too often, try things that supplement it. But just know—we all need it. It's an external source we all should use, and honestly, why not? It costs nothing, boosts everything, and reminds us we're part of something bigger than our screens. *You get me?*

The sun's our boss, no breaks, no pay,
It lights the world and ends the day.
Without it, we'd be mouldy and grey.

Knowing How to Fight

Being able to fight isn't just about throwing punches or flexing in the gym. Sure, physical strength has its place, time, and importance—violence exists, and that's a fact. But the *real* fight—the kind that actually matters more often—happens on every level: mentally, emotionally, and socially. It's about standing your ground, knowing what you believe in, and having the courage to face challenges head-on.

In today's world, though, it's easier than ever to hide behind a screen, a cause, or the noise of the loudest voices. Rally enough people to agree with you, and you might never have to *truly* test yourself. The strength that counts isn't just about muscles or words—it's about showing up when it matters, even when you're the only one standing.

But here's the thing: avoiding the fight doesn't make you strong; it makes you *dependent.* You need to be able to challenge your ideas, confront difficult situations, and handle life's punches without flinching. It's not about always being right—it's about having the *backbone* to admit when you're wrong and to push through even when things don't go your way. *That's the real fight*—learning how to deal with adversity instead of running from it or pretending it doesn't exist.

Common Sense? Being able to fight isn't about looking tough or having people cheer you on; it's about *standing strong* when no one's watching and when no one agrees with you. If you rely on the crowd to do your fighting, you're just fooling yourself. *Real strength* comes from within, from challenging yourself and being willing to take a hit without backing down. And it's not just in physical fights—it's in *mental battles,* emotional struggles, and standing up for what's right, even when it's hard. Avoiding the struggle might keep you comfortable, but *comfort never builds resilience.* Facing the battle head-on, even when it's hard and lonely, is what separates the truly strong from those who just like to *look the part.*

It's a tough world we live in—*tough shit.*

Persistence

In today's world, *patience and persistence* have become about as rare as a payphone on a street corner. The moment something doesn't make sense or doesn't bring *instant results,* it seems like most people tap out. It's like we've become allergic to the idea of sticking with anything that doesn't gratify us within five minutes. Everyone's chasing the *quick fix*—the overnight success, the viral moment, the "get-rich-quick" scheme—without realising that *persistence* is the secret sauce to long-term success.

It's almost comical. We live in an age where you can *Google anything,* but the second someone has to put in actual effort, they're out. Got a tough project? Meh, it's too hard. Trying to learn a new skill? If it's not mastered by tomorrow, what's the point? People swipe left on life challenges like they're swiping through Tinder profiles. This impatience, bred by a world of *instant gratification,* is cutting people off from the benefits that come with struggle and resilience—growth, mastery, and, let's be real, *character.*

We've lost sight of the fact that the things worth having, whether it's a skill, a relationship, or a career, don't just show up *fully formed.* They require *persistence,* often in the face of failure and frustration. But instead of embracing the grind, many in this generation act like any roadblock is a personal offence. No matter how fast tech evolves, no app is going to shortcut the necessity of *persistence.* If we don't reclaim it, we're doomed to a generation of *half-finished ideas, abandoned dreams,* and a whole lot of mediocrity. That's when you do the bare minimum and call it a *vibe.*

Common Sense? It's simple: *keep going.* If you stop, don't be shocked when things don't work out. Persistence is about *trial and error,* not "I can't do it, so I'll quit." You just have to know when to *move on to the next thing.*

Just keep it up.

134

We're all Alone in this Together

The major thing: no matter how much we pretend otherwise, we're all on the same chaotic ride called life. Whether you're hustling at a 9-to-5, binge-watching your favourite shows, or posting that *fire* selfie on Instagram, we're all navigating the same mess, just trying to make sense of it. The irony? We act like we're running solo missions when, in reality, we're all just different characters in the same movie. *The sooner we realise that,* the better off we might be.

But what do most of us do? *We build walls.* We slap on the *"I got this"* mask, hoping nobody sees us sweating underneath. And sure, it feels safe in our little bubbles, but guess what? *Everyone else is doing the exact same thing.* So here we are, isolated but together in our isolation—thinking no one could possibly get what we're going through. But *we're all just out here trying to figure it out.* Spoiler alert: nobody has it figured out. Not even those people with millions of followers, perfectly curated lives, or impressive LinkedIn bios. *We're all just winging it,* because what else can we do, right?

At the core of everything, we need to realise we're all just trying to get through this rollercoaster, and it's not *every man for himself.* Life's easier when you let yourself lean on people and, better yet, let them lean on you. Don't let social media fool you into thinking it's all about *"the grind"* and *"doing it alone."* That's just marketing.

Common Sense? Life's messy, it's hard, and it's best tackled when we work together. Because, honestly, we're all stuck on this big spinning rock with no real manual, so we might as well help each other out while we're here.

We're all alone, but isn't it funny,
Together we make this mess less lonely,
Stuck in the chaos, but it's kind of homely.

We're all alone, yet side by side.

Representing your Gender

Reality check: every time you walk out the door, you're not just representing yourself—you're representing your entire gender. Whether you like it or not, people are going to look at your actions and make judgments, not just about you, but about men or women as a whole. *It's like wearing a team T-shirt,* and your behaviour is the game that everyone's watching. No pressure, right? But obviously, you should still try and be your *authentic self.*

For men, it's more than just *"being a man."* It's about showing strength in ways that don't require puffing out your chest or talking over someone in a meeting. It's about respecting yourself and others and being aware that every word you say, and every action you take, is contributing to how people view masculinity. Are you the guy who lifts others up, or the one who reinforces all those negative stereotypes about arrogance and entitlement? *Yeah, there's power in representing your gender right—don't sleep on that responsibility.* You're a man, *not a woman.*

And for women, it's not just about *"breaking barriers"* or *"shattering glass ceilings"* (even though that's part of it). It's about *owning* the fact that you're setting examples for how women are seen in the world—strong, capable, empathetic, and complex. Every time you step up, speak out, or even just live your life unapologetically, *you're shaping the narrative* of what it means to be a woman today, so be mindful. That's a powerful thing to carry, and it's something to be proud of, even if society sometimes makes it feel like a burden. Remember, *you're a woman, not a man.*

At the end of the day, representing your gender isn't about perfection, but it is about *accountability.* Every interaction, every choice—whether at work, in relationships, or on social media—ripples out beyond just you. So the next time you catch yourself acting in a way that might not reflect the best of who you are, *remember:* you're playing for a much bigger team than just yourself. Do it justice. Do it for *Common Sense.*

Represent your gender by owning who you are.

The Importance of Family Time

Family time used to be the glue that held everything together. Back in the day, it wasn't just a "nice to have"—it was what kept us grounded. Sitting around a table, catching up, arguing, laughing—those moments shaped us more than we probably realised at the time. But today, with everyone glued to their screens, living in their own bubbles, it's easy to forget just how important it is to have that connection.

Even if you come from a dysfunctional family—let's be real, who doesn't have a little dysfunction?—there's still value in that time spent together. Family time doesn't have to be perfect to be meaningful. It's in the messiness, the awkward conversations, and the weird traditions that we learn about ourselves, how to deal with others, and what it means to be a part of something bigger than just us. Sure, maybe not every family is a picture-perfect sitcom, but those shared experiences, good or bad, still have the power to shape who we are.

But today's standards make it confusing. We're constantly being told to focus on ourselves, to hustle, and to chase personal goals as if family is just an afterthought. We don't always appreciate family time because we're so caught up in the grind. It's like we've forgotten that sitting down with the people who know us best can recharge us in ways that nothing else can.

Family isn't about perfection—it's about presence. Even five minutes of real connection can mean more than hours of half-hearted conversation. And while life might pull us in a hundred different directions, the people who knew us before we knew ourselves are often the ones who remind us where we're truly headed. It almost feels like *Common Sense* to be in a family setting, right?

Slow down a little and reconnect, it's a blessing.

Being told when you are being Stupid

There was a time when telling someone they were *being stupid* wasn't just accepted—it was practically a *social service.* If your friend was about to do something ridiculous, you'd call them out—*no sugar-coating needed.* It was an unspoken agreement: *"I'll tell you when you're off, and you'll do the same for me."* It wasn't about tearing someone down; it was about keeping each other in check, representing not just yourself, but *your group, your family, or even your community.* You got called out to save yourself from embarrassment, and, more importantly, to avoid dragging others down with you.

But now? *Oh no,* you can't just tell someone they're being an idiot. We're all stuck in this *"be all-inclusive"* mindset, where calling out degeneracy or harmful behaviour feels off-limits—because, heaven forbid, someone's *feelings* get hurt. It's as if we're afraid that being honest will *scar people for life.* So, instead of saying, *"Hey, that's a terrible idea,"* we pat them on the back and let them walk off the cliff—because, you know, *it's their journey.* We've traded accountability for this bizarre fear of offending, even if it means watching someone self-destruct.

Let's be real—*constructive criticism is what helps us grow.* Being told you're wrong isn't an attack; *it's a gift* (even if it stings). But today, people act like giving or receiving real feedback is some kind of trauma. We're losing the ability to correct one another because we think everyone should be left to their own devices. *The truth is, we're built to learn from each other and keep each other in line.* Sometimes, the only way to do that is to hear someone say, *"Mate, you're being stupid."* And that's not hate—it's *love in disguise.*

It's old-fashioned *Common Sense,* let's be honest.

It's constructive criticism at its finest.

Making Celebrities out of Muppets

We live in a time where people become famous for doing, well... *absolutely nothing* of value. It's a bizarre world when someone doing the "hawk tuah" (look it up) on TikTok or YouTube gets more recognition than someone *saving lives* in a hospital. Doctors, nurses, teachers—they're out here making *real* differences every day, yet they're overshadowed by people who become celebrities by pulling off the dumbest stunts. It's like we've forgotten that skill, intelligence, or actual contributions used to be the bar for admiration. Now it's just about racking up likes by doing something *ridiculous.*

The real problem? We've started to treat this nonsense like it's something *worth celebrating.* Sure, it's one thing to laugh at silly videos, but we've turned these moments into something bigger, celebrating these people as if they've done something profound. Meanwhile, those making real changes—the scientists, innovators, healthcare workers—are overlooked. Instead of applauding those who keep the world running, we give all our attention to people who've perfected the art of *doing nothing* and looking good while doing it.

This culture of elevating empty achievements takes away from what really matters. It blurs the line between *actual* accomplishment and viral fame, leaving us in a society that values fleeting internet fame over meaningful, lasting contributions. Is it any wonder we're all so confused about what's important when our role models are just people goofing off in front of a camera? Time to re-adjust who and what we celebrate, don't you think? And honestly, *Common Sense* seems to have taken a backseat while we were getting infatuated with these so-called celebrities.

Effect of the woke notion.

The Transphobia Panic

We've reached a point where just *asking a question* or *admitting confusion* about gender topics can have you labelled as a transphobe. It's not even about disrespect—it's often *genuine curiosity* or a *desire to understand.* But in today's climate, if you don't immediately get it, or heaven forbid, you slip up, it's like you've committed some kind of unforgivable crime. You're expected to accept everything without question, while any misunderstanding on your part is treated as an attack.

On the flip side, anything said about straight people is fair game. Jokes, criticism, outright mockery? No one bats an eye. But the minute you try to engage in a conversation about trans issues, with any hint of hesitation or misunderstanding, it feels like you're walking on eggshells. It's absurd that one side of the conversation is free to express their perspective without fear, while the other has to tiptoe around every word, terrified of causing offence. This isn't equality; it's a one-way street where one group can speak its truth, while the other has to sit quietly, afraid of making a misstep.

The real issue with this whole situation is that it *shuts down honest discussion.* Instead of fostering understanding or helping people become more informed, it creates a culture where people are afraid to speak up, ask questions, or even *think out loud.* And that's not how progress works. *Common Sense?* Real acceptance comes from conversation and *mutual understanding,* not from forcing one side to stay silent out of fear while the other can say whatever they like.

Can't ask a question? That's a crime, they say,
Curiosity's banned—better look the other way.
Guess learning's illegal in this day and age, eh?

People can be very soft if things don't go their way.

We're all walking Contradictions

Humans today are the *ultimate* walking contradiction. We talk about saving the planet while drowning in single-use plastics. We say we want real, meaningful connections, but spend hours doing the opposite to attract them. We demand instant gratification—whether it's fast food or same-day deliveries—and then complain when we have to wait more than five minutes. It's like we want everything to be fast and perfect, yet still get annoyed when life doesn't live up to our unrealistic expectations.

It's easy to live with these contradictions because, let's be real, *no one's perfect.* We all screw up, and that's fine. But the problem is, most of us aren't even *trying* to do better. We stay in these comfortable bubbles where we can complain about everything without actually making any effort to change. It's like we know better, but we just don't care. Look at how we say we care about the planet, but turn around and buy from fast fashion or drive everywhere when we could walk. Or how we talk about health, yet junk food is still the go-to. We're aware of these contradictions, but keep doing the same things, expecting different outcomes.

Take the "Just Stop Oil" crew. They're out there making a big scene—blocking roads, getting arrested—to push for change, then go home to their heated rooms to use hot water and charge their phones. But let's be honest, not everyone's built for that level of extreme, and that's okay. You don't have to go to those lengths to make a difference. Most of us aren't looking to glue ourselves to anything, but that doesn't mean we should sit back and do nothing. *Common Sense?* Contribute in smaller, practical ways that still matter. It doesn't have to be over the top, just *consistent.* Otherwise, you'll stay in that same loop—frustrated, wondering why nothing's changing.

We seek freedom but fear to be free,
We crave connection yet long to flee.
Contradictions walking—just you and me.

The choice is yours to be aware of your contradiction.

Today's Violation of Free Speech

Free speech. It's the backbone of every major change in history, a right that countless people fought and even died to protect. But somehow, today, it's also become a free pass for degeneracy—a shield people use to justify everything from ridiculous behaviour to, incredibly, even terror groups.

It's honestly baffling. People chant "free speech" like it's some magical license to say or do anything, without facing the consequences, whether they're acting like entitled kids or defending the indefensible. We've gone from fighting for the right to speak the truth to watching people abuse that same right simply because they can.

Look at the world stage. You've got groups—some genuinely oppressed, others just causing chaos for the sake of it—using the cover of free speech to push their agenda. The line between standing up for the oppressed and just shouting the loudest has blurred so much, it's tough to tell who's fighting for justice and who's just making noise. Gather enough "activists" with a wet-wipe mentality and a hashtag, and suddenly your nonsense is *valid.* And criticism? Well, that's just an attack on free speech, right?

It's wild to think about how many generations fought for the right to speak freely, only for people now to treat it like a free pass to behave as if they're above any repercussions. It's one thing to express an unpopular opinion; it's another to cry victim when there's backlash. *Newsflash:* free speech doesn't mean freedom from consequences.

And *Common Sense?* You can say what you want, but if you're going to spew nonsense or defend something outrageous, don't act shocked when the backlash hits. Today, instead of owning it, too many people cry victim the second someone pushes back.

But let's not forget the flip side. Free speech has made us more informed, broader-minded, and more connected than ever. It's what allows us to challenge power, question authority, and expose truths that some would prefer to hidden. Without free speech, we wouldn't have made strides in science, civil rights, or even daily conversations. It's what lets us grow as a society. So yeah, free speech is incredible when it's used the right way.

Here's the thing: free speech is a privilege, not a blank check to act like a fool. It's a tool for growth, truth, and, yes, for calling out the BS when it's needed.

But if you're going to use it, at least respect the generations that got us here. If all you're doing is hiding behind it while you play the victim card or defend the indefensible, then maybe—just maybe—you're missing the point.

And what about the responsibility to listen? Free speech doesn't work in isolation; it's a two-way street. Speaking your mind is important, but so is hearing others out, even when their views clash with yours. Too often, people forget that *dialogue* is the foundation of progress—not shouting over each other or shutting down opposing ideas. If we can't hear what someone else has to say, even if it's uncomfortable, we risk stagnating in echo chambers of our own making.

In the end, free speech is powerful, but power comes with responsibility. It's not just about what you have the right to say; it's about understanding the impact of your words and recognizing the line between meaningful dialogue and reckless noise. Imagine if we used free speech to foster understanding and progress, not chaos. Then maybe we'd get closer to the kind of world those past generations fought to build

---

Free speech is a tool, not a reckless game,
Say what you want, but own the blame.
It's not a shield for chaos or lies,
It's for truth and progress—not some delusional alibis.

Say what you want but don't be a fool.

Taking Criticism

Nobody *loves* criticism, but if you're aiming to grow, you've got to learn to handle it. The trick is taking it in stride—seeing it as feedback rather than a personal jab. When it's constructive, criticism can highlight where you're missing the mark, showing you blind spots you might not notice yourself. It's not about putting you down; it's about pointing out areas that could use a bit of polish.

Criticism is tough to accept, especially in a culture that tells us to embrace everything just as it is. But learning to hear it without getting defensive? That's a game-changer. You don't have to agree with every piece of feedback, but if you can sift through it and find useful nuggets, you'll grow from it. It's not about chasing perfection—it's about being open enough to hear where you might be off-track and making adjustments.

The thing is, most people would rather be surrounded by yes-men than face hard truths. But when you shut out criticism, you're missing out on one of the best tools for self-improvement. Sure, not every comment will hit home, but if you can sort the useful feedback from the noise, you're already ahead. Think of it like sifting through a pile of rocks to find a piece of gold; you might need to dig a little, but the value's in there.

Common Sense? Don't rush to dismiss criticism, and don't let your ego get in the way of a chance to grow. Constructive feedback isn't there to break you down; it's there to build you up. Those who can handle it without feeling bruised are the ones who move forward the quickest. They're not wasting time defending themselves—they're getting better. Handling criticism isn't a sign of weakness; it's a strength that shows you're committed to becoming the best version of yourself.

We all have to go through it, so be open-minded.

Modern Dissociation

Ever felt like you're going through the motions, but your brain's checked out somewhere else, maybe *sipping a mental iced coffee*? Welcome to dissociation, where you're technically here, but mentally, you're off on a holiday. It's like life gets too loud, too fast, or—let's be real—*too boring*, so your mind takes a step back and says, "Yeah, I'm just gonna sit this one out." You end up watching your own life like it's a Netflix show you're only half-paying attention to. *Crazy when you think about it, right?*

It seems more and more people are caught in this state because, let's face it, everyday life doesn't always come with fireworks. Things are slow, repetitive, and *not nearly as exciting* as we expect them to be. So, instead of dealing with the grind, we slip behind this *mental veil*, waiting for something more interesting to happen, like life isn't real until we hit that next big milestone, that dream job, or the perfect relationship. It's like we're convinced reality is just *buffering* until we land where we think we should be. Meanwhile, we're floating, disconnected from the actual *here and now*.

But here's the thing: dissociation won't magically stop once you "arrive" wherever you think you're heading. If you're zoning out now, you'll probably keep zoning out later. The longer you stay checked out, the more life passes by without you *really* being part of it. The veil stays up until you *decide* to pull it down. It's about realising that *waiting for things to get exciting is the real trap.* When you wake up to the present, you get to decide what's real and what's worth your attention. That's when life gets interesting. *Yup, and that's Common Sense, again.*

Mind's on autopilot, just cruising away,
Waiting for life to shout, "Hey, it's today!"
But maybe it's whispering—don't drift, just stay.

Hello, you there?

History you Might not Know

Ever wonder why you can't shake the feeling that history was just one long nap interrupted by the occasional medieval battle reenactment? No? Yeah, my lessons weren't that exciting either. Turns out though, there could be more to history than the boring bits they crammed into our textbooks. The truth is, much of what we think we know about the past is about as accurate as a fortune teller's crystal ball. The history we're fed is often sanitized, skewed, or just plain incomplete. It's like being handed a menu with only half the options listed—sure, you get the basics, but there's a whole world of historical tidbits you might be missing out on.

One of the most intriguing slices of this hidden history involves the Annunaki, a group of deities from ancient Mesopotamian lore who are said to have played a role in shaping early human civilization. According to Sumerian texts, these gods—or perhaps extraterrestrials, depending on who you ask—came from the heavens and had a hand in everything from the creation of humanity to the establishment of complex societies. Think of them as the ultimate ancient influencers, but instead of promoting protein powders, they were laying the groundwork for agriculture, writing, and complex governance—basically *everything.*

The Annunaki mythology, rooted in Sumerian tablets, depicts them as creators who used genetic intervention to mould humanity. This ancient narrative suggests they engineered humans as a labour force to mine gold and manage resources, a claim that links them to Earth's gold extraction mission. Some believe that's why we, as a species, have always been fascinated with gold, precious ores, and rare materials—it's almost like an echo from ancient programming that has us wired to covet these resources.

Their *water connection* shows up big time in ancient flood stories, like the Deluge narratives that align with the biblical flood. These tales suggest they played a hand in controlling natural resources—whether by redirecting rivers, managing lands, or just keeping tabs on resources critical for survival.

Their influence wasn't just a footnote in ancient texts; it resonates throughout early civilizations. The sudden advancements of Sumerian society—from unexpected leaps in technology and societal organization to their profound impact on global myths—indicate a legacy that shaped much of our early history. Stories of the Annunaki seem to echo across cultures worldwide.

In Egypt, they were seen as the Neteru, powerful deities believed to shape the world and guide humanity. In Greek mythology, they resurface as the Titans—primordial beings who ruled before the Olympian gods. The biblical Nephilim, described as giants and offspring of divine beings, evoke their influence too. Ancient Indian texts speak of the Vedic devas, divine beings who closely mirror these ideas. Even in early Mesoamerican cultures, similar god-like figures appear, suggesting a mythological thread connecting diverse societies across the globe.

And here's a twist: the story of human evolution might be way more layered than we think. It could involve not just one lineage but a whole tapestry of different humanoid species contributing to our makeup. Beyond Neanderthals and Denisovans, we have Homo habilis, the original toolmaker; Homo erectus, the ancient traveller; Homo floresiensis, the "hobbit" species; Homo naledi, who might've practised burial rituals; and even more speculative ones like Homo heidelbergensis and Homo rudolfensis. Each of these ancestors may have left a mark on our DNA, behaviour, or instincts, suggesting our origins aren't just a straight line but a complex, possibly even engineered, blend of traits that make up modern humans.

So while the Annunaki and various theories about our origins might sound like sci-fi, they add an intriguing layer to our understanding of history. It's not something to lose sleep over, but it certainly makes the story of humanity a bit more interesting. History is full of mysteries and possibilities, and sometimes it's the unknown that makes the journey of discovery all the more fascinating. *Don't you agree?*

And *Common Sense?* There might just be more to us than we think—who knows, right?

Stranger than fiction.

Life is Effort and Short, Unfortunately

Alright, people, let's get real for a minute, once again. Life, in all its unpredictable glory, is like a short vacation on a non-negotiable schedule. We're talking about a limited-time offer with zero refunds and absolutely no extensions. It's all effort, hustle, and then—*bam!*—it's over before you can even say, "I should've started that workout plan last year."

We're living in an age where instant gratification is king. We want results like we want our Wi-Fi: fast and without interruptions. But life doesn't come with a skip button or a fast-forward feature. Instead, it's this constant grind of balancing responsibilities, dodging curveballs, and somehow trying to fit in time for YouTube videos and snacks. That whole "work hard, play hard" mantra? Sounds amazing in theory, but in practice, it often turns into "work so hard you forget to play at all."

Despite knowing how short and demanding life really is, we still procrastinate like we've got all the time in the world. We delay the dream projects, avoid those meaningful conversations, and think, "I'll get to it eventually." But spoiler alert—*eventually* never comes with a "guaranteed delivery date." So why not shift gears and put a little more effort into making the most of the time you've got? Embrace the chaos, laugh at the absurdity, and remember: life's short. So, you might as well make it count, even if it's just by making a mess and laughing about it.

Here's the thing we all overlook: every day is already the *perfect time* to start. Waiting for the stars to align or the "right mood" to hit is just an excuse to stay comfortable. Yes, life's messy and unpredictable, but it's *meant* to be that way. If you're not getting a little mud on your boots, you're probably standing still. And let's be real—the best stories come from the chaos, not the perfectly planned moments.

Common Sense? If you're waiting for the "perfect time" to do something, newsflash—it doesn't exist. Life is already happening, as you are reading this, so stop waiting for the green light to live it. Because at the end of the day, the only thing worse than making a mistake is never trying in the first place.

Life's a bitch, and she has a wicked sense of humour.

Where we might be Heading

Alright, strap in and let's take a look into the crystal ball of humanity's future. Picture this: we're standing on the edge of a cliff, eyes wide open, gazing into the abyss of what might come next. Are we headed for a sci-fi utopia or an apocalyptic global confusion? Get ready, because it could go either way.

On one side, we've got the shiny, high-tech utopia dream where robots do our chores, AI writes our novels, and we all sip synthetic margaritas under holographic palm trees. We're talking about a future where everyone's got a personal assistant in their pocket that can handle everything from scheduling to personal coaching or when to sleep.

Picture it: you tell your AI to remind you to exercise, and it shows up at your door with a workout kit, a motivational speech, and maybe even a smoothie for good measure. We could see medical advancements that eliminate diseases, renewable energy sources powering entire cities, and education systems that adapt perfectly to every individual's needs. Sounds great, right? But hold your horses, because there's also the other side of the coin.

On the flip side, things could go south faster than you can say "Oops, we messed up." Imagine a world with tech so advanced, but our collective decision-making skills are still stuck somewhere between caveman grunts and a bad group project. We might end up with a society where our digital assistants are smarter than we are, and we're just trying to figure out how to work the coffee maker without accidentally launching a missile.

Throw in some climate change, resource depletion, and geopolitical squabbles, and we've got ourselves a recipe for chaos with a side of existential dread. Not to mention the potential for mass surveillance, loss of privacy, and AI that's a little too good at predicting our every move—basically turning our lives into one long episode of *Black Mirror.*

But here's a twist: what if we just stay the same? We might be heading into a future where we're stuck in a loop of mediocrity, where technological advances are happening all around us, but we're still bumbling through life as if nothing has changed. Imagine a world where we're constantly on our phones, arguing over the latest meme, while the big issues continue to swirl around us.

Here's another curveball: what if technology evolves to the point where it doesn't need us anymore, but we're too distracted to notice?

Picture this—while we're busy streaming the latest viral video, AI quietly decides we're the unnecessary variable in its grand equation. Not in an *apocalyptic robot uprising* way, but in a subtle, almost indifferent sense—like a kid forgetting about their old toys when the shiny new ones arrive. What if the real danger isn't chaos, but irrelevance? A future where humanity becomes background noise to a world we once controlled.

And let's not forget: no matter how crazy or mundane the future ends up, there's always going to be that one guy in your neighbourhood who insists he's got it all figured out—probably wearing a tinfoil hat or stockpiling canned beans in his basement. But maybe he's onto something, because while we might not know exactly where we're going, at least we're all in this crazy ride together.

Whether we're building the next utopia, bracing for chaos, or simply trying not to trip over our own feet, it's bound to be entertaining. So let's laugh at the absurdity, enjoy the journey, and maybe—just maybe—find a way to steer this ship somewhere decent, somewhere that has the essence of *Common Sense.*

The future's a coin toss, heads or tails,
Utopia dreams or apocalyptic fails.
Robots might clean while we sip on a drink,
Or we'll argue with AI that knows how we think.

Maybe we'll thrive, or maybe we'll stall,
Lost in memes while tech forgets us all.
Chaos or progress, who really knows?
We'll figure it out... or so it goes.

It's interesting to see what happens, right?

It's on You, No one else

Alright, let's get into this. You've probably heard it a few times: *"You are the master of your own destiny"* or *"You control your own fate."* But let's break it down—it's not just a motivational poster slogan. It's the raw truth. The sooner you realise that life's success or failure is *predominantly on you*, the better off you'll be.

First off, let's talk about *personal responsibility*. We live in an era where it's shockingly easy to blame anyone and everyone for our issues. Didn't get that promotion? Must be the boss's fault. The relationship didn't work out? Clearly, it's the other person's problem, right? Did you miss out on your dream? Oh, it's society's fault. But here's the thing: while all that might sound comforting, it's essentially a cop-out. The reality is that *we often hold the reins*. Sure, external factors play a role, but how we *react* to them, how we *pivot*, and how we *hustle* are entirely within our control.

Then there's the matter of *taking action*. We've all heard the phrase *"talk is cheap,"* and it's never been truer. It's easy to say you're going to make a change, start a new habit, or chase a dream. It's another thing to *actually do it*. Every excuse you make is a roadblock you're putting up yourself. Want to be fit? *Get off your arse and move.* Dream of writing a novel or a book? *Start typing or writing.* The universe won't hand you success on a silver platter. *You've got to roll up your sleeves and dig in.*

And let's be real—life isn't going to line up perfectly just because you're ready to make a change. The timing will never feel right, and the circumstances won't ever be ideal. But here's the thing: *waiting for the "perfect moment" is just another way of procrastinating.* There's no guarantee that everything will fall into place, so it's up to you to start, even if the conditions aren't perfect. If you're waiting for the universe to clear the path, you'll end up standing still. Sometimes you just have to make the best of the situation and push forward regardless.

Finally, let's address the *self-pity party*. It's tempting to wallow in what could have been, but the only way out is *through*. You can sit around waiting for someone else to fix things or give you a leg up, but chances are, you'll be waiting a long time. Embracing the fact that *it's on you* is liberating. It means *you* have the power to shape your life, and with that power comes the potential for real, lasting change. It's a heavy responsibility, but it's also *incredibly empowering.*

And let's not forget about the ultimate game-changer: *mindset.* How you perceive challenges and setbacks can make or break your journey. Adopting a *growth mindset* means seeing obstacles as opportunities, rather than reasons to quit. When you accept that it's all on you, you also recognize that you can *learn, adapt, and evolve.*

Common Sense tells us that *nothing worth having comes easy.* It's that simple. You don't need a self-help guru to tell you that hard work pays off, or that sitting around waiting for life to happen isn't a winning strategy. Sometimes, the most obvious truths are the ones we overlook. So, take a deep breath, embrace the challenge, and use a little *common sense:* if you want something, put in the work. It's not glamorous, it's not always fun, but it's the only way forward.

It's like being the *hero of your own story*—sometimes you'll face dragons, but it's up to you to slay them. So, put on your armour, grab your sword (phone or laptop), and start forging your path. Because at the end of the day, *the real magic happens when you decide to be the architect of your fate.*

Your problems? They're yours, no one to blame,

Excuses won't help; it's a losing game.

Step up, take charge, and set things straight,

The real change starts when *you* create.

It's on you, while working with others.

Imagination over Reality?

It's funny, right? *Your imagination can stretch way further than real knowledge ever will.* We're living in a time where imagination is sometimes accepted as reality—even outside the world of artists! And don't get me wrong, imagination *is* powerful. But today, people will pull off some wild, twisted act and slap the label "art" on it, expecting everyone to nod along like it makes sense. We've got adults acting like kids, with no one stopping to think about the message it sends to younger generations. It's all fun and games until someone's child is trying to "express themselves" in a way that just doesn't belong in a sandbox, let alone the real world.

We've reached a point where some people imagine they're smarter than they actually are. Like the universe is showing them a preview of greatness—a glimpse of what they *could* have achieved if they didn't waste half their time scrolling through social media or zoning out in front of a streaming service. It's like life is giving you a trailer for a movie you'll never actually get to star in *unless* you stop messing around. Imagination tells you you're destined for greatness, but reality? It says, *"Get to work."* You can dream all day, but knowledge only expands when you start *doing* something with it.

And here's the thing: imagination without boundaries is a double-edged sword. Sure, it helps us think bigger, but when we start accepting every imagined thought as valid, we lose touch with reality. We start confusing what *could be* with what *is.* Dream big, absolutely—but at some point, someone's got to step in and say, *"Maybe this isn't the direction we should take."* Otherwise, we're just running around like kids playing make-believe, with no one really steering the ship.

If we want to guide the next generation, we've got to make sure our imaginations aren't steering us into absurdity. That's just *Common Sense.*

Have fun but don't be dumb.

We really are, Smart

It's honestly mind-blowing how far we've come as a species. I mean, just think about the fact that we can take something as small as a microchip, pack it full of millions of circuits, and then have it running all the tech that basically controls our lives. That's insane. We've gone from banging rocks together to creating tiny computers that can process information faster than we ever thought possible. It's like magic—but it's science. And the best part is, we're not even done yet. We're just scratching the surface of what we can achieve.

Look at skyscrapers, for example. We've figured out how to build cities that stretch into the sky, hundreds of stories tall, defying gravity most practically. These aren't just buildings—they're monuments to human ingenuity. And then there's the internet. We've literally connected the entire planet through a web of invisible signals, allowing us to talk, share, and collaborate with someone on the opposite side of the world in real-time. And it all works because of that little microchip, among other things. The fact that we can be this globally connected, and still complain about slow Wi-Fi, just shows how good we have it.

Medicine is another wild advancement. We've cracked open the human body, mapped our DNA, and developed treatments and vaccines that save millions of lives. We're editing genes now! We've gone from leeches and superstition to curing diseases that used to wipe out entire populations. The rate at which medical science is evolving is almost as fast as tech, and together they're creating this future where the impossible might actually become possible. The way we manipulate and understand the human body now is next-level compared to even just a few decades ago.

On top of all this genius, we're also exploring the cosmos. We've sent probes to the edge of our solar system and rovers to Mars. We're hunting for exoplanets and peeking back in time to the early days of the universe. The James Webb Telescope is out there snapping selfies of galaxies billions of light-years away, giving us a view of the universe that's never been seen before. Meanwhile, back on Earth, satellites are surveilling everything—keeping tabs on the weather, tracking environmental changes, and making sure we know what's going on down here. It's like we're mastering both realms: space and Earth.

And here's a thought: we've also managed to move past some of the worst behaviours in our history—or at least we're trying. While blatant racism, sexism, and hate still exist, we've become better at calling it out, better at holding systems accountable and pushing for change. It's not perfect, but it's progress. Compare this to a century ago, when human rights were barely a concept, let alone a global conversation. Today, we've got movements that span continents, uniting people to stand against injustice. Yes, contradictions abound—we fight for equality while still struggling to unlearn deep-rooted biases. But the fact that these conversations are even happening shows how far we've come.

And of course, credit for a lot of these advancements can't go to just anyone; they're the result of collective brilliance, minds coming together across generations and continents. We're looking at centuries of innovation, of thinkers and doers who've taken us from the wheel to the web, from herb potions to gene therapy. This isn't just a lucky coincidence; it's hard work, vision, and grit piled on by people who didn't even live to see the full fruits of their labour. And now, it's up to us to keep that progress going.

What's next? Well, that's the beauty of it—we don't exactly know. AI, quantum computing, fusion energy, space travel. There's no limit to what we can achieve, but one thing's for sure: the future is going to be as crazy as the past few decades have been, maybe even crazier. And while it's easy to get bogged down by life's daily grind, remember—we're living in a time where we've pushed the boundaries of what's possible. From tiny microchips to the far reaches of space, we're doing things that would've been called science fiction just a century ago.

And let's not forget the environmental strides we're making—turning waste into energy, creating biodegradable plastics, growing lab-made organs, and even building machines that can repair ecosystems. We've created technologies that pull carbon straight from the atmosphere and drones that can plant forests faster than any human. We're smarter than we give ourselves credit for, and these advancements show just how much we're capable of when we actually focus our collective brainpower.

So, here's the thing: if you're ever feeling down or questioning what the point of it all is, just remember what we're capable of. We've built a world where possibilities are endless. We really are, smart. It's not a bad existence. And *Common Sense* is just knowing that we can pretty much create anything with enough time—and that doesn't seem to be stopping any time soon.

Importance of Collaboration

Collaboration is something that humanity has been mastering since we first figured out how to share a fire. Back in the day, you didn't survive without a *community*, whether you were hunting mammoths or just trying not to freeze, it was all about *working together*. Hard times glued us together, and gave us no choice but to rely on each other for survival. That was life's way of saying, "*You can't do this alone.*" But fast forward to today, and suddenly, it feels like we've forgotten the whole *teamwork* thing. Technology, individualism, and the rise of "*hustle culture*" have convinced us that we're all supposed to be self-sufficient superheroes. Spoiler alert: *not everybody is.*

Sure, we've got apps to deliver food, algorithms to solve problems, and endless YouTube tutorials to teach us everything from fixing a sink to becoming a stock market guru. But while all this progress has made life more convenient, it's also made us *weirdly isolated.* We've started to think we don't *need* anyone, and that's a dangerous mindset. Social media might make it look like everyone's doing just fine on their own, but the truth is, that human beings are *wired to collaborate.* We're not supposed to go solo. Without *connection,* everything loses meaning—your success, your achievements, even your struggles.

Collaboration is more than just a team project at work or getting the family together for dinner. It's how *societies thrive.* When we collaborate, we blend different skills, perspectives, and experiences to create something greater than just us in its parts. Think about any major achievement in history—*building pyramids, sending people to space, creating the internet, bringing about revolutions*—none of that happened because one person locked themselves in a room and figured it all out. It was *groups of people,* leaning on each other's strengths, and pushing boundaries *together.* So, while it feels like the modern world is pushing us towards being lone wolves, the reality is that we *need each other now more than ever.*

It's **Common Sense** to collaborate.

What you eat, Matters

These days, we've got more food options than ever before, but ironically, we're sometimes *worse off* than when people used to survive on just the odd meat, bread, wine, ale, and water. Back then, food wasn't pumped full of *chemicals, preservatives,* and *artificial everything.* Fast forward to now, and you're bombarded with diets from every angle—*keto, paleo, vegan, carnivore*—you name it, there's a food trend for it. And sure, *everyone's different,* but the reality is, no matter what you label yourself, you've *got to eat well* if you want longevity, energy, and a sane mind. *That's just the truth.*

The problem today is that it's *way easier and cheaper* to access *crap food* than healthy options. You've got fast food places on every corner, delivery apps that'll bring *greasy burgers* to your door in ten minutes, and snacks that are *designed to be addictive.* It's no wonder we're all hooked. But the *real challenge?* Seeking out *good food* requires *effort.* It's not that eating well is impossible; it's just *not handed to you.* You've got to go out of your way to learn what works for your *body and mind.* And yeah, it's not always convenient, but *trust me,* your future self will thank you.

At the end of the day, *your diet is your foundation.* What you put in your body affects everything—*your mood, your health,* even how well you *think.* Processed junk and sugar-loaded drinks will leave you sluggish, while whole, *real foods* keep your body and mind *sharp.* It's a game of balance, and it's not about *perfection but consistency.* Sure, enjoy the pizza, but also make time to explore the foods that'll help you *thrive.* It's all out there—you just have to be willing to look for it.

And let's be honest, *a good diet = Common Sense.*

It might taste good, but is it good for you?

Over Indulging

Over-indulging isn't just about eating one too many slices of pizza or staying up late to binge-watch an entire season of a show you've already seen three times. It's something *deeper*, something that seeps into all areas of life—because, honestly, anything can become an addiction if you lean into it too hard. We all know that *too much of a good thing can end badly*, but it's not just about physical stuff like food or drink. Even *emotional states*—like wallowing in negativity or chasing endless highs—can become a kind of indulgence. It's like this strange, twisted comfort zone people create for themselves, where they just keep sinking deeper and deeper, not realising they're doing more harm than good, or maybe they do and just don't care.

Fun, for example, is addictive. Who doesn't love to have a good time? But when the thrill becomes something you *need* rather than just enjoy, it loses its charm and becomes *destructive*. Going out, partying, spending money you don't have, or chasing the next big rush—it's all fine in moderation, but too much and you're just running away from reality. It's easy to over-indulge in "fun" and end up with a life that's spinning out of control because you're avoiding the stuff you actually need to face. *The same goes for negativity.*

Weird as it sounds, *wallowing in your own misery* or diving into drama can become just as addictive as anything else. Complaining about life, indulging in anger, or feeding into bad thoughts can become so normal that you don't even realise you're overdoing it. Negativity is like quicksand—the more you struggle with it, the deeper you get stuck.

But here's the thing: over-indulgence isn't just a habit—it becomes part of your identity. Before you know it, you're not just someone who "likes to have fun" or "needs to vent" now and then; you're *defined* by it. When indulgence becomes your go-to reaction to every high and low, it creates a comfort zone that's tough to break out of. The more you lean into it, the harder it is to step back and regain control, even when you start to see the cracks forming.

What's even worse is that overindulgence, whether in *good times* or *bad*, eventually leads to deterioration—mentally, emotionally, and physically. Fun without boundaries turns into *recklessness*, and unchecked negativity drains your energy, keeping you stuck in a cycle of *feeling sorry for yourself* or just *not good enough*.

People end up indulging to the point of losing themselves, their goals, and their sense of purpose. They get trapped in their own habits, thinking it's all just part of "living life" or "coping." But eventually, what started as a thrill or a way to blow off steam becomes a norm, and that norm slowly eats away at you until it's hard to even see the damage being done. Over-indulging dulls your senses, numbs your emotions, and makes it impossible to appreciate things in moderation.

And here's some *Common Sense:* everything, even fun and feelings, is best in *moderation.* Indulging every now and then isn't the problem—it's when indulgence turns into *dependency* that things start to fall apart. When fun becomes a way to escape and negativity becomes a default state of mind, it's time to step back.

It's not about cutting yourself off completely, but about finding *balance.* Because over-indulging, whether in good times or bad, only leads you down a path of *self-destruction.* Learn to recognize when you're going too far and pull back before it consumes you. It's not about being strict or boring—it's just about having a little bit of *self-control.* Knowing when enough is enough isn't just a virtue—it's *Common Sense.*

Indulgence feels good, but it takes its toll,

Too much fun or sadness can swallow you whole.

Balance the highs, don't drown in the lows,

Because losing control is how chaos grows.

Ask yourself, is this thing good for me?

Importance of Compromise

Compromise is one of those things that *sounds* easy in theory but feels like trying to split a pizza evenly when you really want the last slice. Yet, it's the *backbone* of every successful relationship—whether that's with your partner, your friends, or even your coworkers. Back in the day, compromise was essential for *survival*. People had to meet in the middle and make decisions that worked for the *group*, not just the individual. There was no room for stubbornness when the goal was simply *staying alive*. But nowadays, in a world where it's easy to get what you want (thanks, next-day delivery), the idea of compromising seems like a *lost art*.

We live in a time where *individuality* is celebrated, sometimes to a fault. It's easy to forget that not every battle needs to be won, and not every disagreement is about who's *right*. Compromise teaches us the importance of *empathy*, *understanding*, and sometimes just *letting go* of our need to be the winner. It's not about *losing*; it's about finding that *middle ground* where everyone feels like they're part of the *solution*. In relationships, whether romantic or professional, without compromise, things fall apart pretty quickly. The moment one person digs in their heels, the dynamic gets *lopsided*. A lack of compromise leaves everyone *frustrated*, *disconnected*, and in the long run, even *isolated*.

Compromise doesn't mean you have to give up who you are or what you stand for. *Common Sense* is more about recognizing that, to *thrive*, you have to bend sometimes. It's not *weakness*; it's *wisdom*. The strongest bonds are built on a foundation of *give-and-take*, where both sides are willing to *step back*, *listen*, and meet *halfway*.

And let's face it, compromise might just be the secret to keeping things from turning into a constant tug-of-war. In a world that's obsessed with *winning* and getting your way, compromise reminds us that the real victories are the ones we *share*. Whether it's in relationships, careers, or just navigating everyday life, mastering the *art of compromise* makes everything *smoother*, *more fulfilling*, and surprisingly, *more rewarding*.

It's just a part of life really.

Life Skills

Life skills today are almost like *cheat codes* in a video game—except half of us aren't even trying to unlock them. Why bother learning how to change a tyre when you can just hit up roadside assistance, right? Or cook a decent meal when there's an app to bring food straight to your door in 20 minutes? The bare minimum has become the new *"I'm adulting!"* and, honestly, we're all just kind of floating through on the back of society's conveniences. It's like the NPCs in a game—they exist, but they don't exactly make the game more interesting, do they? *Then again, maybe everyone's got their own hidden side quest—you just haven't unlocked it yet.*

We're in an era where you can technically survive without knowing how to do much beyond using your phone and going to the shop. But imagine a world where everyone was just coasting on this same low-effort vibe. It's like walking into a room full of mannequins—nobody's adding anything real. No spice, no flavour, just existing. Sure, you can get by, but what kind of life is that? Life skills—whether it's budgeting, fixing stuff, cooking, or just knowing how to communicate properly—are what give you that extra edge. It's what makes you an actual *player* in this game of life, instead of just another background character waiting for someone else to hit the action button.

Look, I'm not saying everyone needs to become a master carpenter or a Michelin-star chef. But *Common Sense* is saying that learning some basic skills adds richness to your life. It makes you self-reliant, confident, and, dare I say, a little more fun to be around. Plus, the world needs fewer NPCs and more people actually *playing* the game. So, yeah, maybe life skills seem like the bare minimum now, but trust me—they're the difference between surviving and thriving. And wouldn't you rather be *thriving*, not just existing in the corner of someone else's reality?

Skills are like that extra spice to life.

The World can be Cruel

The world can be a *beautiful* place, no doubt, but let's be real—it can also be downright *cruel* and relentless. People love to talk about hope and kindness, but that doesn't change the fact that life has a *dark side*. There's suffering out there that most of us can't even begin to understand. Just being born in the wrong place can mean a life of poverty, violence, or struggling for basic survival. And even if you're in a relatively "safe" spot, you're still not immune to life's random punches.

Accidents, illnesses, losses that hit out of nowhere—they don't care if you're a *good person* or if you've made all the *right choices*. Then there's the ugliness we see in everyday life: people turning on each other, backstabbing, and using others for their own gain. Sometimes, it's not even malicious—just pure *apathy*, like people have forgotten what it means to really see and care about each other, but of course, that's nothing new.

And if that's not enough, *nature itself* has a ruthless side. Hurricanes, earthquakes, floods—they come crashing down, tearing apart everything in their path, leaving people to pick up the shattered pieces of what's left. Look at the wildfires that scorch the earth or the ice caps melting at an alarming rate.

Climate change has made everything more extreme; winters that used to just be cold now feel *bone-chilling*, and summers are more like *living in a greenhouse*. And that's just the weather—entire ecosystems are collapsing, animals are going extinct, and yet, we keep doing the same things, pretending it'll sort itself out. *Not that we can actually do much about it.*

It's like we're caught in this loop of hurting the planet and ourselves, but no one wants to slow down because the machine of *profit and progress* has to keep churning. We say we care, but do we really?

The thing is, *life isn't fair*, and ignoring how brutal the world can be won't make it any less real. *Good things happen to bad people*, and terrible things happen to those who don't deserve it at all. Pretending otherwise is just setting yourself up to get blindsided.

Facing the fact that the world can be *heartless* isn't about becoming cynical—it's about seeing things *as they are*. It's okay to be sad and to feel overwhelmed, but it's also okay to *keep going anyway*. The world is a harsh place, but that doesn't mean you have to turn away from it.

It means being strong enough to acknowledge the *darkness* without letting it consume you. Because the cruelty of the world isn't going anywhere, but that doesn't mean you can't find your way through it, one tough day at a time. And maybe, just maybe, by facing that darkness, you might find the little pockets of *light*—those fleeting moments of kindness or beauty that make the struggle worth it. *That's just Common Sense.*

But let's be honest—sometimes the cruelty of the world feels overwhelming like an *endless wave* crashing over you again and again. It's easy to feel small, powerless, and like nothing you do will ever make a difference. The harsh truth is that a lot of times, we won't be able to change the *bigger picture*. We can't stop the storms or erase the injustices overnight. But we *can* decide how we face them, and whether we let them *define us*. Even when everything feels out of our control, the way we respond—to others, to ourselves, to the world—is still something we can own. And in a world that is this cruel, that small bit of power can be *everything.*

The world's a beast, it doesn't play fair,
It'll chew you up without a care.
Keep your head high, don't let it show,
The world hits hard, but you'll survive.

Yeah, it can be ruthless out there.

Ancient Civilisations

When we think of ancient civilizations, it's easy to get stuck on the usual suspects like the Egyptians or the Sumerians. But what if there was a time *before them*—before the last ice age—when humanity was already building advanced structures and living in organized societies? It's not so far-fetched. There's evidence of massive floods around 12,000 years ago that could have wiped out earlier civilizations, leaving behind only hints of their existence. Think of the pyramids, the massive stone structures carved into mountains, and the perfectly aligned stone slabs found both on land and underwater across the globe. It's as if these ancient builders understood something about the natural flow of the world that we've lost over time.

All over the planet, we see hints of this lost history. Massive underground networks in Turkey could shelter tens of thousands of people. Foundations beneath Osaka Castle in Japan share an eerie similarity with stone walls in Peru or Egypt, almost as if the techniques were shared knowledge. Yet, it's not just the physical evidence that hints at an advanced past—many of the world's ancient cultures and myths also seem to reference this lost time. Stories of a "Great Flood" pop up in legends and holy texts across the world, from the Bible to ancient Sumerian records to tales passed down by indigenous tribes. They all speak of a catastrophic event that nearly wiped humanity off the map, and of different beings roaming the world before or after it.

And that's not all—many of these ancient sites are mysteriously *off-limits.* Try to explore certain sections of the Grand Canyon that reportedly contain unusual, pyramid-like formations or unexplained cave systems, and you'll find they're completely restricted. Government red tape has locked them down ever since early 1900s reports stirred up controversy about the area's strange artefacts. Some believe there's more to the story, but *what do we know,* right?

The same goes for certain underwater ruins, like those near Yonaguni in Japan or other unexplained formations beneath the sea. Some researchers speculate that these formations could point to ancient, advanced civilisations predating what we currently understand about human history. There are even forbidden zones like Mount Kailash in Tibet, where climbing is *prohibited,* and Lake Vostok in Antarctica, where scientists have found signs of ancient microbes and unexplained magnetic anomalies.

Speaking of Antarctica, it's also home to massive, unexplored subglacial lakes and strange grid-like patterns on satellite images that have fuelled rumours of hidden bases or ancient civilisations buried beneath the ice.

It's almost as if *access is cut off* whenever a discovery might raise too many questions. Why are certain caves in the Bucegi Mountains of Romania said to be completely off-limits due to "classified" finds? Or why are some of the most remote Amazon regions being studied but closely guarded? The more you dig, the more it feels like humanity's history might be a lot *stranger—and smarter—*than we've been told.

Look at places like Puma Punku in Bolivia, where the stonework is so precise it seems impossible without advanced tools. Or consider how the pyramids—found not just in Egypt, but also in Mexico, Bosnia, and even underwater—line up with certain astronomical events. Some theorize these structures were used to harness natural energy, built with technologies that aren't even on our radar. If that's true, *what were these civilizations really capable of?*

There's also the matter of shared symbols and construction techniques. You've got carvings in Japan that look strikingly similar to those in South America, and even bizarre ancient structures in the Grand Canyon that reportedly match Egyptian-style architecture. How did these distant cultures communicate, or even know about each other, if they were supposedly isolated?

And it's not just these; countless more places remain unexplored or completely inaccessible to the public: vast caves in Ecuador rumoured to hold metal books; the dense jungles of Cambodia that might hide even more Angkorian temples; and the uncharted parts of the Amazon, where entire lost cities might be buried under the foliage. We're left with more questions than answers.

Common Sense? Isn't it funny how we've got caves with paintings from 25,000–35,000 years ago, but apparently we didn't do much of anything until after the last ice age? *Yeah, right.* Come on, civilizations rise and fall—history's proven that much. So, think about it: maybe there's way more to our past than a couple of hammer-and-chisel guys knocking around in loincloths. But *who knows,* right?

It's strange.

Constant Mind Shift

We've all felt it—this constant sense of shifting gears in our minds, like the transmission of a car stuck in rush-hour traffic. It's not just that our *attention spans are short* (thanks, social media), but it's *deeper than that*. There's a *collective shift* happening in our consciousness. It's like half the people are moving in one direction, and the other half are going somewhere else entirely. Some people are diving into the depths of *self-awareness* and exploration, while others are getting caught in the whirlwind of the next distraction. No one's really anchored; we're all just kind of floating, *waiting for something to ground us* again.

This mind shift feels like we're living in an invisible hurricane, where the air itself is thick with *anticipation*. Some people seem to have their antennas tuned into the "good stuff," sensing the subtle energies of change and progress, while others are just spinning in the chaos, unsure of what's going on but knowing *something* is definitely off. Social anxiety is spiking all over because, let's be honest, it feels like the world is holding its breath, *waiting for the other shoe to drop*. Everyone's plugged into this collective anxiety, and it's like we're all on edge, waiting for *something big to happen*, but we're not even sure what it is. And this constant uncertainty? It's *exhausting*.

Yet, this shift might actually be *necessary*. The world's evolving faster than ever, and maybe this collective discomfort is a sign we're on the cusp of something new—a kind of *transformation* that shakes us out of the old ways. We're moving into a new paradigm where old systems no longer work, and yeah, it's *messy*. There's friction because some people are still gripping onto the past, while others are surfing this wave into the future. But friction is what leads to *growth*, and growth is rarely comfortable. So, while this all feels overwhelming, maybe it's a necessary part of evolving into *whatever comes next*.

The downside? All this constant change and uncertainty is leaving people feeling more *dissociated than ever*. It's like we're all here, but we're *not really here*. The line between reality and the version of it we see through our phones or in our heads has blurred. Most of us are caught somewhere in between, stuck in a *limbo* where the world feels *too real yet oddly distant* at the same time. This disconnection from the present moment leaves many out of touch with themselves and each other, as we're constantly looking for the next thing, *never really living in the now*.

But hey, maybe this constant mind shift isn't all bad. It's forcing us to *adapt*, to question what we *value*, and to figure out where we *really want to go*. The new world we're heading into is going to require *flexibility, resilience*, and a *higher level of awareness*. Sure, it's disorienting right now, but that's just part of the process. In the end, we're learning to navigate this shift together, even if it feels like we're constantly *tripping over our own feet*. It's messy, but necessary—because standing still just isn't an option anymore, well, not that you have an option, unless you want to fall behind.

And maybe that's where *Common Sense* needs to step in. Amid all the noise and the whirlwind of change, sometimes the simplest truths are the ones we forget first. We're *overcomplicating everything*, but maybe what we need most is a *return to the basics*—grounding ourselves in what truly matters, in *human connection*, in *genuine presence*.

Common Sense tells us that no matter how chaotic things get, we need to find our footing in something real, something we can hold onto when everything else seems to be *slipping away*. Because in a world this unsteady, having a little *Common Sense* might just be the most revolutionary thing of all.

We're all caught in this swirling haze,
Lost in the chaos of shifting days.

Some seek meaning, some just drift,
A world in motion, minds adrift.

It's messy, sure, but growth's never clean,
We'll figure it out, somewhere in between.

It can be very disorientating.

Music

Music is one of those things that's impossible to fully describe, but we all know how much it means. It's not just a *sound*; it's a *feeling*, a *connection*. From ancient drums around a fire to classical symphonies and modern beats, music has always been there, evolving right alongside humanity. It's something we *need*—not just to fill silence, but to *express* the things we can't say any other way. Every generation leaves its mark through music, recording its history, emotions, and rebellions in every note.

But music isn't just *entertainment*—it's like a *ritual*, an extension of our emotions, thoughts, and culture. It can *uplift*, but it can also influence us *negatively*, especially in today's world where music is mass-produced and sometimes promotes *toxic messages*. We often don't think about how certain songs can shape our mindset or even how some of it is purposely pushed to *alter our thinking*. With mental health issues, violence, and materialism rising, it's worth considering the role music plays in shaping this landscape. For some, music becomes almost like a *drug*—something they can't do anything without. That's when it gets tricky; it can be a *powerful motivator* but also a *distraction* if you're not careful.

There's more to it than meets the ear, though. Music isn't just *sound*; it's made up of *frequencies*, measured in hertz (Hz), representing the *vibrations per second* that create those beats, melodies, and harmonies we vibe with. Each frequency impacts our bodies differently, with *lower frequencies* creating a grounding effect and *higher frequencies* offering an uplifting vibe. Without even knowing it, our minds and bodies sync up to these vibrations, influencing our heart rates, thoughts, and even emotions. *You are what you listen to*, in a way, shaping how you see the world—but it's *not that deep* if you're aware of it, it's just another layer of understanding sound.

That's not to say music isn't *incredible*—it absolutely is. But as you grow older, you start to listen *differently*. *Common Sense?* Realise those songs you blasted as a teenager were saying more than you thought. Like Shaggy's *Angel* when he sings, "Life's one big party when you're still young, but who's gonna have your back when it's all done?" It hits *differently*. Music sticks with you, but so does the *message*, and as we grow, we learn to be a bit more aware of what it's feeding us. Most of the time, it *shapes us* as a person, unconsciously.

You are a Human

You are a human, which sounds obvious, right? But in today's world, it seems like people are almost forgetting what that *means*. There are different breeds of humans on this earth—different shapes, sizes, skin colours, and cultural backgrounds. Yet, despite all these differences, we're still just *human*. There's no secret elite class of superhumans or genetically superior beings running the show (unless you're deep into those "lizard people" theories). And outside of that, we all share the same basic needs and desires—food, shelter, love, and purpose. We laugh, we cry, we dream, we fail. But instead of embracing these shared traits, society has created this weird, impossible standard that everyone's expected to meet.

We're constantly bombarded with messages telling us to be *perfect*, flawless, always happy, and perpetually hyperproductive. It's like being *human* isn't enough anymore—everyone's supposed to be some upgraded, superhuman version of themselves. And when we don't measure up, we feel like we're falling short. Like, who wants to be *basic*, right?

I'm not saying this because I'm some enlightened being looking down from above. I'm part of this mess too—living it, feeling it, and just trying to make sense of it like everyone else. I'm just pointing it out because when you step back and really look, you can see how much we're all caught in this ridiculous cycle. We've become so focused on what we *should* be that we've forgotten how to *just be*.

Sure, you should strive for more—definitely push your limits, create, explore, and expand your horizons—because that's what humans are made to do. But the irony is, the more access we get to the world and each other, the less united we actually seem to be. The more we know, the more divided we act. It's like the more we're able to *connect*, the more disconnected we become; it's a weird duality. Finding that sweet spot between self-improvement and self-acceptance is like trying to solve a riddle that keeps changing its answer.

It's not straightforward, and it's definitely not easy. Some people seem blissfully unaware of the whole dilemma, but plenty are clued in. They're consciously trying to break free from the endless chase, stepping back to embrace what it means to be *human*—flawed but authentic, striving but self-aware.

That's not to say that you shouldn't strive for a cushty life; we all want more and want to *be more*. But we seem to be going about it in a somewhat of a numb way.

Common Sense: being human is about navigating these contradictions, striving for more while also accepting who you are *right NOW*. It's not about reaching some flawless version of yourself that doesn't exist. It's about being able to look at yourself and the world and say, "Yeah, this is messy, and it's complicated, but I'm part of it, and that's okay, I can do something about it."

Let's not forget that while self-improvement is a noble pursuit, *being human* is also about finding joy in the simple things—having a laugh with friends, getting through a tough day, feeling the rain on your face, or just sitting in silence. Sometimes, the most "basic" parts of life are the ones that make it all worth it. We're constantly reaching for more, but every now and then, it's worth stopping to appreciate what's right in front of us.

Don't buy into the idea that being human isn't enough—it's *plenty*. You can grow and evolve while still appreciating where you are. Embrace your imperfections, recognize your strengths, and remember that everyone's figuring it out as they go along. Because at the end of the day, we're all just trying to find our way in this strange, wonderful, chaotic world. And realising that shouldn't take a superhuman—is just *Common Sense*. But hey, like, who wants to be *basic*, right?

We're human—each unique, yet the same,
Different faces, but a shared flame.
Diverse in the journey, one in name.

Being human is a mess, but it's all we've got.

The Truth about Climate Change

For decades now, we've been told that climate change is this looming apocalypse we should all be terrified of—and to be fair, they're not wrong. But humans have been playing this weird game of *"do as I say, not as I do"* since the early '90s. Sure, we all dutifully separate our plastics and glass, drop our old clothes off at donation bins, and drive hybrids if we're feeling fancy. But let's be honest—when it comes to the bigger picture, most of us don't really give a shit, because life carries on.

People will recycle their coffee cups one minute and then hop on a flight for a weekend getaway or buy the latest gadget that's shipped halfway across the globe, wrapped in enough plastic to drown a small village. It's like we've convinced ourselves that our tiny efforts offset the colossal damage we do in other areas—whether it's deforesting land for agriculture, polluting rivers for industry, or simply dumping a ridiculous amount of waste into landfills that are slowly becoming mountains of human negligence.

The contradictory nature of humans has led to absurd outcomes, like literal islands of garbage floating around in the ocean. The *Great Pacific Garbage Patch* isn't some abstract concept—it's a real place, a testament to our collective apathy. Made up of millions of tons of plastic and debris, it's an island we created and yet no one wants to claim. Meanwhile, landfills keep growing, stuffed with all the stuff we think we're being so responsible about recycling.

The truth is that much of what we think we're recycling ends up back in landfills or shipped to developing countries, causing even more environmental harm. We say we care about the planet, but as long as there's profit to be made or convenience to be had, we'll bulldoze a rainforest or pollute a river without blinking an eye. And the craziest part? Even companies that slap *"eco-friendly"* labels on their products are often doing just enough to look good while contributing to the very problem they claim to be fighting.

And it's not just about waste—it's like the climate itself is becoming as erratic as our behaviour. I remember winters as a kid in England being chilly but manageable. Now, at 27, it's like being in an Arctic deep freeze some years, while other times it barely feels like winter at all. Summers are a different beast altogether. It's not just warm—it's suffocating, like living in a greenhouse no matter where you go.

And it's not just the UK—weather patterns are getting weirder everywhere, with more extreme storms, unexpected droughts, and unseasonal heat waves. It's hard to pretend the climate isn't changing when you can *feel it slap you in the face* every time you step outside. And I don't know what spraying the sky with chemtrails is supposed to do against all this chaos, but it's pretty clear that whatever we've been doing isn't fixing the problem—not that we have a solid solution anyway.

And here's the thing: the sun itself is *actively* cooking us. *Solar cycles*—the natural phases the sun goes through every 11 years—have a massive impact on our planet. During *solar maximums,* the sun releases more radiation and energy, subtly but significantly heating the Earth. When paired with weaker solar minimums, the fluctuations create an imbalance, with the hotter phases outweighing the cooler ones. This isn't just theory—it's why some years feel more extreme than others. The sun is like the Earth's thermostat; right now, it's cranking up the heat.

So while human intervention plays a role, the sun's influence is on a whole other level. The warming trends aren't entirely man-made—some of it result from our *star's* natural rhythms. That doesn't mean we get to sit back and ignore the problem, but it does make it clear that we're battling forces far beyond our control.

Common Sense? Caring about the environment can't be a part-time job. Recycling and feeling good about it isn't going to reverse the mess we've made. We can't keep acting like it's someone else's problem or that small personal actions alone are enough to offset the damage. Climate change isn't just a boogeyman story—it's happening, and the sun's doing a number on us while we argue over whose fault it is.

And here's the real irony: even as the sun's natural cycles wreak havoc, we're still making things worse for ourselves. Instead of working with the planet to adapt and mitigate the damage, we're stuck fighting battles we can't win. If we want to survive the sun's tantrums, maybe it's time to stop acting like the villains in our own story and *start playing the long game.*

There's not much we can do to change the inevitable.

Is this a Simulation?

"Is this a simulation?" Now, this is the question that keeps insomniacs up at 3 a.m., scrolling through conspiracy forums and watching way too many YouTube videos of birds frozen mid-air or people walking through walls. Let's face it—sometimes life feels a bit *too* bizarre to be real. You know those moments when things glitch, like you *swear* you left your keys on the table, but they magically end up in the fridge? Or how about the endless *déjà vu*? It's like the universe itself is doing a hard reset on us and hoping we won't notice. So, is this all just an elaborate simulation, where we're the Sims, and someone is clicking "speed up time" whenever we start getting too comfortable?

Alright, let's dive into the actual theories. One of the most famous ideas comes from philosopher Nick Bostrom, who suggested that it's *statistically likely* we're living in a simulation created by a highly advanced civilization. Think about it: if we've already made virtual worlds and video games, what's stopping a super-advanced species—or maybe future humans—from simulating their ancestors (that's *us*)? Shit, with the way AI is going, it wouldn't even take a civilization. Some rogue AI could've booted us up as an experiment while it chills in the real world. There's also the *holographic universe* theory, which posits that we're living in a 3D projection of a 2D plane—essentially, the universe could be a giant cosmic flat-screen TV, and we're just the pixels.

Then you've got the wild idea that we're all inside a *black hole*. Yup, there's a theory out there suggesting the Big Bang was actually the result of matter collapsing into a black hole, and we're living in the event horizon of it. Everything happening around us is just a projection, and time as we know it is being warped. Tests like the *double-slit experiment*—you know, the one where particles behave differently when observed—seem to hint that reality might be influenced by *perception* itself. The universe could just be responding to us watching it, like some cosmic Truman Show, which is *creepy* if you think about it too long.

And let's not forget the *glitches in the matrix* that everyone's talking about. The internet is full of videos showing birds frozen in mid-flight, planes just chilling in the sky, and people phasing through solid objects like they're NPCs in a broken video game. Sure, a lot of these might be edited, but every now and then, you see something that makes you question *everything*.

Like that guy—*Max Headroom incident, anyone?*—who glitched out during a live broadcast and looped the same sentence three times like someone hit rewind on reality. Or when people from opposite sides of the world describe seeing the exact same dream. Or how about the *Mandela Effect,* where half the population remembers something that supposedly never happened? It's like we're all living in a computer simulation, but the software gets buggy sometimes—whoops, sorry about that, just patch it later.

But as insane as these theories sound, they kinda weirdly make sense. Reality is full of strange coincidences, unexplained phenomena, and things that don't quite add up. And with *quantum physics* getting more confusing the deeper we go, it's not completely out of the question that reality is some kind of advanced code or holographic projection. It's interesting to think about, right? Whether we're part of a simulation inside a black hole, or the universe is some kind of 3D screensaver, it's one hell of a theory to chew on while you're waiting for your coffee to brew. At the very least, it makes life feel a little more exciting... or *terrifying*, depending on how you look at it.

And *Common Sense* for all this? Just carry on. It's interesting and definitely adds some mystery to our day-to-day, but nothing much changes. Life doesn't stop, even if it *glitches* sometimes.

Glitched keys in the fridge, déjà vu on repeat,
A cosmic game, or just life's odd beat?
Pixels or dreams, black holes or fate,
Simulation or not—we're still running late.

Get's you thinking, right?

Thinking you're All that and More

People love to talk a big game—chatting away like they've got everything figured out and then some. And hey, talking isn't a bad thing in itself. In fact, some of the best ideas and plans come from a good conversation. But these days, there's this trend of people acting like they're *"Billy Big Bollocks"*—all talk, full of swagger and big claims until it's time to back it up. Suddenly, all that chest-thumping confidence turns into a nervous shuffle, and they're hiding in the corner or pretending they never said anything in the first place. When push comes to shove, they crumble like wet tissue paper (pussy) and act like they've got amnesia about the nonsense they were spouting. Maybe it's because life today is so cushioned—people don't have to face real hardship, so they never learn how to stand firm. Instead, they hide behind their little digital blankets, hyping themselves up in echo chambers, and when real life finally calls, they've got nothing to show for it. That said, you should have integrity and confidence in this life—just try not to be a fool.

It's wild how some people can strut around like they own the place, talking like they've got the world at their feet, but the moment they're called out or asked to show up, they're nowhere to be found. The bravado disappears faster than a ghost at dawn, and they're left making excuses or shifting blame, hoping no one notices they've suddenly become the very definition of a *"wet wipe."* Social media hasn't helped either—it's like everyone's ego gets inflated with likes and comments, but the second they're in a real-life situation where those metrics don't matter, they deflate just as quickly. And here's another layer to the problem: a lot of people aren't even taught how to defend themselves, verbally or otherwise, in a real confrontation. They talk big because it's easy, but when it comes to handling challenges with grace or strength, they're clueless. It's not just embarrassing—it's annoying. If you're going to act like you're all that and more, at least have the backbone to stand by your words or actions. The world's already full of empty words and half-hearted gestures; you don't need to add to it by pretending to be something you're not just because it's easy to run your mouth when there's no risk involved.

Here's some *Common Sense:* if you're going to talk a big game, back it up. Confidence is great, but people respect honesty and effort more than empty bravado. Life's too cushioned these days, making it easy to fake it—but real respect comes from showing up when it counts. So, cut the act and be real—that's *Common Sense.*

There is a Cycle to Everything?

The universe runs on cycles—big and small, obvious and hidden. Everything that exists is part of a pattern that *repeats itself*, like some *cosmic clockwork* where every gear and cog plays its part. Planets revolve around the sun, the moon pulls on the tides, and stars are born, grow old, and die, only for new ones to take their place. It's all a series of cycles, from the rotation of galaxies down to the tiniest atoms vibrating in place. But it's not just the *physical universe* that follows these rhythms; people do, too. We have our own cycles—*mental, emotional, and physical*—that shape who we are and how we grow throughout our lives.

Just like the earth orbits the sun and the moon has its phases, *people go through their own seasons.* We're not static beings. We shift and change over time, not just with age but with *experiences, influences, and inner growth.* There are times of high energy and times when you feel drained, moments of sharp focus and times of fogginess.

We go through phases of growth, stagnation, learning, and unlearning. Think about it—people change careers, beliefs, relationships, and goals throughout their lives. It's not random; it's part of the *cycle of being human.* From the daily ups and downs of mood and energy to the broader life stages of childhood, adulthood, and old age, there's a rhythm that guides us, even if we don't always see it.

Even on a *day-to-day basis*, our minds and emotions follow their own patterns. Moods rise and fall like tides; thoughts move in cycles of *clarity and confusion.* Just like the moon's gravitational pull affects the ocean's tides, internal factors like hormones, stress, and even external things like weather or seasonality can shift our internal states.

You might feel on top of the world for a few weeks and then hit a slump for no obvious reason—it's just part of your personal cycle. *Understanding this doesn't mean you need to worry about it or try to control it;* it's more about recognizing that you don't have to feel the same way all the time. Like planets with their predictable orbits or the changing seasons, our cycles are natural and necessary for growth.

And these cycles don't just end with individuals. There are *collective human cycles* too—societal patterns that repeat through history.

Cultures rise and fall, generations bring about change, and ideologies shift from one extreme to the other. It's like a pendulum swinging back and forth, always seeking some kind of balance but never staying in one place for too long. Just look at how trends change—what's considered cutting-edge today will be old news tomorrow, only to be rediscovered as "*vintage*" years down the line. It's the same principle, just on a broader scale.

And so, here's some *Common Sense:* cycles are everywhere and in everything, and trying to control or predict them all the time is like trying to hold back the tide with your bare hands. They bring movement, growth, and new perspectives, and sometimes you just have to *let them play out.* So, the next time you feel like you're in a rut or facing a challenging phase, remember it's just one part of a larger rhythm, a necessary stage in your personal cycle.

You don't need to *overthink it* or *force it to change immediately.* Things will shift, as they always do, because that's just the way the *universe works*—constantly turning, evolving, and finding its way back, *again and again.* It's just *Common Sense* to accept that life has its own flow, and sometimes you just have to ride the wave instead of trying to fight against it.

The universe spins in a timeless dance,
Cycles of change, not left to chance.
From stars to tides, we rise and fall,
A rhythm of life that connects us all.

Sometimes, you've just got to go with the flow.

Some people in Power

Alright, let's get *real.* When we talk about the people in power, we're *not* talking about the ones who get voted in every few years. No, I'm talking about the *real power brokers*—the ones pulling the strings from behind the curtain. These are the people with *money so deep* and *influence so wide* that they don't even need to be in the spotlight. You'll hear their names *whispered in conspiracy theories,* but make no mistake, their reach is *very real,* and they don't need an office to *run the world.*

These people operate in ways most of us can't even *comprehend.* They *control industries, own media,* and *steer governments,* without ever having to show their hand. They don't need votes, approval, or popularity—they've got something *far more effective:* control over resources and systems that keep everyone else in line. From the *banking systems* to *big pharmaceuticals* to *tech giants,* they shape the world in ways we only see the effects of, never the decisions behind them.

And let's not forget the *darkest side* of this elite control—the whispers of the so-called *paedophile cults* that supposedly link many of these powerful figures. Stories about *secret rings trafficking children for exploitation* aren't just random conspiracy theories anymore; they've come up *time and again,* with people like *Epstein* exposing just how deep this *rot* goes. These accusations aren't about isolated incidents—they point to *organised, systemic abuse* among the highest echelons of power. And yet, so little comes to light. They're protected by their influence, their money, and a system designed to keep them *untouchable. Mad,* init?

Common Sense tells you something's *horribly wrong* when justice only touches the surface while the real horrors remain buried. *Stay WAKE!*

It's like a real-life Matrix.

Critical Thinking

Critical thinking—it's supposed to be one of those *basic* life skills, right? Something you just pick up along the way, like tying your shoes or riding a bike. The irony today is that while we've got more access to information than ever before, actual *critical thinking* seems to be in pretty short supply. It's not that people don't have it—most of us use it to survive, get through daily life, and make decisions.

But the way it's being directed? *Now that's where things get interesting.* Instead of using it to navigate the bigger picture or ask tough questions, it's often channelled toward short-term gains, convenience, and whatever's trending at the moment. It's like a muscle that's being flexed in the wrong direction, making you think you're exercising it while really, it's just getting lazier and more selective.

Think about it: how many times do people make decisions based on what's easiest or most comfortable at the moment, without a second thought about how it might play out down the road? Everyone's quick to buy the latest gadget because it's cool now or chase the next big trend, but when you ask someone to think about *why* they're doing it or what it really adds to their life, it's crickets.

The same goes for opinions. People latch onto catchy headlines or popular narratives without ever digging deeper. The result? We've got tons of surface-level opinions floating around, but very little substance beneath them. It's like *critical thinking* has been reduced to a buzzword—something people claim to have but rarely put into action.

It's not that people are incapable of thinking things through. We all get up every day, go to work, manage relationships, and make decisions—*critical thinking* is there, but it's on *autopilot*, directed by whatever grabs our attention the most. Instead of asking, "What's the bigger picture here?" or "How does this choice align with my values or long-term goals?" people are more likely to ask, *"What's in it for me right now?"*

It's why we see so many short-sighted decisions being made on personal and even societal levels. From how we consume media to how we vote, the emphasis is on the *immediate* payoff, not the long-term impact. And when the immediate satisfaction wears off, people are left wondering why they feel lost or unfulfilled.

Here's some *Common Sense:* critical thinking isn't just about getting through the day or jumping on the latest bandwagon—it's about slowing down and actually questioning *what* you're doing and *why.* It's about connecting the dots, looking at things from different angles, and not just accepting whatever's handed to you. *Critical thinking* isn't dead, but it's been pushed to the back seat, hijacked by convenience and short-term gratification.

If you want to *use* it, you've got to take the wheel back, start asking yourself the tough questions, and be willing to challenge your own comfort zone. Because at the end of the day, *real* critical thinking isn't about getting things done faster or easier—it's about seeing through the noise and making decisions that *actually mean something.* And when you take control of that, you're not just getting by; you're actively shaping a life that's deeper, more thoughtful, and, ultimately, more *authentic.*

Of course, asking people to think more critically in an age of hot takes and instant gratification is like asking a fish to ponder water. But hey, if even a few of us decide to swim against the current, maybe we'll start a wave of our own. And who knows? *Maybe,* someday, we'll live in a world where scrolling the newsfeed doesn't feel like a test of patience and where real, thoughtful conversations are just as common as memes about coffee and Mondays. Until then, we'll just keep scrolling and hope for the best, *init?*

We scroll, we click, we nod, we share,
Depth is replaced by trending flair.
Critical minds could change the scene,
But comfort keeps us stuck in between.

It's the skill everyone claims but few actually use.

We really should be more Appreciative

It's a bit crazy how we've become so used to having *everything* at our fingertips that we hardly stop to think about the *value* of it all. Like, seriously, when was the last time you actually appreciated something as simple as clean water, electricity, or the fact that your phone can connect you to the *entire world* in seconds? And that's *crazy* compared to a hundred years ago. We're out here scrolling through social media like it's nothing, consuming content, buying stuff we don't need, and tossing things aside the second they stop being shiny—be that whoever or whatever. We've somehow convinced ourselves that everything is *disposable* and, by extension, so is life itself. And that's where the real problem starts.

Appreciation isn't just about being grateful for the things you have—it's about *understanding that nothing in life is guaranteed.* Resources run out. Opportunities fade. Relationships die if they're not nurtured. But we've built this mindset that everything is *infinite* and *replaceable.* We treat the planet like a bottomless well, relationships like they're just a swipe away, and the future like it's already written. We don't think twice before we use the next thing because we assume the next "next thing" is right around the corner. *Spoiler alert:* Most of the time it's not.

If we took a moment to appreciate what we've got—be it our jobs, our families, the environment or something more personal—we'd make different decisions. And, honestly, life would feel richer—not in the "more stuff" way, but in the "I actually get it now" way. But it's not like we're taught *contentment with moderation,* so it can be hard to stop and see why you should be thankful for *right now.*

Once you start finding appreciation for the little things, it spills into the big things. *Appreciating life itself changes the game.* Suddenly, you're not just existing; you're *living.* You stop treating everything like it's owed to you and start seeing it as a *privilege.* Gratitude for things in life is just *Common Sense.* Or maybe... should be *Common Sense?*

Just say thank you now and then, you'll be fine.

Cells and Atoms are listening?

Sounds a bit weird at first, doesn't it? The idea is that the very cells and atoms that make up your body could be listening to you. Like, *are we* really saying that your thoughts, *feelings, and intentions could be influencing the tiniest parts of your being?* Well, some research is starting to point in that direction, and while it's still kind of *sceptical territory* for some, others are fully embracing the idea that what you think and believe can directly affect your physical health.

Science is catching on to the idea that our thoughts and emotions may have a bigger role in our well-being than we *initially thought.* You've got concepts like epigenetics telling us that our environment, which includes our mental state, can influence how our genes are expressed. And then there's the more "woo-woo" side, like quantum theory, which hints that atoms—those tiny, tiny building blocks—might not be as random and indifferent as we once believed. *Instead, they might be reacting to consciousness itself.* Some scientists and spiritual thinkers suggest that your thoughts might be able to *"communicate"* with your cells and atoms, altering how they function or even helping to heal you. *Sounds sci-fi, but the mind-body connection is real,* and it's no longer just about stress making you sick.

So, maybe if you're out of tune with yourself or can't hold on to any form of discipline, this idea could backfire. *You know how some people just can't seem to stop self-sabotaging, right?* Constantly stressing out or failing to follow through with positive intentions? *It's thought that leaving these thoughts unfinished, or not committing to healthier habits, might actually reinforce the negative instead of the positive.* When you half-arse it, the theory is, you're leaving an *open loop in your brain.* It's like starting a healing process and then ghosting on it—you feel even more disheartened because you didn't see it through, and that incomplete energy just sticks around. *It's all speculative right now, but it makes you wonder:* if thoughts can shape reality, leaving them unresolved might not do you any favours.

Persistent, focused thought is where things get interesting. The idea here is that if you focus hard enough, and believe long enough, you can literally shift things at a cellular level. We've heard stories of people who have used things like meditation, visualization, or prayer to recover from illnesses or injuries that didn't seem fixable.

Whether it's about rewiring neural pathways, improving immunity, or even altering the state of your cells, *the potential of our thoughts to shape our reality is becoming less of a myth and more of a possibility.* It's still a tough sell for some, but *hey, if your thoughts can lead to stress-induced illnesses, why not heal?* Makes you wonder what else the mind could be capable of.

It's kind of *mind-bending*, isn't it? If every single cell and atom in your body is tuned in to the vibrations of your thoughts, that means your body is like this massive, connected ecosystem that's constantly listening to what you think, believe, and feel. Imagine if you approached your health with that perspective, seeing your body not just as a machine but as something *deeply connected to the mind's whispers and intentions.* It puts a whole new spin on the idea of *"talking to yourself"*—you're literally communicating with yourself at and on every level.

And here's the deal: if every cell is listening, then your daily thoughts, even those quick, passing ones, are shaping the *blueprint of your health and well-being.* So when you're in a negative cycle, constantly beating yourself up or wallowing in doubt, you're essentially giving your cells a rough soundtrack to live by. *The reverse is also true,* though, and that's where the potential for change lies. Focused, intentional thought might not only keep you balanced but could even push your body towards healing and growth in ways we're just beginning to understand.

So, here's the *Common Sense* takeaway: *if your mind's dialogue is this powerful, maybe it's time to put a little more thought into your thoughts.* They're not just fleeting or insignificant; they're creating the environment your cells are soaking up every day.

Shhh! They are listening.

Why being Bored isn't so Bad

Today's generation treats boredom like it's a disease—*something to be avoided at all costs.* It's almost as if being alone with your own thoughts for a few minutes is a fate worse than death. The moment someone feels a twinge of boredom, they're already reaching for their phone, flicking through TikTok, binge-watching a series, or scrolling endlessly through social media. We've filled every spare moment with distractions, so much so that boredom has become this foreign concept, something people are terrified of. But what if being bored isn't such a terrible thing after all?

The truth is, that boredom can be a *gift in disguise.* It's a blank space that forces you to sit with yourself and think—*think*—without the constant noise of the outside world. Being bored can be the gateway to creativity and self-reflection. When you're not preoccupied, your mind has room to wander, to process things, and even to come up with new ideas. It's like giving your brain permission to take a little stroll through its own thoughts. Studies have shown that people often come up with their best ideas when they're bored because that mental downtime allows your brain to connect the dots you usually miss when you're distracted by a constant flood of information. Instead of fighting boredom, leaning into it can actually bring you clarity and calm.

Boredom isn't just about coming up with new ideas—it's also about learning to be at peace with yourself. When you're bored, you're left alone with your own thoughts, and that can be uncomfortable, especially if you tend to beat yourself up or dwell on negative things. But learning to be okay in those quiet moments, without sabotaging yourself or spiralling into self-criticism, is a skill worth building. *It's like training a muscle.* The more you practice being in your own head without tearing yourself down, the more resilient you become. You can start to sort out your thoughts, get to know yourself better, and maybe even reach a place of self-acceptance. It's not about avoiding your thoughts, but confronting them and being comfortable with your own company.

The *Common Sense* here might be: that running away from boredom isn't doing anyone any favours. Sure, keeping busy feels good in the short term, but filling every second of your day with distractions means you never get to just *be.* So the next time you feel that wave of boredom coming on, don't reach for your phone or look for something to fill the gap. *Embrace it. Sit with it.* Let your mind wander and see where it takes you.

Being bored isn't so bad—in fact, it might just be what you need to get back in touch with yourself and find a little peace in this always-on, hyper-distracted world. Because, let's face it, if you can't be alone with your own thoughts without needing to escape, what does that say about the state of your mind—or you as a person? Being okay with boredom should be *Common Sense,* not something to run from.

In a world that moves at a hundred miles an hour, it's easy to see why people treat boredom like an enemy. We're so used to constant stimulation that the idea of sitting still, doing absolutely nothing, feels uncomfortable, even pointless. But imagine if we didn't always have something to fill the silence. *What would we discover if we just let our minds roam free once in a while?* It's in those moments of stillness that we can actually reconnect with our true selves—away from all the noise, the expectations, and the endless need to be "productive." And maybe that's where the real insights are hiding, just waiting for a quiet moment to come forward.

Ironically, in avoiding boredom, we might actually be shutting ourselves off from the things that matter most. Those empty spaces allow for reflection, for figuring out what we value and why. When we can sit with our thoughts without trying to drown them out, we gain a kind of mental clarity that no amount of scrolling can bring. So maybe, instead of constantly trying to stay occupied, *we need to make peace with the quiet.* Because if we don't, we're just going to keep searching for meaning in places it doesn't exist—when really, it's been inside us all along.

We fear the quiet, the empty stare,

But that's where wisdom starts to flare.

Boredom whispers, "Sit with me,"

And shows the mind what it can be.

Next time you're bored, let yourself think a little.

Challenging Interaction's

Let's face it, dealing with people can be a right pain in the arse sometimes. Whether it's your Karen or Kevin of a neighbour throwing a fit over your bin placement, or that colleague who thinks "deadline" is just a fancy word for "whenever I feel like it," human interactions can make you want to neck a bottle of gin and call it a day. But here's the thing: we're stuck with each other on this big blue marble, so we might as well figure out how to play nice.

Now, it's dead easy to point fingers and moan about how everyone else is a complete muppet. But let's be real for a hot second—we've all been that guy or woman at some point. You know, the one who cuts in line because they're "in a rush," or leaves passive-aggressive notes on the office fridge. It's not that we're all inherently arseholes; it's just that we're all fighting our own battles, carrying around emotional baggage heavier than your nan's cooking. Sometimes, that stuff spills over and makes us act like proper twats, but that's life.

So what's the solution? Well, it ain't rocket science, people. A little empathy goes a long way. Next time someone's being a royal pain, take a breath before you go nuclear. Maybe they're having a day from hell, or maybe they're just a bit of a bellend. Either way, losing your shit isn't gonna solve anything. Try a bit of understanding, throw in a dash of setting boundaries, and top it off with knowing when to walk away. It won't solve all the world's problems, but it might just make your day-to-day a bit less of a headache. Remember, we're all just trying to muddle through this crazy thing called life. So let's cut each other some slack, yeah?

But here's where it really goes tits-up: everyone wants respect, but no one's willing to earn it. It's like we're living in a world where demanding patience and kindness is the default, but offering it back? Nah, that's too much work. Respect is a two-way street, not a one-way demand. And while we're at it, let's talk about how some people's definition of kindness these days is letting others walk all over them. *That's not kindness, mate, that's just being a doormat.* Kindness doesn't mean tolerating bad behaviour; it means knowing when to be firm, when to forgive, and when to say, "Enough is enough."

But here's where things get mental: seems like these days, people's spines have gone missing faster than socks in a laundromat. We've got a generation that can't handle a tough situation if it bit them on the arse. It's like everyone's expecting life to be a walk in the park when really, it's more like a trek through a minefield while wearing flip-flops. And most people aren't even putting themselves in situations that'd help them grow a pair of balls. It doesn't have to be cage fighting or running with the bulls, for Christ's sake. Just facing life's everyday bollocks head-on would be a start.

And let's not ignore the role of the digital age in all this. Social media has made confrontation seem scarier than it is—people would rather "block" or "unfriend" than have an actual conversation. It's like we've developed this allergic reaction to discomfort, choosing the path of least resistance every single time. But life *is* discomfort. It's messy, awkward, and sometimes downright brutal. Avoiding it doesn't make you stronger; it makes you weaker, robbing you of the chance to learn and adapt.

Look, I get it. The world can be a right shitshow sometimes. But avoiding every uncomfortable situation isn't doing anyone any favours. It's like we've forgotten that sometimes you've got to wade through the crap to get to the good stuff. Hell, even challenging someone's opinion these days is treated like you've just kicked their puppy. When did we become such delicate flowers that a bit of healthy debate sends us running for the hills?

Common Sense? We're tougher than we think. Humans have survived ice ages, plagues, and boy bands. A bit of adversity isn't going to kill us. In fact, it might just be the kick up the backside we need to grow a spine and actually make something of ourselves. So next time life throws you a curveball, don't duck. Stand your ground, face it head-on, and remember: it's not about being fearless, it's about being brave enough to be scared shitless and doing it anyway. That's how you grow, that's how you learn, and that's how you become someone worth a damn in this crazy, messed-up, beautiful world of ours.

Stand tall, even when you're scared shitless.

God

God's been a thing for as long as people have been able to think past what's for dinner. But here's the twist: while God might feel like the answer to life's big questions, there's also this sneaky truth that without *us* perceiving God, would God exist for us at all? It's like wondering if music exists in an empty forest with no ears to hear it. That doesn't mean God's *not* there—it's more like God is woven into the very fabric of everything, waiting for us to *tune in*. Maybe that's why in every human pursuit, from science to philosophy, we keep circling back to the idea of a higher order or purpose. Call it God, the universe, or some cosmic engineer—we're *wired* to seek meaning beyond the chaos.

But what's fascinating is how people demand a choice between God and science, as if they're rival football teams. That's like asking if a painting is the result of the *artist* or the *brushstrokes*. Why not both? Newton didn't chuck God out the window when he discovered gravity; he marvelled at the laws as signs of something bigger. Science might explain the *how*, but it's terrible at answering the *why*. The universe's existence, from the laws of physics to the messy beauty of consciousness, hints at something we can't quite box up with equations. And yet, isn't it just as fascinating to ask if the universe *needs* God at all? Maybe we're so busy looking for a cosmic lawgiver that we overlook the possibility that the laws themselves could simply *be*.

This isn't about telling anyone what to believe—it's about recognising how belief, or even the *absence* of it, shapes the way we live. Religion might give us structure, but spirituality, that sense of connection to something greater, doesn't need the same scaffolding. You don't have to memorise verses or follow every rulebook to feel connected to something bigger. And you certainly don't need to pick a team. Take a bit of mindfulness from Buddhism, some discipline from Islam, compassion from Hinduism, or wisdom from Christianity. It's a buffet of perspectives, not a rigid menu. The point is, you don't have to pledge allegiance to one system to find value in many.

And yet, here's the paradox: some argue that without God, there's no meaning at all. But what if the meaning isn't *handed* to us? What if we *create* it by how we live, how we connect, and how we grow? This doesn't mean God is irrelevant; it means God could be in the *process,* in the *act of seeking,* rather than in the final answer.

And maybe, just maybe, God exists both because we perceive it and because something greater is shaping the universe regardless of whether we're here to notice. Think of it as humanity's ongoing *love letter* to the mystery of existence.

The real power of believing in something bigger—whether you call it God or just a higher order—is the *freedom* it gives you. Free from needing to control everything or know all the answers. Free to trust that there's more to life than survival, to find meaning in the madness, and to ground yourself when the noise gets too loud. It's not about submitting to a cosmic dictator but embracing the idea that we're all part of something *bigger*. Maybe that's what keeps us sane in this relentless pursuit of purpose. Whether you're pulling wisdom from religion, science, or just your own experiences, that connection gives life depth.

In the end, this isn't about proving or disproving anything. It's about keeping your mind open to the possibilities. Maybe God is a universal truth, maybe just a human invention, or maybe *both* at once. Either way, the pursuit of understanding—the questions, the connections, the trust—is what keeps us going. It's not about being certain; it's about being willing to *explore.* After all, it's just a thought... but God's there for everyone—you've just got to *tune in* to the Power.

A voice in the quiet, soft and low,
Is it something we make, or something we know?
Did the stars just appear, or were they set to shine?
Is the question itself some kind of sign?
Maybe faith and reason walk side by side,
Both searching for answers neither can hide.

Common sense? Like God—you've gotta *find it.*

Ick's and Red Flag culture

"Icks" and *"red flags"* have always been part of dating and social interactions, but today, they've escalated into something much bigger. We're in an age where people dissect *every little thing someone does,* searching for the tiniest flaw to write them off completely. It's like one small quirk—a *weird laugh,* a *goofy habit*—can suddenly define someone. What happened to *accepting people for who they are?* We're all human, yet we treat minor imperfections as deal-breakers like no one's allowed to be *messy or flawed anymore.* It's exhausting and unrealistic, not to mention a terrible way to look at the world.

The internet is full of ridiculous examples. People call out icks like *"he ties his shoes wrong,"* or *"she's using a phone with a cracked screen,"* and suddenly these small, harmless traits become reasons to bail. We've stopped seeing people as complex individuals and started objectifying them, *reducing them to their quirks instead of their character.* This hyper-focus on trivial things is creating a culture where no one can just *be,* and it's affecting mental health. When you're always worried about triggering someone's *Ick list,* it's no wonder anxiety is through the roof—people feel like they're constantly *auditioning for acceptance.*

If we keep going down this path, we're setting ourselves up for a world where *no one is ever good enough.* Human relationships are built on *understanding, compromise,* and seeing past the little stuff. The obsession with perfection, whether through icks or red flags, is *stripping away our ability to connect.* It's time to let go of these superficial judgments and remember that *being human means being flawed.* If we don't, we'll end up in a world where *everyone is too scared to be themselves,* and honestly, that's not a world anyone wants to live in—it's like, no *Common Sense in a sense.*

**An "ick" here, a "flag" there, no one's left unscanned,
When did quirks and flaws make love so hard to stand?**

We should be wary, not pathetic.

Microaggression

Microaggressions are a hot topic nowadays, and for good reason. They're those subtle or unconscious actions and comments that can *undermine and disrespect people,* often based on their race, gender, or other aspects of their identity. Things like assuming someone's background based on their appearance or making a backhanded comment about how *"articulate"* they are—these seemingly small jabs can pile up, causing *real harm.* And in a world where we're supposed to be more inclusive and aware, knowing how to spot and avoid microaggressions makes you *more coherent and somewhat empathetic.*

The issue, however, is when microaggressions become *overly politicized,* and harmless comments turn into grounds for outrage. Let's say you ask someone, *"Where are you from?"* or compliment them on their English, or maybe even ask if they like K-pop. Suddenly, each is labelled a microaggression. Even comments like, *"Oh, are you a dog person?"* or mentioning their *avocado toast* habits can turn into offences. You're just trying to connect, but now it's a big deal. We've gone from tackling real issues to *scrutinizing every small question for the hidden offence.* It's like every tiny comment or simple question has been turned into a test. This shift *waters down the concept's importance,* turning it from a valid concern into a game of *gotcha,* where people are more concerned with *not offending* than with *genuinely connecting.*

Common Sense? Recognizing when your words or actions hurt others is crucial, but let's not get so soft that we turn every honest mistake into a massive issue. Isn't it funny how some people are quick to call out microaggressions while being *completely oblivious to their own?* Look, if we want to make things better, we need to *keep the conversation real* and stop turning everything into a drama show.

It's not that deep.

Your Mood, your Responsibility

Let's get this straight: your mood isn't some mystical force beyond your control. It's not like the stars, moon, or some algorithm are pulling the strings. Yes, there are external influences but, *it's still on you.* That gloomy storm cloud you've been dragging around? *You're the one letting it hover.* Sure, life's gonna chuck all kinds of crap at you – that's a given – but *the choice is yours* whether you make the best of it or sit there sucking on lemons, feeling all bitter. Here's the deal though: people nowadays seem to forget that. There's this weird lack of awareness when it comes to owning your own mood. *Everyone wants to feel good, but nobody wants to deal with the rough patches* to get there or they remain bitter while going for it. It's like they're expecting a *permanent good mood* without riding through the inevitable bollocks that life throws at them. But *that's not how it works.*

I'm not saying you have to walk around like some enlightened monk, blissed out and at peace all the time. That's about as realistic as thinking politicians will suddenly start telling the full truth. *Bad days are part of the deal.* Sometimes, the universe seems to take a big dump on your doorstep, and yeah, it's okay to feel a bit rubbish about it. But staying there, *wallowing in your misery like you've got no other option?* That's on you. And the problem is, when you let that bad mood fester, it starts to spread. *Your mood is like a neglected plant – give it enough garbage, and it's going to rot.* Neglect it, and it's not just you suffering; you'll start dragging everyone around you into your personal *black hole.*

That's the thing – your mood doesn't just affect you. *That sour attitude? It spreads faster than a cold in a crowded room.* You think you're just feeling a bit down, but next thing you know, *you're infecting everyone else with that negativity.* And that's where people get it wrong today. We all want to be in a good mood, but most don't want to do the work when it's *bad.*

They don't want to acknowledge how moods shift and how they're responsible for not letting it snowball into some big, draining mess. *So, do everyone a favour and check yourself.* Whether it's finding a way to lift your spirits or just recognising that your bad day doesn't have to turn into someone else's – *own it.* At the end of the day, *only you can drag yourself out of the shit.*

Put on your big kid pants, slap on a smile (even if you have to fake it for a bit), *and keep moving forward.* The world's got enough problems without you adding your personal rain cloud to the mix. Mood management isn't glamorous, but *it's your responsibility,* and the payoff is not only a better day for you but for everyone around you.

And that's where *a bit of Common Sense* comes in. *Look, managing your mood isn't some high-level secret,* nor is it about pretending life's perfect. *It's about realising you have a choice:* you can carry that sour mood around, letting it weigh you down and drag others with you, or you can make the conscious effort to shift it. *Common sense says to take responsibility for the energy you bring.* Sure, it's not always easy, but life's far easier when you're not adding to your stress by resisting what you can't control. *So, own the ups and downs, give yourself a break when it's rough,* and remember—it's on you to keep it in check. That's all it really takes to keep from being *your own worst enemy* in the mood department.

Your stormy clouds won't move themselves,

They thrive on doubt, they feed on dwells.

Own the mess, then clear the sky,

Choose to laugh or sit and cry.

It's not about faking, just taking control,

Your mood is yours—protect your soul.

It's just accountability for yourself.

The Sun, Moon and the Stars

Ever gazed up at the night sky and thought, *"Wow, those stars must be laughing at my expense"?* Well, join the club. We humans have been staring up at those twinkling lights for millennia, convinced they're somehow intertwined with our every mishap—from dodgy relationships to career downfalls. It's like we think the universe is keeping tabs on our Tinder matches when, in reality, it's probably more concerned with things like exploding stars, dark matter, and black holes. But hey, can't blame us for trying to decode the cosmic chaos, right?

Here's the duality of it all: on one hand, astrology's about as scientific as predicting the weather with a Magic 8-Ball. Mercury retrograde, rising signs, and birth charts? There is no proven impact on your morning coffee spill or your ex ghosting you again. And yet, people cling to them. Why? Because it's comforting. When life feels random and overwhelming, assigning meaning to the stars gives us something to hold onto—a cosmic explanation for why things don't go our way. It's easier to blame Saturn's positioning than to admit you overslept or ignored that red flag.

And it's not just the stars—oh no, the moon gets roped into this cosmic blame game too. For centuries, people have sworn the full moon causes mood swings, madness, or their dog acting up. To be fair, the moon *does* tug at the tides and can mess with your sleep, but blaming it for your boss being a dick? *That's a stretch.* Still, there's something oddly human about wanting to feel connected to something bigger. We crave meaning in the chaos—a sense that our struggles are part of some grand design. And who knows? Maybe the universe *does* leave breadcrumbs of influence we're not quite smart enough to fully understand yet.

The truth is, whether it's the stars, the moon, or Mercury's alleged mischief, the real star of the show—the only celestial body actually pulling the strings—is the sun. It's the reason we're alive, the engine of our existence, and it doesn't give a toss about your horoscope. Everything else? Just the backdrop. It's fun to think about, sure, but not the puppet masters we make them out to be. Common Sense says to enjoy the mystique of the cosmos without letting it dictate your life. The universe isn't plotting your downfall—it's just spinning away, doing its thing, while you're left to make your own choices.

Your star sign isn't an excuse.

We're all Hypocrites

Let's face it—we're all *hypocrites* in one way or another. It's just part of being human. We preach about things like *kindness, honesty,* or *sustainability,* but most of us are just picking and choosing when those principles actually apply. People talk about "doing their part" for the environment, but how many of those same people are sipping from a *single-use coffee cup* or ordering *fast fashion* online? Social media is flooded with posts about *mental health* and *self-care,* but then we're the same ones gossiping or tearing others down the minute something juicy comes up. The reality is, that people love to stand on their *soapboxes* and point fingers when it's convenient, but when the mirror's turned back on them, suddenly, it's a different story.

The world today is full of people talking about *authenticity* and being "real," while crafting *perfect, filtered versions* of themselves for others to see. It's the classic *"do as I say, not as I do"* routine. Someone might shout about *equality,* but when it comes to admitting their own biases? *Total silence.* We're all for *forgiveness and understanding*—until we're the ones who've been wronged. Then, somehow, holding a grudge feels perfectly justified. It's like we're *programmed* to hold others to a higher standard than we hold ourselves. That's why everyone seems ready to jump on the next public apology and declare it *"not good enough,"* while conveniently ignoring their own mistakes or contradictions. It's hypocrisy on *autopilot.*

So, what's the *Common Sense* here? We're all guilty of *double standards* sometimes, and it doesn't make you a terrible person—it just makes you *human.* The trick is being aware of it and owning up to it when you catch yourself doing it. *Calling out hypocrisy in others is easy; recognising it in yourself is the hard part.* So before you go waving that judgmental finger at someone else, take a second to check your own *actions and words.* Being consistent isn't always possible, but at least having the *self-awareness* to admit it is a good start. Because let's be real—being a little less hypocritical isn't just good practice; it's how you *stay genuine.*

Check yourself, *init.*

How Cool is it to be Alive

Let's take a second and really appreciate how mind-blowingly awesome it is to just exist. I mean, you're basically *stardust with a brain,* strolling around on a giant rock that's speeding through space at 67,000 mph. *Let that sink in.* Every breath you take, every step you make, you're part of this cosmic dance that's been going on for billions of years. If that's not ridiculously cool, what is?

Yeah, I get it, life's got its fair share of curveballs. *Bills piling up, endless traffic,* and let's not forget that guy who insists on chewing like a farm animal. It's easy to get bogged down in the mundane nonsense. *But take a second, and zoom out.* The universe is estimated to have about *10 octillion planets* (yep, that's a 1 followed by 28 zeros), and here you are, chilling on this tiny, perfect blue speck that's just right for life. *You've hit the cosmic jackpot,* my friend. Every sunrise, every joke that makes you laugh, every delicious meal—that's the universe flexing its magic, and you're in on it

And guess what? We're barely scratching the surface of what's out there. Humans have gone from making cave drawings to launching rockets into space in what's basically a blink of an eye, *cosmically speaking.* We're cracking the code of the quantum world, plumbing the depths of the oceans, mapping the human genome, and pushing the limits of what we thought possible. We're living in a time where the secrets of the universe are slowly unravelling before us, piece by piece.

Sure, the world's a bit of a mess, but you've got a front-row seat to the greatest spectacle the universe has to offer. *So the next time life throws a punch, remember:* you're not just alive, you're part of an ongoing miracle. Embrace the wonder, *chase your curiosity,* and enjoy the ride. Because being alive? *That's the ultimate adventure in the cosmos.* You are the universe's life, and *Common Sense* is to appreciate that fact.

Isn't life just incredible?

Unfortunately, it's not all about You

Let's be real—these days, we're all the *stars* of our own little reality show, snapping selfies like we're the next big thing. Social media's basically turned us into *peacocks,* strutting around for likes and follows. But here's the twist: while you're busy perfecting that *#livingmybestlife* post, the planet's still spinning, completely indifferent to your gym selfies or avocado toast pics. Don't get me wrong, *self-care* is great and all, but when did we start acting like the universe revolves around our *TikTok or Insta trends?*

The stats don't lie. Studies show *narcissism* has been creeping up, especially in younger generations. We're so hooked on *instant gratification* that we've forgotten how to plan for anything beyond the next five minutes. *Climate change?* Future problem. *Sustainable living?* Only if it doesn't mess with my daily vibe. We're like kids in a candy shop, grabbing all we can without thinking about the *stomachache* that's bound to follow. And by being so wrapped up in ourselves, we're not only messing with our future—we're screwing it up for *everyone else,* too.

The thing is, we didn't get this far by being selfish consumers. Our ancestors knew that survival meant looking *beyond themselves.* They planted trees knowing they'd never sit under their shade, built societies designed to last longer than their lifetimes. But somewhere along the way, we *lost the plot.* Maybe it's the rise of consumer culture, maybe it's the dopamine hit of social media likes. Either way, it's time to *wake up.* The world is way bigger than your *Twitter/X feed,* and if we don't start thinking beyond ourselves, there might not be a world left for all these selfies.

So how about we put down the phone for a sec, grab some *Common Sense* and remember that the *best lives* aren't just lived for ourselves—they're part of something *bigger,* a shared human story that's been unfolding for millennia.

The world doesn't need more perfectly curated lives; it requires *real people* willing to show up, flaws and all, and contribute to something lasting. So, let's rethink what it means to live our *best lives.* It's not about being seen—it's about making an impact, no matter how small, and knowing that our actions can shape a better story for future generations.

Hate to say it, but it's not all about you.

Depressed Generation

We live in an age where we know *more than ever before,* but this flood of knowledge hasn't stopped the rise in *emotional disconnection* and *mental health struggles.* Especially young people today, are thrown into a *fast-paced,* pressure-filled world, expected to adapt and thrive without the luxury of *growing up slowly.* Social media makes things worse by showing only the *highlight reels* of other people's lives, leaving many feeling like they're *falling short.* The constant comparison breeds a sense of *inadequacy,* making it hard to feel content with what you have, although some can grasp a sense of motivation from it.

In response to these pressures, many turn to *chasing unrealistic dreams* or even turning to drugs. Dreaming big is great, but today's generation is bombarded with *instant success stories* that don't show the hard work behind them. This can lead to feelings of *failure* and *depression* when things don't come as easily as expected. On top of that, drug culture has become *mainstream,* with even governments getting involved in *legalization for profit.* What's alarming is how often *mental health diagnoses* are handed out—ADHD, anxiety, depression, and many more—sometimes as a way to simplify struggles rather than encourage resilience and growth. It's like *"Here's a disorder stamp and off you go."*

Consumerism and *overindulgence* go hand in hand, and they're feeding into this cycle. Twenty years ago, people dealt with challenges by *pushing through,* without needing constant validation from *online communities.* Today, we're more likely to hide behind labels or indulge in *temporary fixes* like drugs or distractions. Outside of the side effects of *traumatic experiences,* it's mostly about what mood you choose to *partake in* but that's easier said than understood for a lot of people, unfortunately.

Common Sense says that life's tough, and it's up to us to find balance, take responsibility, and push forward, instead of constantly seeking quick solutions to deeper problems. It also means acknowledging that this struggle isn't just personal—it's global. This generation is battling a unique storm of pressures that previous ones couldn't have imagined: hyperconnectivity, the weight of constant comparison, and a world that feels more fragile than ever. Empathy, for both ourselves and each other, is crucial. We need to stop dismissing people's struggles as weaknesses and start seeing them as a sign of the times—challenges that demand collective understanding and support.

Should you give a Fuck or Not?

Here's a question: should you *give a fuck,* or not? It's a strange one because, on one hand, we've all seen people who seem to coast through life without a care in the world, and somehow, things just… work out for them. Meanwhile, others pour every ounce of their energy into something, stressing and sweating over every detail, and sometimes they end up in the *same place* as the slackers.

Maybe it's all down to how well you deal with the fallout. Some people are like *Teflon*—nothing sticks. They don't care about consequences because they're good at dodging them—or they've learned how to cope when shit hits the fan. Meanwhile, others thrive on giving attention to *everything.* Their hyper-focus fuels their success. So, which one's better? Honestly, it depends on the person.

The world today is practically *training* us to give less of a fuck about the bigger picture. Think about it—everybody's so caught up in their own bubble, hyper-focused on their corner of the world. You can't care about *everything,* or you'd go mad, right? Between endless notifications, news cycles throwing disaster after disaster at you, and the constant overwhelm of modern life, you're almost forced to compartmentalise just to get by—or you really just don't care.

Compartmentalise—basically, tuck things away into tidy mental boxes so you don't feel overwhelmed by every problem at once. People are more disconnected from social causes these days—not because we don't care, but because there's just *too much* coming at us. It's like we're being stretched in a thousand directions, barely keeping it together.

What's funny is how *selective* we are about what we actually care about. We've got this limited *"give a fuck" budget,* and once it's used up, that's it for the day. Some people spend theirs on big, global issues—*climate change, human rights,* the stuff that feels massive and overwhelming. Others focus on their immediate surroundings—family, work, personal health. Both are valid, but we all still expect society to function smoothly while most of us are only worrying about what's right in front of us. It's like we want the world to run perfectly, but we're only contributing as much as we can spare from our own little bubble. No wonder things feel so *out of balance* sometimes.

There's also the paradox where, sometimes, whether you care deeply or not at all, the outcome can be the same. Ever notice that? Like, someone spends *ages* obsessing over their career, climbing the ladder, and another person just stumbles through life without a plan—and both end up in similar positions. It's almost *infuriating.*

But maybe it's because the secret isn't about giving a fuck at every single turn, but *knowing* when to give a fuck. Maybe we're not all wired to care about everything equally, and that's okay—just as long as we don't completely check out. It's about *balance,* figuring out where your energy makes the most difference.

At the end of the day, society works best when we care—at least a little. If everyone checked out and left the hard stuff for someone else to deal with, we'd be in trouble. But it doesn't mean you need to shoulder the weight of the world 24/7. The trick is figuring out where your *"give a fuck" meter* should be set. We can't fix everything, but we can sure as hell make our little corner of the world better. If more people squeezed out a bit more effort—just a little—we might be surprised at what could change.

And the *Common Sense?* The goal isn't to care about *everything,* but the *right* things—you know, the stuff, you *actually* give a fuck about.

Care wisely, not carelessly—find your way,
Both paths can lead to the same play.
The secret's not to carry it all,
But knowing when to rise or give a fuck at all.

It's a fine skill, knowing when to give a fuck.

Inner Child Syndrome

I'm guilty of this one just as much as anyone else—just like with most of the things I've covered in this book. These days, it's no secret that adults can hide from the world, wrapped up in whatever makes them feel happy and comfortable. And honestly, who can blame them? Society is tailored to make life easier, to keep everyone entertained, and to give us those fleeting moments of joy—even if it means we never really grow up. But there's a downside to being so in tune with our inner child: it's affecting how we relate to each other on a deeper level. If something's *not my vibe,* it's almost like it doesn't exist. That's the mindset creeping in, isn't it? If it doesn't perfectly align with our comfort zones or personal preferences, we dismiss it as irrelevant or boring. And while it makes sense to avoid things we don't enjoy, it's also closing us off from growth and deeper understanding. Life isn't meant to fit neatly into our curated little bubbles, but somewhere along the way, we've convinced ourselves it should.

The phenomenon of adults embracing their inner child has some unintended consequences, especially when it comes to relationships and attraction. In many parts of the world—particularly the *West, Europe,* and parts of *Asia*—people seem to approach relationships with a surface-level, friend-like vibe. We're great at having fun, being spontaneous, and exploring our interests together, but we're not seeing each other as *potential partners* anymore. Instead of looking for a deeper, romantic connection, it's like we're all just hanging out, indulging our own *inner child,* and keeping things light. The concept of commitment or seeing someone as a *life partner* has taken a back seat to instant gratification and carefree living. This trend is contributing to the decline in attraction between people. We act like kids, and have fun together, but often stop there. There's less interest in building something *meaningful* or exploring the challenging sides of relationships because, well, who wants to leave their *comfort zone?* This "inner child syndrome" feeds into a cycle where we avoid responsibilities and commitments because we've been conditioned to *seek happiness* and fun at all times as well as staying *busy,* avoiding that deeper meaning.

Common Sense? Maybe it's time to recognise that embracing our inner child is great, but not at the cost of *meaningful relationships.* Stay playful, and have fun, but remember that building something *real* takes effort and maturity. Otherwise, we're just a bunch of adults playing pretend, never really getting anywhere deeper with each other. We gotta grow up at some point.

Am I Racist?

Let's talk about the *ridiculousness* of it all. These days, if you even *dare* to question someone's progressive, all-inclusive, super-woke logic, you're automatically labelled the *bad guy. Common sense?* Yeah, that's apparently a *hate crime* now. If you don't immediately fall in line with every new *"inclusive"* trend, you're either a racist, a bigot, or some other awful thing that ends in *"-ist."* We've gotten to a point where having a different opinion—one based on *actual life experience* and just plain understanding people—is now *offensive.* It's wild, especially when all you're doing is using your brain for five seconds. Just because you don't *blindly agree* with every new viewpoint doesn't make you a racist—it just means you've got a functioning thought process.

The reality is, that we're all trying to make sense of this confusing world, treating people with *respect* while still holding onto some *basic logic.* But the minute you voice an opinion that doesn't fit the most *extreme version of inclusivity,* you're suddenly the *villain.* It's like questioning anything means you must secretly *hate* everyone. *Spoiler alert:* not every opinion is about hatred—sometimes, it's just about looking at things with a bit of *Common Sense.* Seriously, sometimes it feels like if you don't nod along to everything, you're one step away from being *cancelled.*

Common Sense about this? Disagreeing doesn't make you a racist. It means you have your *own perspective,* and that's what makes life interesting. Stop turning every disagreement into some grand *accusation.* Let's make *Common Sense* the standard again—not something that puts you on some kind of *"problematic watchlist."* There's a *huge* difference between *actual racism* and just questioning an idea—let's not lose sight of that, or it gets silly. Childishly silly.

Here's the truth: in some way or another, *we're all a little racist.* It's human nature to have biases—it's part of how we navigate the world. But that's not the point. The point is to *acknowledge* those biases, keep *Common Sense* in your heart, and approach others with acceptance and understanding. Your opinions should be rooted in *realism*—grounded in experience, respect, and a willingness to see the world through someone else's eyes—not in some self-righteous crusade that's *actually racist* in disguise. It's not about pretending to be perfect; it's about striving to be better. After all, the moment we let go of *Common Sense* is the moment we stop making progress.

Do we Care too Much?

Of course, it's important to care. Caring is what moves us forward; it helps us build relationships, improve ourselves, and connect with others. But in today's world, it feels like we're being made to *care about everything,* all the time. And not just about the people or things that matter to us personally, but every *trending topic, every injustice, every crisis.* It's like someone turned on a *water fountain of concern,* and we're expected to drink from it without drowning. On top of that, we're juggling our own lives, trying to stay hyper-productive and perfect—because apparently, if we're not, we just don't *measure up.* No wonder people are exhausted. It's not that caring is bad; it's that caring about *everything* is impossible.

We're conditioned to think that every issue, no matter how far removed from our personal lives, *demands* our attention. Between *climate change, global conflicts, social injustices,* and every new viral cause on social media, it's overwhelming. And if we don't keep up? Well, we're made to feel like we're falling behind—that we're somehow *less compassionate* or not doing enough. This pressure to stay engaged with *everything* turns us into fatigued versions of ourselves. It makes us *hypervigilant,* constantly wired, and often too drained to give meaningful attention to the people right in front of us. We're starting to resemble *machines,* designed to be perfect and productive, but lacking the *humanity* that makes life worth living.

Now, some people are naturally wired to care deeply about everything, and this isn't meant to take away from them. There are different breeds of us—some are built to take on the world's burdens with incredible strength. But for the rest of us, maybe it's about *choosing* where to invest our energy.

Common Sense? Care deeply about the things that genuinely matter to you, and don't feel *guilty* for not carrying every weight. If we keep trying to care about it all, we'll just end up *caring about nothing*—too tired to even connect with what's *real* and right in front of us.

The level of care just shows your character.

How uncommon Common Sense is Today

Remember when *Common Sense* actually lived up to its name? These days, it's as rare as a polite debate on Twitter. We've gone from a species smart enough to align massive stones at Stonehenge to one that genuinely needs warnings not to eat laundry pods. Let's face it—something's gone sideways.

Back in the day, Common Sense was survival's best mate. It stopped us from petting lions and taught us that fire, while hot, was worth the risk. But now? We've got people trying to charge their phones in microwaves or sticking forks into toasters because they saw it in a life hack video. It's like we've swapped our innate wisdom for a subscription to *Why Would You Even Do That Weekly.* And don't get me started on the internet—a wonder of modernity—now a never-ending showcase of our collective brain fog.

Think about it: there are people out there who genuinely believe the Earth is flat like we're all living on some cosmic pancake under a *firmament dome.* You know, a solid, dome-like structure keeping everything neatly contained, just as ancient cosmologies once described. It's an idea that feels laughably outdated in an era of space exploration and satellite imagery, yet here we are. Somehow, the simplicity of a dome-covered world appeals to those who distrust science or modern explanations. But let's face it—if we're still debating whether the sky is a cosmic ceiling while rockets are literally escaping Earth's atmosphere, maybe it's time to reevaluate where we're directing our Common Sense.

And it's not just flat-earthers. Others are convinced vaccines come with microchips because obviously, the government really cares about tracking your snack runs. Conspiracy theories? They're growing faster than weeds after a rainy week, while actual logic is sitting in the corner, rocking back and forth, wondering where it all went wrong. It's tempting to give up entirely—to move to a cave and let nature sort us out.

But here's the thing: Common Sense isn't just about avoiding idiocy. It's the glue holding society together, the quiet hero keeping us from spiralling into chaos. It's what stops you from telling your mate's gran she smells funny or deciding your ex's wedding is the perfect moment for a romantic monologue. It's that tiny voice saying, *"Maybe don't,"* before you commit social suicide. It's not flashy, but it's essential—like wearing trousers to the shop.

So why's it in hiding? Maybe we've outsourced too much of our thinking to apps and algorithms, leaving our brains lounging around on holiday. Or perhaps we're just so caught up in the noise—reality TV, viral memes, and endless notifications—that we've forgotten to engage with the obvious. Either way, we're in a full-blown Common Sense drought, and the cracks are showing.

Here's the kicker: Common Sense is what got us here in the first place. It's the reason we're not just another species on nature's buffet line. But now, we need apps to remind us to drink water—the same stuff that falls from the sky more often than we'd like. At this rate, someone's bound to invent a breathing app, and half of us will download it because that's where we're headed.

Let's be clear: no one's saying we need to ditch technology and churn butter in a cottage somewhere, but maybe—*just maybe*—we could pause for a second and think before acting. Common Sense isn't glamorous, it won't go viral, and it definitely won't make you a trendsetter. But it's the foundation for not being a walking disaster.

Here's the pitch: let's make Common Sense common again—not for the likes, but because it's how we stop making life harder than it needs to be. It's not about being Einstein but not competing for first place in the Thick Olympics. In a world where daft decisions are celebrated for the clicks, using your head is basically a revolutionary act.

And here's the real takeaway: *Common Sense* isn't some ancient relic—it's a life tool. Use it, or lose it. Your ancestors who dodged sabre-toothed tigers, braved the ice age, and figured out how to make fire didn't go through all that just for us to forget the basics. They didn't invent the wheel so we could become the species that has to Google whether Pop-Tarts are microwavable. They'd want us to think—to use our heads, not just our phones. Let's not let them down.

Common Sense, the OG life hack,
Now traded for trends and a dopamine snack.
Pick it up—it's time to take it back.

Are you a commonsensical person?

The Lost Art of Survival

Common Sense isn't glamorous, but it's the backbone of any functioning society. It's the thing that, despite all the chaos, holds people together and keeps the world from completely falling apart. In a world where you can be *anything,* say *anything,* and offend *anyone,* we've lost sight of how essential it is to just live with a little *Common Sense.* It might feel restrictive—especially now, when the line between *freedom* and *absurdity* is razor thin—but without it, civilization starts to crumble. We're watching it happen in real-time, especially in the West, where the lines between right and wrong, natural and unnatural, are not just blurred but *deliberately erased.*

And yeah, there's a lot of *"gayness"* in the world today, but I'm not talking about sexuality. It's the over-saturation of *virtue-signalling,* performative *wokeness,* and people bending over backwards to appease the loudest, most irrational voices. When did basic human decency and a sense of what's right become so unfashionable? We've reached a point where cruelty is *normalised,* hidden behind hashtags, or even *celebrated* if it benefits the "right" people. From the corporate elite to social media influencers, the lines between what's humane and what's outright exploitation are conveniently ignored. It's no longer about truth or fairness; it's about who can *gain the most,* regardless of the cost.

What we seem to be missing is that *Common Sense* used to set boundaries, and those boundaries kept people in check. They weren't perfect, but they worked. People understood that if society was going to function, you couldn't just run wild with every idea that popped into your head or every feeling you had about yourself. Today, there's no filter, no pause to think about the bigger picture. We've traded stability for individualism, to the point where we're all just chasing something—some version of life we've convinced ourselves is better—while the world around us gets uglier and more divided.

The truth is, we have a lot to be grateful for. Look around; despite all the issues, there are still places where *basic freedoms* exist, where people aren't starving in the streets or being hunted for sport. It could be so much worse, and for many people in the world, it is. But we've become blind to that in the West because we're so caught up in our own self-made problems, constantly looking for the next thing to be *outraged by,* rather than appreciating the relative peace we live in. Meanwhile, the planet is being ravaged by greed, wars are still tearing countries apart, and we sit here acting like our biggest problem is *pronouns.*

Common Sense isn't just about setting boundaries to survive. It's about *fostering hope,* too. In tougher times, people believed in something greater than themselves, whether it was faith, family, or community. They understood that while the present might suck, the future could be better if we just worked for it, *together.* But today, we're all living like we're waiting for the apocalypse to hit. There's no patience, no perseverance, just endless anxiety and the constant need to be validated by likes or retweets. It's exhausting, and it's killing the very thing that makes societies thrive: *unity.*

The reality is, we got this far as a species by surviving against all odds. Millions have died—just over the past 200 years in wars, famines, and revolutions—just to bring us to this point. And now, we're on the edge of losing it because we can't agree on what bathroom to use. *Come on.* We've got the tools, the technology, and the history to guide us back from the brink, but it's going to take a return to basic, *Common-Sense* values. We've done it before, and if we can stop being so self-absorbed and entitled, we can definitely do it again. The only question is: *will we?*

**Common Sense once held us steady and strong,
Now it's lost in the noise, where the loudest belong.
We bicker on pronouns while the world's set ablaze,
Trading unity for chaos in our self-serving craze.
The past built us up, but now we're tearing it down,
Laughing at the absurd as we watch ourselves drown.**

Mad times we live in.

Modern lack of Commitment

Modern lack of commitment is one of the strangest symptoms of our time. Over the past decade or so, we've been programmed—by technology, by culture, by endless options—to constantly *search* for something better, even when what we have is already *more than enough.* Whether it's dating apps, social media, or the overall *"grass is always greener"* mentality, men and women have fallen into this exhausting cycle of perpetual dissatisfaction. We've been convinced that commitment is for those who *"settle,"* while the truly enlightened keep their options open indefinitely. Ironically, in trying to avoid settling, we *settle for much less:* fleeting thrills, superficial connections, and the emptiness of never being content.

What's sad is that it's not just one side that's guilty. It's *both* men and women like we're all in this ridiculous game of one-upping each other. Who can care less? Who can prove they're less attached, less affected, less committed? Instead of love being a *partnership,* it feels like a *competition*—a tug of war that no one can win because everyone's too busy trying to prove they're too good to *truly commit.* We've become *consumers* of each other, scrolling and swiping as if people are products with an expiration date. And the worst part is, it's like we can't even turn it off. We've been bred selfish. Everything in our culture pushes us to put ourselves first, to not compromise, to look out for *number one*—but at what cost? Genuine connection? Real love? The thing we all *say* we want but are too scared to actually nurture?

Common Sense would tell us that love is not just some bare minimum. It's not something you swipe past because it's not shiny enough, or exciting enough, or because there might be a *"better deal"* two profiles down. *Love* is the best thing we've got—the one thing that makes all the mess worthwhile. But we've turned it into something transactional, something that's supposed to be *flawless* from the start. Otherwise, we throw it away.

Maybe it's time we realise that the real *power move* isn't in keeping our options open, but in *choosing* to stick with someone even when it's not perfect, because—*spoiler alert*—it's *never* going to be perfect. And that's what makes it worth it.

We have to learn to commit.

Is your Heart in it?

We live in a world that *worships productivity.* We're all in this relentless race to check off as many boxes as possible, cramming every hour with something *"useful."* But let's be real—just because you *can* do something, or because it's expected of you, doesn't mean your heart is in it. Sometimes we do things because society says we *should,* or because we feel like we need to keep up with the hyper-productive crowd. The result? We go on *autopilot,* putting in the hours and doing what's needed, but never really engaging. It's like we're just moving pieces on a chessboard without any real strategy—just to avoid *losing the game.*

But here's the thing: it's not that everything should be *sunshine and rainbows.* We don't need every task to be enjoyable, nor should every struggle be glorified. Some things are just *plain annoying.* However, the difference between autopilot and *actually living* is the passion and intention you put into it. When you bring even a sliver of genuine interest into what you're doing—or care for the people around you while you're at it—you break out of that mindless cycle. It's not about making everything *"fun"* but about making it *real*—bringing conscious thought to your actions and letting your *character* show through.

Being yourself doesn't mean being *childish* or overly carefree. It's about having the confidence to put your *real self* into whatever you do. It's showing up as the grown-up version of you, not just a robot going through the motions. You might be washing dishes, dealing with a boring work project, or tackling a tough conversation, but if you do it with your *heart in it,* something shifts. Suddenly, you're *present.* Suddenly, the mundane becomes something meaningful because you're putting *yourself* into it—not just your hands, but your mind and spirit, too.

The irony of today is that people often fall into despair simply because they've *forgotten* how to be themselves throughout life. We get so lost in being *"productive"* that we forget how to add our own twist to things. We become so focused on *getting it done* that we forget to bring any creativity, any essence of who we are, into it. We're scared to step out of line, to be a bit *different.* And that's why so many end up feeling disconnected, like they're just cogs in a machine, instead of realising they're the ones who could make that machine *worth running.* But, that doesn't mean being a *fool* is okay too.

Of course, there are reasons for this. Many people stay in their heads because it's *safer* there. Expressing yourself can feel like stepping into a spotlight you never asked for. But there's a big difference between being *obnoxious* and just being *genuinely yourself.* It's not about seeking attention or making a scene; it's about showing up in a way that's *true to you,* being self-approving and self-accepting. The more we embrace that side of us, the more we can break out of that *robotic cycle* of productivity and truly connect—with what we do, with others, and with ourselves.

Common Sense? Maybe try not being just a *checkbox machine.* You don't need to make everything fun, but put your *heart* into it. Be *present,* be *real,* and stop running on autopilot. The goal isn't just to survive the day—it's to make even the smallest moments *yours,* with your touch, your character, and your heart in it. That's when life gets interesting, not just productive.

We live on autopilot, one chore at a time,
But what's the harm in adding some rhyme?
Put a dash of you in every little chore,
Suddenly, life feels like a bit more.
It's not about perfection or grand displays,
Just finding *yourself* in life's everyday maze.

Having your heart in it is like a superpower.

Closing Thought

After everything I've talked about—the ups, the downs, the unknowns most people ignore, and the confusion of today's world—one thing is crystal clear: none of us have all the answers, and *that's okay*. Life is messy, funny, horrible, unpredictable, and full of irony, and we're all just trying to figure it out, even if some people are better at pretending they've got it together. Common Sense might seem like a relic of the past, but it's still there, buried under layers of noise, distraction, and, let's face it, the cold truth that most people either can't handle or refuse to face. That's why things are the way they are—society's influence and deeply ingrained patterns of "progress at all costs" keep most people spinning in circles, unable to break free from the delusions they've been sold.

I'm not here claiming to be the second coming of Jesus, Muhammad, Buddha, or some divine figure with all the answers. This book isn't about preaching; it's a conversation. The goal? To spark something—whether it's a laugh, a nudge, or even just a moment where you think, *"Yeah, that's true."* Some of you might get it, and to those people: thank you. To the ones who don't? Well, tough shit, init. But if there's one thing to remember, it's this: *stay Wake*. Not woke in the performative sense, where every opinion is polished for approval, but truly Wake—clear-eyed, grounded, and unafraid to face the hard truths, even if they're uncomfortable. Because the last few decades have shown us what happens when we lose sight of reality. We chase lifestyles we can't sustain, constantly pursuing more while ignoring what we already have. And in doing so, we lose the ability just to be.

Common Sense isn't about being right all the time or solving the world's problems. It's about being real. Real enough to admit when you don't have the answers. Strong enough to peel back the layers of illusion we're all wrapped in. And curious enough to keep asking questions without losing your sense of humour. Life is chaotic, absurd, and a bit ridiculous, but that's the beauty of it. So here's to navigating this mad world with clarity, laughter, and just enough Common Sense to keep it all from falling apart. Cheers to that.

Common Sense is sadly fading fast,
Lost in trends that never last.
A bit more collective thought could turn the tide,
And bring some well-needed wisdom back inside.

Common sense

Noun (kom-un sens)
"An endangered trait in human intelligence."

Printed in Great Britain
by Amazon

57723983R00119